THE HEIR

(Kelderan Runic Warriors #3)

JESSIE DONOVAN

The Heir
Copyright © 2018 Laura Hoak-Kagey
Mythical Lake Press, LLC
First Edition

Cover Art by Clarissa Yeo of Yocla Designs
ISBN: 978-1942211587

Books by Jessie Donovan

Asylums for Magical Threats
Blaze of Secrets (AMT #1)
Frozen Desires (AMT #2)
Shadow of Temptation (AMT #3)
Flare of Promise (AMT #4)
Whirlwind of Change (AMT #5 / TBD)

Cascade Shifters
Convincing the Cougar (CS #0.5)
Reclaiming the Wolf (CS #1)
Cougar's First Christmas (CS #2)
Resisting the Cougar (CS #3)

Kelderan Runic Warriors
The Conquest (KRW #1)
The Barren (KRW #2)
The Heir (KRW #3)
The Forbidden / Kalahn & Ryven (KRW #4 / July 2018)

Lochguard Highland Dragons
The Dragon's Dilemma (LHD #1)
The Dragon Guardian (LHD #2,)
The Dragon's Heart (LHD #3)
The Dragon Warrior (LHD #4)
The Dragon Family / Finn & Ara (LHD #5 / May 2018)
The Dragon's Discovery / Alistair Boyd (LHD #6 / Fall 2018)

Chapter One

Twenty-Three Years Ago

Azalyn Rippak rubbed the material of her skirt between her fingers and resisted peeking out of the storage room once more. Keltor would come as soon as he could. After all, he was a prince with a lot of boring tutors and instruction from his father, King Kastor, and his schedule left little room for meetings with her.

If only their time together didn't have to be so short, let alone secret. But she was a shop assistant's daughter and nowhere near the same station as a prince. Keltor had assured her that next year, when he turned twenty and inherited more responsibilities from his father, he could start finding councilors sympathetic to his desire to take Azalyn as his bride. Once he had enough support, he could announce his intentions publicly, but not before.

Why politics had to be so complicated, she didn't know. At seventeen, she'd never really thought about them before meeting Keltor. She knew her extended family's merchant business like the back of her hand, but none of that would help in her current situation. Or, so Keltor had said. She hated relying on him for matters related to the palace. She really needed to study a bit more about how it all functioned.

Steps echoed down the hallway. Her worries melted away and her heart skipped a beat. Her prince had finally come.

Yet in the next heartbeat, doubt crept up her spine. What she had planned was a big step for both of them, one from which there was no return.

Maybe she should rethink it.

However, as soon as Keltor entered the room and locked the door, his eyes met hers and the world melted away, as did her doubts. He already risked everything to spend time with her. She trusted that he wouldn't abandon her and disregard all his promises to date.

Jumping into his arms, she kissed him. She wasn't an expert on the subject, but as his lips devoured hers, she couldn't help but sigh.

Keltor chuckled and broke the kiss. "What happened to making me work for everything? Giving in so easily strokes my ego, and I know you try not to do that."

She frowned. "Excuse me for missing you. It's been two weeks, Keltor. That's a long time."

He gently placed her on the floor and lightly stroked her back. "I know, love. My father is growing suspicious, which means I have to be even more careful." He took her chin in his hand. "But everything I do is for us. If I could resign my place as heir today and run away with you, I would."

She finished his thought. "I know, but Kason is in the army now, and your sister can't rule because of the law. I still think that's stupid. Females are just as smart. You've said so yourself."

"Yes, but remember Kalahn isn't more than a baby right now. Father announcing the heir is a toddler—and a female one no less—won't help anything, especially with the recent end of the war with the Brevkan. He has to be focused on healing and rebuilding Keldera."

She noticed the worry in his eyes. "What aren't you telling me?"

He shook his head. "I'd rather not waste what time I have with you talking about serious matters. I'm more interested in what you have planned for today's adventure."

If it hadn't been so long since she'd seen Keltor, Azalyn might've pushed. But she'd worked hard at finding a new surprise for her prince, and was anxious to get started. "Come. The guard rotation change will happen soon, and if we miss the small window available to leave the palace grounds, we won't have another chance for hours."

Keltor took her hand and motioned in front of them. "Then lead on, my lady."

She flashed a grin, opened the door to peek out, and tugged him behind her. When she'd met Keltor by chance a year ago, he'd been dressed as a commoner and had been roaming the streets of the capital. It was still hard to believe that the male she'd castigated for stepping on her foot had ended up being the future king of Keldera.

Not that it had mattered to her at the time, nor did it in the present. All she wanted was to become his bride and live out a future with her best friend and counter-balance.

Strange to think a prince helped to tame her impulsiveness, let alone the fact a shop assistant's daughter was able to show a new side of the world to a crown prince.

Squeezing Keltor's hand, she led them through one of the service tunnels and toward the palace's side exit. She was aware that Keltor's future wasn't his own. Still, she believed in their love. He would find a way for them to be together.

Some might say she was foolish for such thoughts, but stubbornness was Azalyn's middle name. Her father had never believed she could apprentice to an acquisitions' assistant before her eighteenth birthday, and yet she'd done it at sixteen.

Becoming Keltor's bride and one day the queen of Keldera might be a little more difficult, but she never said never.

They reached the end of the service tunnel and checked out the area, from the perfectly laid out garden to the surveillance stations posted at regular intervals around the palace grounds. The guards would be gone from this section for the next five minutes. She whispered, "Run."

Never releasing her hand, Keltor ran and took her with him. His long legs made it difficult to keep up, but Azalyn pushed to run faster.

Once they reached the tree cover at the edge of the grounds, next to the crumbling palace walls that still hadn't been rebuilt after the war, they stopped to catch their breaths.

At the flush on Keltor's cheeks and his hair slightly disheveled from the wind, his handsomeness made her ache. "You're beautiful."

He snorted. "Males are not beautiful." Before she could state her case, he reached out and ran his finger down her neck. "The flush on your lavender skin is splotchy."

"Keltor," she growled.

"Let me finish. The patterns remind me of distant galaxies. One day, I want to show you them from a spaceship and maybe even some of the nearest planets. The shape and colors of them are unlike anything you've ever seen. You'd love it, Aza. I know you would."

Her anger eased a fraction. "Now who's planning adventures?"

"A certain female opened my eyes to the world." He reached out and pulled her up against his body. "She has also taught me a thing or two about life outside the palace and how much more there is to see. Learning to be king is important, but I'll never be a good one if I don't know how people are living elsewhere in the world. Meeting you was a gift and one I'm never going to take for granted. I hope to prove it to you. We're going to have amazing adventures, Azalyn. Just wait and see."

While many of her friends said males just told females what they want to hear in order to get them naked, Azalyn believed Keltor was different. His passionate words did something to her heart.

Any lingering hesitations she'd had about her plans for the night vanished. She wasn't going to back down. "Then hurry up and kiss me so I can show you our latest destination. I have a surprise waiting for you once we get there."

"I used to hate surprises, but if you're doing it, then I can't wait to find out what it is." He kissed her once more before releasing her. "Lead on, my lady. The heir to the Kelderan throne is at your command."

It was difficult, but she kept her face serious. "I sure hope so."

"Cheeky female."

He reached out to tickle her side and Azalyn had to bite her lip to keep from squealing. "Stop it, or someone will hear."

Leaning down to her ear, he whispered, "Then I hope our destination is isolated because I want to kiss and tease you without fear of being discovered."

"Oh, it is. Now, hop to it, Prince. See if you can keep up."

Azalyn dashed along the wall to the jagged opening big enough for them to sneak through. Having done it countless times before, she was careful to make as little sound as possible. As expected, Keltor easily followed her lead.

Just the idea that someone as powerful as a prince wanted her made her smile.

Then she remembered what she was determined to do

later. Her family would call her a fool, but Azalyn knew Keltor would do anything to keep her.

And so she was going to offer her body to him later in the evening and allow him to claim her.

Glancing at Keltor, she waited for hesitation or doubt to rush forth like earlier, but it never did. No one accepted her rashness or tendency to defy expected female norms as much as Keltor. She loved him.

And together they would change Keldera for the better.

Picking up her pace, she enjoyed the wind rushing against her skin and the sound of her male right behind her. Tonight would be the start of her future and Azalyn couldn't wait to see what it held.

Chapter Two

Present Day

Prince Keltor tro el Vallen stared down at Azalyn's unconscious body and willed for her to wake up. It'd been over a week since he'd had to watch the dishonorable Tallarian male assault her in front of his eyes. True, her lip had healed and the bruising on her face was fading, but he was far more worried about her internal injuries. Not even the doctors knew what the long-term effects might be.

Even though his political skill had ultimately saved her, it didn't seem enough. And not just because he wanted to hear her voice again, either.

No, the son Keltor hadn't known about until last week was anxious to talk to her, too. The boy was nearly as difficult to read as Keltor's younger brother, Kason. And considering Keltor had no idea how to act around his newly discovered son, they had barely managed anything beyond a few civilities. The boy was more concerned with his research work than what his future entailed as a Kelderan prince and heir to the throne.

Not that Keltor could blame him. After all, Keltor had been young once, too, and had wanted to carve his own path. But Kelzal's heritage had been confirmed—he was

Keltor and Azalyn's son. There was no going back. He would formally announce the boy as his heir in the coming weeks.

After all, Keldera needed reassurance about the succession. Maybe one day Kelzal would recognize the importance of his existence and stop disliking and avoiding him.

As Keltor stared down at the lavender skin of Azalyn's neck, he decided that she might be able to help him sway Kelzal toward accepting his fate.

She just needed to wake up first.

One of Keltor's personal royal guards, Xerlig, cleared his throat and brought him back to the present. The sound meant Keltor should consider leaving for his next task.

Sometimes, all he wanted was for people to speak freely with him, like Azalyn had done when they were younger.

Not wanting to think of what he had easily given up over twenty years ago, Keltor turned toward Xerlig. "Inform those who should know that I'm headed for Kelzal's quarters."

To his credit, the guard didn't so much as blink at the change in Keltor's schedule. "As you wish, your highness."

After one last look at Azalyn's still form, Keltor strode out of the room. Guards walked in front of and behind him, but he paid them little attention. They were as familiar a sight as his own face in the mirror.

When they finally arrived, the guards in front of him stopped to the left side of Kelzal's door and the ones behind him to the right. He looked from one set to another as he said, "I'm going in alone."

Ervan, the highest ranking and most trusted guard assigned to Keltor, clenched his jaw a fraction but remained silent. He would air his grievances in private later; he wouldn't question the prince's authority in front of the others.

While tempted to use the override code to enter Kelzal's

room, Keltor forced himself to press his finger to the chime touchpad.

One second passed and then another. The computer would've identified Keltor via his fingerprint and the thought that Kelzal didn't want to see him sat heavy in his stomach. The boy was much more than security for the Kelderan throne; Keltor wanted to know his son. He'd never admit it aloud, but he desperately wished he could rewind the clock and raise the boy with Azalyn.

To be the father he had always wanted to be, but at age forty-two, had thought would never happen.

However, time travel wasn't possible, and he couldn't change the past. All Keltor could do was try to make a better future for all, starting with Kelzal and Azalyn.

The door finally opened to reveal Kelzal's golden-skinned face. The boy's green eyes met Keltor's dark brown for a second before looking off to the side. "What do you want?"

Since the royal guard already knew about Kelzal's heritage, they didn't ask the boy to speak with respect to the future king.

Keltor gestured inside the room. "May I come in? I have something I wish to discuss."

"You can have five minutes, but then I have to go back to work," Kelzal replied.

"I will take whatever you give me, Kelzal."

The young man met his gaze again before turning away. "Then hurry up. The clock has started."

Keltor moved inside. The instant the door closed, he spoke again. "Have you received everything you need in order to continue your work?"

Kelzal focused on a disassembled device on a table. "Why ask me that? I'm sure you receive reports about my requests."

A snarky comment was on the tip of Keltor's tongue, but

he ignored it. "Data doesn't tell me everything. I'm trying to ensure you're comfortable."

"Odd, considering I'm a prisoner."

"You're here for your protection. While the formal announcement of your heritage is scheduled for a few weeks from now, rumors have started about who you are. Even if you've buried your nose in your work for years, you should still know about the antimonarchy factions. You're now a target, Kelzal. You must accept that your life will never be the same."

Kelzal tossed down the electronic components he'd been studying and met Keltor's gaze. "I never asked for this."

"And neither did I."

Kelzal blinked. "What?"

Since politeness had gotten him nowhere, Keltor was going to be blunt. "I wasn't much younger than you when I wanted to run away with your birth mother and live a normal life. But believe it or not, it was Azalyn who convinced me that leaving would hurt too many people. We don't always ask for certain responsibilities, but if you're anything like me, then you know that sometimes you must give up your own wants for the greater good. For you, the greater good is developing technological research that can eventually save lives. For me, it's keeping the world in one piece. And for better or worse, you're now a part of that."

"But why? You have a brother and he has a pregnant bride. The succession is all but guaranteed."

Keltor raised an eyebrow. "I commend your initiative in gathering that information, but yet again, the data doesn't tell you everything. Kason would never leave his human bride, and she will never leave Jasvar. Not to mention the fact that most Kelderans would never accept a half-human ruler. Unless I'm fortunate enough to have more children, you are key in keeping Keldera from civil war."

"Not true. Disband the traitors and it will ensure peace."

"Unless you have a foolproof plan, that isn't possible right now."

"So if I find a way to disband the threats, I can go back to my old life?"

Keltor had no right to expect anything of Kelzal, but the male's fervent desire to leave twisted his heart a little. "Perhaps. I'm not about to agree to anything until Azalyn wakes up."

The anger in Kelzal's eyes faded to concern. "Is she worse?"

"No."

Nor was she better, but Keltor wasn't about to say that.

Silence stretched. He wanted to ask his son about his work, his childhood, and a whole lot more. He was hungry to learn about the son he'd sired.

And yet, Keltor's father was waiting for him. If the Kelderan king were healthy, he might ignore the meeting. But King Kastor was closer to death every day. While they had never been close, he and Kastor had started to talk more as of late. Considering Keltor would be ascending the throne soon, he needed all the wisdom he could glean from his father while he still had the chance.

Keltor nodded at Kelzal. "I'll let you know if Azalyn's condition changes. Regardless, I want you to have dinner with me later."

"I'm busy."

"Then work harder to make up for the lost time. Dinner is not a request."

Before Kelzal could reply, Keltor exited the room and headed in the direction of his father's quarters. His guards accompanied him.

The end of his conversation may not have gone the way Keltor had envisioned, but he didn't regret it. The young man had a bit of Azalyn's temper and stubbornness, which meant sometimes Keltor would have to be firm.

He only hoped that the next time he saw Kelzal, he could sound a little less like his own father and more like the father Keltor wished to be.

✴ ✴ ✴

Azalyn Rippak Sulani heard the whirring and beeping of the machines. The only problem was that no matter how hard she tried, she couldn't move her body, let alone open her eyes.

Yes, there was also dull pain emanating from her jaw, ribs, and abdomen, but she could handle that. Her injuries would heal.

Lying still and being powerless, on the other hand, was going to drive her crazy.

Of all the possible futures she'd imagined, being trapped in her own body hadn't been one of them.

Enough. It was time to stop whining and do something, anything, to pass the time. Because if she had to count the beeps of her heart one more time, she might go mad.

More than that, if she couldn't wake up, she would never get to talk with her son again.

Thinking of her intelligent, handsome boy, Azalyn decided to forget about opening her eyes and focus on something easier, such as moving a finger.

After who knew how many minutes or even hours had passed, she still hadn't wiggled the digit. There had to be something else she could try.

As she lay there, thinking of a new plan, male voices filled the room.

The first one was a doctor she'd heard earlier in the day. "I'm not sure if this will work, your highness. I'd rather run more tests to ensure the proper dosage."

Azalyn wasn't surprised to hear Keltor's deep voice state, "I trust the Jasvarians and their recommendation. Despite her better judgment, my sister already used herself as a guinea pig so we know it's safe for Kelderans."

Wait, how had they received something from Jasvar? Unless it had been sent via an express delivery pod. But that would've cost Keltor a small fortune.

The doctor interrupted her thoughts. "Ms. Sulani could still be allergic, and it could kill her. Since her files were scrubbed from the Kelderan database, I don't know anything about her medical history."

Keltor's father had erased Azalyn from all Kelderan records, she was sure of it.

Keltor hesitated before replying, "She had no allergies in her youth. Unless she developed new allergies in adulthood, she would want to chance it."

"That's dangerous, your highness."

But exactly what I'd want to do. Damn Keltor and knowing her after all these years.

For a split second, nervousness gripped her heart. If the remedy worked, she would soon be face-to-face with Keltor. He'd probably dismiss the doctor so that he could speak with her alone.

Over the years, she'd thought of plenty of things to say to him. Part of her wanted to scold him for what he'd done, but another part was curious about the male who had orchestrated her rescue.

As much as she hated to think rationally, she and Keltor had been teenagers when her life had come crashing down. If he'd known about Kelzal, she didn't doubt that Keltor would've done right by her. Marriage might've been out of the question, but he would've kept her safe and provided for her.

And yet, she hadn't wanted him to "do right" by her because of a surprise pregnancy. All she'd ever wanted back then was Keltor the male. Her foolish, teenage self had wanted him to want Azalyn for herself, too.

Not that it mattered. Given the state of Keldera and the growing antimonarchy faction, Keltor would never risk taking a commoner with no wealth or advantageous connections as his bride. On top of that, Azalyn had no wish to deal with the platitudes and geniality required of prominent public figures.

The sooner she could tell him that, the better.

Keltor's commanding tone broke through her thoughts. "I will take full responsibility for what happens. I refuse to wait, especially as each day lessens her chance of waking up. Or, so you've said."

"But your highness, Jasvar is a primitive culture compared to our own. I'm not sure we should trust their strange medicinal plants."

Keltor didn't miss a beat. "Prince Kason and Princess Kalahn recommended this medicine. Unless you're questioning the entire royal family—my father would agree with me—then I suggest you give Ms. Sulani her injection."

The doctor's commanding tone was replaced with a complacent one. "Yes, your highness."

While Azalyn had noted Keltor's self-confidence and ease with command briefly back on board the Tallarian ship, when he'd been communicating with her captor via the video comms, it was strange to hear it again in person.

Keltor was indeed a grown male and not the unsure teenager of their youth, who had struggled to find his place in the world.

Something pricked her skin. A few seconds later, a burning flood of fire rushed through her body and forced her to gasp. Without thinking, her eyes popped open.

But she didn't have a chance to revel in that fact. Her entire body screamed in pain. Arching her back against it, she couldn't control her own voice.

As soon as her cries filled the room, a strong, warm hand cupped her cheek. "Just a few more seconds and it will pass, Azalyn," Keltor said.

Tears streamed down her cheeks, and she was about to stop fighting against the pain to welcome oblivion when it vanished as quickly as it had come. Slumping onto the bed, she tried to catch her breath.

Keltor's face appeared above her own. She tried to make her voice work, but all that came out was a croak. He never took his gaze from hers as he said in his infamous calm, princely voice, "Don't try speaking just yet. Let me give you some water."

He removed his hand, and she tried to raise her arm to get his attention. But Azalyn's body was heavy to the point she couldn't do more than raise her fingers a few inches.

The male voice of the doctor filled the space. "May I examine her now?"

Even in her exhausted state, Azalyn easily detected the frustration in the doctor's voice.

"In one second." Keltor gently placed his hand under her head to lift it and put a wet cloth to her lips. "If you can manage it, take as much water from the cloth as you can."

Once a few drops of water slid down her throat, she met Keltor's eyes to say she was done.

However, the fierceness she saw would've made her blink in any other circumstance. Keltor had to fully trust the doctor in the room to reveal so much emotion.

Though why he directed it at her, Azalyn had no idea. If anything, she expected him to be angry at her for keeping their son's existence a secret for over two decades.

Kelzal. She wanted to ask about her son since he hadn't

visited once while she'd been somewhat conscious. Was he okay? Had the Tallarians seen through the threat and killed him? Had everything she'd tried to do been for naught?

The prince murmured, "Kelzal is safe, as is the Barren named Vala. While Vala has already gone to Jasvar, I'll bring Kelzal by later, after you've had a chance to rest."

Vala was Azalyn's friend and had also been a prisoner onboard the Tallarian ship.

Her heart thumped a little slower at knowing both Vala and Kelzal were safe.

Studying Keltor's eyes, she wondered how he could still read her expressions after so many years. He had always been good with languages. Maybe body language was one of his talents as well.

Keltor finally removed the cloth from her mouth and laid her head back on the bed. Once the prince turned away from her, the doctor stepped forward and began feeling and prodding parts of her body.

She paid the doctor little attention. Her gaze lingered on Keltor's back and broad shoulders. At least, until the doctor pressed against her lower abdomen and she winced at the stabbing pain. If she could talk, she probably would've screamed.

The doctor ceased his movements. "Your womb is still tender and swollen. I must run some more tests. I'm afraid your visit must conclude here, your highness."

Keeping his back to her and the doctor, Keltor replied, "I will return soon."

As he walked toward the exit, Azalyn whispered, "Keltor."

His gait paused a split second before he opened the door and left Azalyn alone with the doctor.

Keltor's exit shouldn't bother her. She was nothing to him, and he should be nothing to her.

But even if she'd admit it to no one else, she'd reveled in his gentle touch and protectiveness. Not to mention that at least some of their familiarity from their former years seemed to linger.

She wanted to frown. *No.* She wouldn't wish for anything more than a formal relationship with the prince. She'd been a fool once, and she wanted nothing to do with males. Well, beyond helping her own son.

Azalyn most definitely wouldn't fall for the charms of a prince again. Given how close Keldera sat to a civil war between the pro- and antimonarchy factions, Keltor must find a bride with desirable political connections. Maybe even a female with a wealthy family willing to help fund military campaigns would be acceptable, especially if matters devolved into war.

In other words, not her.

As the doctor called in a few nurses, Azalyn listened to everything they said. For the present, her health was all that mattered. She would heed any and all of their advice. Only then could she see her son and discover a new path for her life. Because as long as Kelzal remained on Keldera, so would she. Her dream of starting over on a new colony was no longer an option.

Chapter Three

Keltor half-listened to one of his councilors as the male recited the daily briefing. While he never enjoyed the dry reports about taxes collected, new diplomatic treaties signed, or the state of agriculture on the planet, Keltor's mind hadn't wandered during a session since his mid-twenties, when his father had asked for him to take over the meetings and pass on only what was relevant to the king.

And yet, all he could think about was the feel of Azalyn's soft hair under his fingertips and her green eyes as he'd placed the wet cloth to her mouth. The pain and exhaustion he'd seen in her gaze had flared something inside him. All he'd wanted to do was hand off all his duties and take care of the brave female who'd endured the Tallarians beating her in order to protect her son's life.

Or, rather, *their* son's life.

To think his father had dismissed Azalyn as an unworthy commoner when Keltor had recently confronted him about sending her away decades ago. But she was braver than most of the people inside his father's inner circle, he was certain.

Even if only for a short while, he longed to see Azalyn awake and out to challenge any who'd face her.

One of the senior councilors, Hinvel Mayta, cleared his

throat. "Your highness?"

Keltor met his former tutor's face. Thirty years ago, Hinvel would've scolded Keltor for his behavior.

Instead, Hinvel danced around him carefully, as did all the councilors. They never truly spoke their minds unless Keltor specifically requested it. They saw it as a sign of respect. Keltor saw it as one of the many layers of isolation in his life.

He never understood why people dreamed of becoming a prince or even a king. Royal life was secluded, full of duty, and usually devoid of laughter. His mother had been an exception to the final point, but she'd died younger than she should have.

Only Azalyn had brought it back for a short while.

Not wanting to think about the happy times of his childhood and adolescence, Keltor noted the time and said, "Send me the reports and I'll reach out if I have any questions. Unless anything requires my immediate attention?"

"No, your highness," Hinvel murmured.

"Good. Then you must excuse me, Councilors. I just remembered there is a matter I must attend to straight away."

The instant he stood, everyone in the room bowed their heads. Not one of them voiced a complaint.

Keltor never thought he'd ever miss his sister Kalahn's outspoken and reckless nature. But with both his siblings currently living as part of the new colony on Jasvar, Keltor had only his father to call family inside the palace. And since his father was gravely ill, not to mention he and Keltor had never been close, there was only one person on Keldera he could seek out and talk with freely.

And Keltor needed to talk about Azalyn so that he could move on. Only then would he regain his wits and be able to focus on his upcoming coronation. Or, rather, he needed Azalyn out of his thoughts so that he could focus on finding a suitable bride. Because if he didn't, his father would never sign the abdication papers and make him king.

The irony of the situation wasn't lost on him. Keltor had never wanted to be king, but now he was doing everything he could to ensure it happened.

He moved to the door. Upon exiting the advisory room, Keltor's guards took their usual positions in front and behind him. Keltor stated, "East Garden," signaling they were to depart.

While the East Garden would always be special to Keltor since it had been his mother's favorite place, it served another purpose. The isolated area allowed him to meet with the only male he called a friend—Veljan Ranna.

And Veljan always tended to the East Garden at this time of day.

After five minutes of going down one corridor and then another, Keltor finally stepped into the bright, open space of the East Garden. Thanks to the clear, glass-like ceiling overhead that allowed the Kelderan sunshine to stream through, the space was warm and inviting.

Keltor stopped. He motioned toward a side door as he ordered, "Wait for me in there."

Since the material overhead was nearly indestructible and the entire garden was well-defended and reinforced, the guards left via the only other exit to the space. They would continue to monitor the area, but wouldn't listen in to whatever conversation Keltor had with his friend.

Walking around the perimeter, he admired the flowers in bloom as well as the bushes trimmed into the shapes of animals. As a boy, he'd spent many hours with his mother in the garden. She'd taught him as much as a mother could teach a little boy about horticulture.

Then she'd died during the Brevkan wars, and it'd taken Keltor many years to set foot inside the East Garden again.

Azalyn had been the one to convince him to visit the garden once more, to honor his mother's memory.

He'd been back at least once a week ever since.

The main door opened, signaling that his friend Veljan was as punctual as always.

Turning around, Keltor walked up to the lavender-skinned male about his own age with magenta eyes and silver hair. "Are any apprentice gardeners with you today?"

Veljan shook his head. "No. They're either spending the day training in a classroom or assisting one of their mentors."

"Computer," Keltor began, "engage level ten security lock on the East Garden."

The computer replied in a flat voice, "Prince Keltor's voice pattern confirmed and protocols implemented. The East Garden is now secure."

Veljan raised an eyebrow. "It's one of those days, then. What's wrong now?"

Most Kelderans would gasp at Veljan's casual nature, but he and Keltor had first met as boys over thirty years ago, when Veljan had merely been following his father, the royal head gardener, around on his duties. Over time, Veljan had not only replaced his father as royal head gardener but had also become Keltor's only friend and confidant. While he would never be as open with anyone as he'd been with Azalyn two decades ago, Keltor was closer to Veljan than to his own brother, Kason. "Don't act ignorant. You know what's going on."

Veljan motioned toward the center of the garden, where there was a complex maze constructed of hedges. "Given how long it took you to get over Azalyn the first time, I wasn't sure if bringing her up would be a good idea."

The pair of them walked toward the maze. "I have every advisor and staff member tiptoeing around Azalyn's presence and all but pretending she doesn't exist. Don't do the same, Veljan."

"Is that an order or a request?" Keltor glared and Veljan chuckled. "I couldn't resist. Maybe one day I'll tire of teasing your princely self, but today is not that day."

Clasping his hands behind his back, Keltor asked, "What the hell am I supposed to do, Veljan? She's lying in a hospital bed because of me. And now her dream of living on Jasvar won't ever happen, either. She will forever be a target. I trust my brother to watch over her on Jasvar, but the trip to the other planet would be too dangerous. She must remain on Keldera. Inside the palace grounds is the safest place for her."

"The palace is a big place."

He narrowed his eyes. "That isn't the point."

Veljan shrugged. "I'm not sure you're ready for my complete honesty on the subject."

"We're the same age, so stop acting like you are so much older and wiser than me."

"Ah, but I am wiser when it comes to matters of the heart."

Warning bells rang inside his head, but Keltor pushed past them. "As long as you don't insult the female, just tell me what you're holding back."

Veljan tilted his head. "All right, then. Here's my question—Do you still love her?"

Keltor replied quickly, "No."

"Your hurried, monosyllabic response is telling."

"Veljan," he growled.

"Well, the real question is whether that's your diplomatic answer, knowing what might happen to Keldera if you took a merchant's daughter as a bride—supposing she wanted you—or is it the truth?"

Stopping in his tracks, Keltor stared at the top of the

fountain poking up from the center of the maze. "Honestly? I long ago gave up loving her. Until recently, I had thought she'd run away from me with another male. And even when my brother told me the truth that he had chased her away, working under our father's orders, there was no rush of tender feelings. There was only guilt and regret, which hasn't dissipated."

That was a half-truth. Not even Keltor was brave enough to admit the rush of heat he'd felt at touching Azalyn's skin. But attraction didn't equate affection. Nor did it erase every potential problem that would arise should he even think about pursuing her.

Because if given the chance, he would like to kiss her again to simply feel something resembling emotion. But that would never be an option.

Veljan placed a hand on Keltor's shoulder. "And that, my friend, is your answer."

"How is that any kind of answer?" He put up a hand. "No, don't elaborate. It's moot anyway. You know I have to find a worthy bride with a family that can help stave off a civil war, through either connections or resources."

"She was adopted by the Sulanis."

The Sulanis were tied for the richest merchant family on Keldera. "Putting aside the fact Azalyn probably hates me for what happened in the past, the head of the Sulanis has his eyes set on the colony on Jasvar. The new enterprise will stretch their resources."

"Perhaps. But it sounds like an excuse to not even try."

"I appreciate what you're trying to do, but in the best interest of Keldera, I must find a bride with a family already offering to support me. That will help ease the transition of power and hopefully allay fears of instability. I may have one heir, but additional ones would better secure the succession."

"You can secure the secession and still allow yourself to love, Keltor. Being royal does not mean one has to live a life where duty extends to marriage and the bedchamber."

An image of Azalyn's naked body below him, as she blushed and revealed herself for the first time, flashed into his mind. He quickly shut a door on the memory. "Keldera was a different place when my father married my mother. No looming wars, there was peace, and the planet overwhelmingly supported the monarchy. He could afford to take a bride he loved."

"If you say so. But regardless of whom you marry, you need to resolve your guilt concerning Azalyn. Only then do I think you'll be able to find a bride with open eyes."

"Are you sure you're a gardener and not a soothsayer?" he asked dryly.

Veljan grinned. "That would make me the soon-to-be king's soothsayer. The 'royal soothsayer' has a nice ring to it." Keltor shook his head, but Veljan continued before he could speak. "Just don't push her away, or your son, and see what happens with them. You've sacrificed much of your life to being the heir to the throne. Don't be afraid to do something for yourself, even if it only results in friendship."

He gave a derisive laugh. "My son dislikes me, and my former lover was fleeing the planet to put distance between us. I'm not sure they want anything to do with me."

"Then show them the male only your sister and I have had the chance to see. It may not work out, I accept that. But don't let the opportunity for others to grow close to you slip through your fingers."

"You are far more optimistic about life than me. I'll do my duty, take care of her, set her up, and then only visit Azalyn when necessary. After that, I'll meet as many of the females on the list crafted by my councilors as I can and select one."

Veljan shrugged. "As long as I still have my job and a safe place to train my fledglings, then do whatever you wish. But just know that if you select a female who does nothing but bat her eyes at you and lacks a brain, you lose the right to complain to me."

Keltor eyed his friend. "It's hard to believe you would give up so easily considering you spent years lecturing me on true love and finding the female who could change my world forever."

"It's your life, Keltor. Do as you wish."

He sensed Veljan was holding back his true thoughts. However, he had another meeting and couldn't afford to linger in the garden any longer. "I must go. I'm afraid our weekly recreation room challenge session will have to wait until everything is cleared up with Azalyn and Kelzal."

Veljan waved a hand in dismissal. "No problem. I have a new flower hybrid idea I want to work on, and I always do my best work when I seclude myself in a lab for a week."

"If flowers could transform into females, you'd probably take one as a bride."

"If only that were a possibility. But, sadly, magic is but a myth. My plants are my family."

While Veljan's tone was lighthearted, Keltor knew it was an act. The female he'd secretly loved for years had joined the colony on Jasvar. "Then tend to them. I'll send a message when I'm free again." Keltor raised his voice. "Computer, end security protocols and unlock the door."

"Action complete."

"Until later, Royal Head Gardener," Keltor stated.

After freeing his face from any emotion, he exited the garden and headed toward one of the meeting rooms. The sooner he finished his duties, the sooner he could check on Azalyn again. Because once she woke up fully and could talk, her disdain would make it easier for him to do his duty and forget about the wild, untamed female he'd once loved.

✵ ✵ ✵

Azalyn opened her eyes and blinked against the lights. She didn't know when she'd dozed off, but at least she'd woken up again. On top of that, the pain hadn't worsened, either, which she hoped was a good sign.

Glancing to the side, she saw Kelzal's head bowed over something in his hands. For a second, she contented herself with watching his deft fingers play with the electrical components. It wasn't hard to imagine him taking apart everything he could find as a boy and attempting to put it back together.

Not wanting to think about all the years her son had lived without her, Azalyn pasted a smile on her face and said, "Hello, Kelzal."

At her voice, Kelzal's green eyes shot to hers. "Are you in pain? Do I need to call the doctor?"

She barely resisted the urge to reach out and take her son's hand. But considering he'd barely begun to talk to her before all hell had broken loose on the Tallarian ship, she wouldn't risk spooking him. "I'm fine, Kelzal. What are you working on?"

Placing the components on a side table, he replied, "It's not important. Taking apart and reassembling things helps to clear my mind."

Silence stretched. Azalyn usually had no issue keeping a conversation going, but she was afraid of pushing Kelzal away. The thought of never seeing him again now that she'd found him made her stomach twist.

Kelzal's voice finally echoed in the small room. "He's going to acknowledge me in a few weeks."

"Keltor?"

He nodded. "And he won't listen to me. I don't want to be a prince. It's hard enough for me to talk with people. Being diplomatic is impossible. I like to speak the truth."

She sighed. "I wish I could change your new path, but I can't, Kelzal. Word has already spread of your existence. You'll forever be a target of our enemies and the palace is the safest place for you."

He stood and turned his back to her. Holding her breath, she waited to see if he'd leave.

As soon as he spoke, she started breathing again. "Is that why you gave me up? To protect me from the life of a royal?"

Azalyn valued honesty above all else. She wouldn't give anything else to her son. "Yes and no. I didn't even know I was pregnant when Keltor's brother and father chased me away. When I discovered that I was with child, all I could think about was sparing you the heartbreak I'd endured. Raising you myself would've brought on too many questions. The best life for you was with a family who wanted a child of their own, a family with no connections to the royal family."

"And so you gave me to the Burrig family."

"Yes. By all accounts, they loved you, Kelzal. And they raised you in a way I never could have."

A few beats paused before Kelzal asked, "Did you ever intend to contact me?"

Emotion choked her throat, but she pushed passed it. "No. Not because I didn't want to, but I didn't want to risk the life you'd built for yourself."

"And yet in the end, none of it mattered."

At his emotionless reply, tears prickled her eyes. She might be losing him. "Kelzal, look at me."

He turned to face her but kept his gaze averted. He seemed to do that whenever strong emotions were involved.

Keeping her voice gentle but firm, she said, "I did what I thought was best. By the time I realized how much I wanted to raise you myself, it was too late. You're my only child, Kelzal. And if the doctor's prognosis is correct, you will always remain so."

His gaze flickered to hers. "What are you talking about?"

"The doctor thinks the damage to my womb is too great and that I'll probably never have another child. Since I gave you up for adoption and by all rights never had children, it means I can be sent away to live with The Barren now."

Kelzal frowned. "In most cases, when it happens later in life because of illness or injury, females are usually granted waivers."

"In most cases, yes. However, if the prince wishes to banish me from his life, he could refuse one. So while I know all of this is painful and you have every right to be angry with me, all I ask for is a chance. Because I may not remain at the palace for long and I want to make the most of what time we do have."

Picking up a small piece from the dissembled device on the side table, Kelzal answered, "I don't think he'll send you away. He came to visit several times while I was sitting with you, before you regained consciousness. Even though I'm not the best at gauging emotions, I know the look of hunger. All people have it for something. And he had it for you."

Shaking her head, she answered, "I doubt it. If anything, I'll be an obstacle to him finding a bride. The rumors say he's to pick one by the time of his coronation."

"Then perhaps I was wrong. But if he tries to send you away, I'll intervene. He needs me more than I need him, after all. I will only stay here if you can, too."

Azalyn tried to think of how to respond to Kelzal's statement when the door slid open and Keltor walked into the room.

✵ ✵ ✵

Keltor had expected to find Azalyn asleep. Instead, not only was she awake with concern in her eyes, Kelzal stood not far from her side.

His first instinct was to demand an explanation about what the boy had said to upset Azalyn. After all, she was recovering, and no matter how strong of a curiosity burned inside Kelzal, he should allow Azalyn to heal first before bombarding her with questions or tugging on her guilt for giving up the boy.

Then he noticed Kelzal's fingers tapping against his thigh and the male's averted gaze. Add in the boy's tense shoulders, and he was upset about something. The question was why. He dreaded to think it was because of him.

Kelzal turned toward him, and the male's gaze turned fierce. "You should leave."

Since he knew how the conversation would go based on earlier, Keltor focused on Azalyn. "What's going on?"

"I think—"

Kelzal cut her off. "If you stay, you might send her away. So, leave. I'll look after her. Since I'm inside the palace, you shouldn't have an objection."

"You're not making any sense, Kelzal," Keltor said slowly. "Without the facts, I can't respond properly."

Azalyn jumped in. "Kelzal, I need to talk to Keltor alone. Can you come back in a little while? For dinner?"

Kelzal grunted. "I've already been ordered to have dinner with *him.*"

"We'll eat together, here. I think that's a reasonable compromise," Keltor replied.

After a few more seconds of the boy glaring, looking away, and glaring again, Kelzal exited the room. Without thinking, Keltor muttered, "He has your temperament."

"Some of yours as well, if you look close enough."

Taking a deep breath, Keltor met Azalyn's green eyes. Whatever emotion he'd seen before had vanished. "Why does he think I'm going to send you away, Azalyn?" When she didn't answer, he moved to her bedside. Even though she didn't back down from his gaze, the heart rate monitor on the other side told him his presence had an effect. He only hoped it wasn't out of fear. "We once pledged honesty to each other, Aza. If nothing else, can we do that again?"

For a second, Azalyn said nothing. While it could only be a few moments of silence, his eyes drifted to the curve of her neck. While he noticed a small scar that hadn't been there when they were younger, as well as a few more lines in her skin, it was as graceful as always.

He wondered if it was as warm and soft as he remembered. Just as he raised a finger, Azalyn turned her head and broke the spell. "Honesty it is. The doctor thinks I might be infertile now, which means you could send me to the Barren if you wish."

He was going to have to visit the doctor and find out more later. "Why do you think I'll send you away?"

"Because we both know that while Kelzal's existence at least secures the succession, only you taking a worthy bride will help tame fears about instability. A male with a family to protect will do whatever's necessary to keep the peace. And no bride is going to want a reminder of your past, and the mother of the heir, living in close quarters."

He raised an eyebrow. "You seem to think you know how I'll act."

"If there's one thing I've learned over the years from the snippets of news and announcements I've read about you, it's that duty is the epitome of your existence. If you weren't about to risk taking a mere shopkeeper's daughter as your bride twenty-odd years ago, then it sure as hell isn't going to happen now when the stakes are even higher."

The right thing to do would be to say Azalyn was correct; duty mattered most to him.

However, as her cheeks and neck flushed with anger, nothing mattered but reaching out a finger and gently running it along her jaw. She had such liveliness, and that was sorely lacking in his life.

She sucked in a breath at his ministrations, and he smiled. "I see that tracing your skin still works as the best distraction." He moved his finger to her neck and traced the shape of one of her markings. "May I talk now?"

Gulping, her voice was still angry when she whispered, "Talk but don't touch. You long ago lost that privilege."

It took every ounce of strength he possessed to remove his hand. Skin-to-skin contact was something he yearned for but rarely had. Unlike most males in his position, Keltor didn't believe in dalliances. At first, he'd told himself it was to prevent scandal. But now, he was starting to think it was because he yearned to touch Azalyn's skin and no one else's.

He nearly frowned at that thought. Azalyn may have been one of his potential destined brides, but after more than twenty years, the pull should've faded.

When Azalyn raised her brows, Keltor focused on the present. Thinking about the past could wait. "You've probably heard the rumors that I'm to take a bride by the time of my coronation. But what you don't know is that I will be making the final choice and no one else."

"If you're about to say that you're going to risk everything and take me as yours, then just stop. I've been swayed by your words before, and I'm not falling for it again."

"I didn't say I had selected you." She opened her mouth, but he beat her to it. "But know that you being safe and involved in Kelzal's life is one of my top priorities. And since words matter so little, I'll have an official, signed document delivered to you later today. There's little I can promise you to make up for what happened in the past, but a safe life with our son is one of them."

"While I appreciate that, Kelzal and I would better enjoy some freedom. I understand the possible danger to both of us, but having our own section of the palace, where not even you have access, would go a long way toward showing me that you're serious. It would also give me a chance to help Kelzal adjust. He's not good with change and needs a new routine established as soon as possible."

"For someone who had only known Kelzal for a short time, you seem to know quite a bit."

She squared her shoulders. "I kept an eye on him from afar. He may not have been mine to claim as blood, but I wanted to ensure his safety."

Before he could stop the words, he murmured, "And yet you were willing to leave him in order to put as much distance as you could from me."

She sighed. "What would you have me do, Keltor? Watching you take another as a bride was something I didn't want to witness. Not because I'm still pining for you. No, I'm not a fool. But to see you have what we could've had constantly taunting me on view screens and ad billboards was something I didn't want to endure. Jasvar was my fresh start. It's gone now, but as long as I have Kelzal, then what you do with your life matters little to me."

Spouting about duty was all well and good when Keltor was talking with Veljan. However, with Azalyn in the room, everything else seemed to vanish.

Before he could convince himself of why not to do it, Keltor leaned close until their faces were a few inches apart. "You're lying."

"Am I?"

"Your eye twitches when you lie, and it's doing it now."

To her credit, Azalyn didn't raise a hand to still the small tic. "I'm not the lovesick seventeen-year-old girl who was swayed by your intelligence and good looks. I've changed, as have you. Don't pretend to know me and my idiosyncrasies. Because we're strangers, Keltor. Just as it should be."

He most definitely didn't like her referring to him as a stranger. "I still say you're lying."

She tilted her head. "Oh? Then prove it, your *highness*."

There were a million reasons why Keltor should walk away and wash his hands of Azalyn. He'd hurt her, and he had no idea if he could ever make up for that pain. In addition, she wasn't born and bred royalty or even a politician's daughter. She'd always speak her mind and push boundaries. The public, not to mention the councilors, wouldn't accept her.

And yet as her hot breath danced across his lips, all he could think about was tasting her wildness. With Azalyn, there wouldn't be any platitudes or false words to mollify a prince. No, she'd let him know what she was feeling and speak her mind, no matter if it'd upset him or not.

A long-buried desire bubbled to the surface. Veljan was the only person to speak freely with him, and Keltor craved more of the directness, so much more.

So for the first time in years, Keltor forgot about being a prince and taking care of the planet. He cupped Azalyn's face and did what he wanted—he kissed her.

Chapter Four

Azalyn had wanted Keltor to both kiss her and to walk out the door. Both outcomes had downsides, but him leaving would be the easiest path for all.

But damn the prince, he took her face in his warm hands and closed the distance between their lips.

She should be angry at him. Abandoning her, all but forcing her to give up their child, and a life of near-exile all traced back to Keltor claiming her virginity and then letting her go.

However, as his firm lips moved against hers, years of pent-up desire rushed forth. More than that, Keltor's taste was familiar. One she'd dreamt of for years before the memories had grown hazy.

His tongue swiped between her lips, and she nearly moaned. While he was more confident and demanding than the last time they'd kissed, she rather liked it. Keltor was no longer a teenage boy. No, he was a grown male.

He took the kiss deeper, with firm strokes and nibbles on her bottom lip. Giving in to the moment, she raised a hand and tentatively touched his hair. The action spurred a growl that sent a shiver down her spine, in a good way.

The rational thing would be to break the kiss and push him away. She had enough complications in her life with

Kelzal.

Then his hand ran over her shoulder and down to her hip. Her skin came alive at his touch. She wanted to feel his skin against hers.

She tried moving so that she could press her chest against him, but a sharp pain erupted in her lower belly and raced through her body. She couldn't help but cry out.

Keltor retreated a few inches and searched her eyes. "What's wrong? Should I call the doctor?"

She took a deep breath, and the pain eased a fraction. "No, I just need to take it easy."

As they stared into one another's eyes, Azalyn willed for Keltor to kiss her again. She wanted her last kiss with him to be free of pain or awkwardness.

Or, if she were completely honest, she wanted to glimpse the old wildness they'd once shared.

However, Keltor stood, putting more space between them. "I'm sorry, Aza. I was selfish. You need to heal. I'll have a nurse check on you right after I leave."

Before she could say a word, Keltor strode out of the room.

The door closed and Azalyn tried to process what had just happened. For a brief second, she'd glimpsed the un-restrained male that was Keltor. Not the prince, not the heir to the throne, but just a hungry male. Whatever else might've changed, one thing was for sure—she was still at-tracted to him.

Yes, that had to be the explanation for her actions—at-traction. There was no logical way to have a future together.

Even if he earned her trust again, which would be a huge undertaking, Keltor would never risk the safety of Keldera. And even if he did, Azalyn would never be able to live with herself if Keltor choosing her resulted in war. The antimon-archy faction grew in numbers by the day and would love nothing more than an opportunity to strike and take down the royal family.

Which now included Kelzal.

No. Kissing Keltor once out of curiosity was fine. But it couldn't happen again. She had a son to protect.

The difficulty would be in keeping her distance and refusing him if he ever tried to kiss her again.

If, and it was a big if, Keltor ever did decide he wanted her, consequences be damned, it was going to take every bit of stubbornness she possessed to ward him off.

But ward him off she would. She'd given up Kelzal and all responsibility once. It was time to put her son first and be the best mother she could. That now meant working toward a peaceful future on Keldera, and that meant helping Keltor to find a bride who could make that happen.

✹ ✹ ✹

Keltor wished he was the sort of male who merely sought out a willing Barren—one of the infertile females who sometimes helped around the palace—when his body demanded sexual gratification.

But since he wasn't, he had spent the last fifteen minutes in his private recreation room, wrestling a computer-generated opponent. In the past, exercise had almost always worked to tame his lust. He found it more fulfilling than pleasuring himself.

However, his hard cock hadn't softened at all. Even as he tossed his opponent across the simulated arena, all Keltor could think about was the opponent morphing into Azalyn and him taking her against the wall.

Her taste had been as sweet as he'd remembered, if not sweeter. Add in her older boldness and fuller form compared to when she was younger, and he'd nearly come from a kiss. His body still wanted Azalyn regardless of consequences, that was for sure.

His opponent raced toward him, and Keltor stepped to the side before jumping the hard-light hologram from behind. A swift tug and they both tumbled to the ground. The opponent managed to flip Keltor over, but then Keltor swung his legs up, wrapped them around the hologram's neck, and reversed their positions. After a few seconds, the opponent yielded.

"Computer, end program," Keltor stated.

The opponent and arena faded to the gray walls of his private recreation room.

Keltor retrieved a towel from a hidden compartment and wiped the sweat from his body. Thanks to the tight trousers worn by all Kelderan males of higher status, each movement caused friction against his cock that made him groan.

"Get a grip on yourself, Keltor. You're a male of forty-two, not a boy of eighteen."

But as tended to happen, his cock didn't care about reason, let alone age.

Since he had to go over a few documents before his scheduled dinner with Kelzal and Azalyn, Keltor was going to have to take care of himself. He didn't have time for his hormones to cool on their own.

Heading into his cleaning room, Keltor stripped and engaged the spray chamber. As he stepped under the hot cleaning solution, he closed his eyes and gripped his pulsing cock. He stroked once and hissed at the sensation.

Drawing on the memory of Azalyn's soft body under his fingers, he increased his pace. Soon his tame memory turned into her on all fours, arching her back as he thrust into her from behind. Unlike his few other experiences, she didn't act reserved around him because he was a prince. In his vision, she moaned for him to take her harder.

He'd barely began to play out his fantasy when his balls tightened and he came. Pleasure wracked his body to the point it was almost painful.

Spent, Keltor braced himself against the spray room wall.

Not for the first time he wondered how fate could've given him a shopkeeper's daughter as a potential destined bride. He'd fought the truth before, but Kelzal's existence proved the point. Very few females could bear the royal line a child because of a genetic defect. Only a potential destined bride had the ability.

However, most of the population didn't know that little secret. And he'd never been brave enough to tell Azalyn the truth since he'd simply wanted her to want Keltor for himself.

He wondered if he had done so, maybe things might have turned out differently. She may have never given herself to him, and then she'd have lived the life she should have done, without him.

Curling his fingers into a fist, he allowed anger and guilt to flow through his body at the thought. Azalyn had been his brief glimpse of happiness. And, he had a feeling, his only chance to have it once again.

The only question was whether he would risk it all to claim her as he should've done twenty-three years ago, or did he take a bride to ease political tensions and never experience the passion he sensed lying within Azalyn.

After all, every royal had more than one potential destined bride. While he hadn't found one among more politically suitable candidates yet, he was certain one existed. Kelzal might be his heir, but the first rule of being in line to the throne was to have several possible successors, to project stability to the people of Keldera.

When his cleaning solution ceased spraying, Keltor exited the room and prepared himself for both his official duties and his upcoming dinner with Azalyn. He could at least enjoy one meal with his pseudo-family before diving back into official duties. After all, he had a rich, well-connected female to welcome to the palace the following day.

Not that he had high hopes for the woman, given what he knew of her father. But as always, duty called.

✲ ✲ ✲

Kelzal Burrig put aside his latest project, an undetectable transmitter that could bypass palace security, and paced the room.

He was due to leave and have dinner with his birth mother and the prince in the next few minutes. But as he walked the length of his quarters and turned back again, he had something more pressing on his mind than even how behind he was in his research.

A few weeks ago, he wouldn't have thought twice about sharing his deepest, dearest secret. But with the possibility looming over his head of his birth mother being sent away and Kelzal losing the chance to better know the female who had given him life, he was starting to think Azalyn needed to hear the full truth.

Because while she'd known and kept track of his existence, there was more to it.

Per Kelderan custom, females who decide upon giving their child up for adoption were denied both ultrasounds and to hear fetal heartbeats. And in Azalyn's case, the birth had been difficult, and she'd been unconscious during her surgery to bring Kelzal into the world.

Except it had been more than just Kelzal—Azalyn had carried twins.

During that time, her new foster family—the Sulanis—had made a decision about Kelzal's twin sister. She'd been given to a distant Sulani relative and continued to live with them to this day, never wiser as to the true identity of their mother. Kelzal wasn't sure of the reason why Azalyn had never been told of her second child, but no doubt the head of the Sulani family had his reasons, as he always did.

While Kelzal had never been able to find a picture of his birth mother, let alone her name, his sister had sought him out a few years ago.

She hadn't known Azalyn's details, either, but her adopted family had explained to her on her eighteenth birthday that she had a twin brother and had shared Kelzal's information. Strange that he had never received the information; maybe his personality and tendency to speak the truth had made the Sulanis wary to share it.

Regardless, the first meeting with his sister was a memory he thought about often. He hadn't believed her, of course, since she'd had lavender skin and golden hair and looked nothing like him. Granted, fraternal twins often didn't look alike, but Kelzal never trusted a statement until it could be proven.

And once the DNA test had done so, he'd tried his best to form a relationship with his sister, Toralyn. Kelzal had a hard time reading social cues or emotions, but Toralyn didn't seem to mind. She'd simply loved having a sibling. Over the last four years, they'd shared monthly video chats, and his next scheduled one was due in two days.

Hence trying to find a way around the palace's security. Kelzal didn't want to be a prince or to be forced into a political world that would cause anxiety as he struggled to determine who was truthful or deceitful. But to force that life on Toralyn would be even worse. She was female and princesses were often treated as property, to be married off and form alliances.

His smiling, bold sister didn't deserve that life.

The decision to keep Toralyn's existence a secret should be an easy one. However, Azalyn had risked her life back on the Tallarian ship to protect Kelzal. Not only that, she had nearly died as a result. To not tell her about her other child sat heavy in Kelzal's stomach. He would always love his adopted parents, but they were both dead. Azalyn might be his only chance to have a family again and keeping secrets wasn't the best start to building a relationship.

His notescreen chimed its alarm, telling him it was time to leave for dinner.

As he made his way toward Azalyn's hospital room, Kelzal made his decision. He'd tell Azalyn and only her about his sister's existence, but she first had to promise to keep it from the prince. Kelzal refused to give that male another pawn to use in his game.

Some might say his hatred was overblown. But he'd seen his fair share of females tossed out of families because of one dalliance with a male that had led to an unwanted pregnancy. Even employers overlooked the qualifications of such females and focused only on what was considered disgraceful in Kelderan culture.

Kelzal hadn't been aware of the problem until one interview several years ago. The female had been intelligent and easily the most qualified for the position. So when she'd cried at the news of being selected, even he had sensed something was wrong. Her story had come out about her illegitimate son and her struggle to find work.

After that, Kelzal had dedicated his tech firm to hiring qualified females, regardless of what had happened personally in their pasts. SHIELD Tech was one of the few companies that even considered females for higher-level positions. From Kelzal's point of view, genitals or gender made little difference. Skill and ability were all that mattered. So if other firms were too ignorant to realize that, it was his gain. And since everyone decried him a genius, SHIELD Tech allowed him to do what he wished as long as it increased profits.

Arriving outside Azalyn's room, he pressed his finger to the touchpad scanner. He was going to do everything he could to drive the prince out of the room so that he could talk with his birth mother. Because he wanted to share his secret with her. Azalyn had experienced a lot of hardship in her life, partially because of him. He wanted her to smile since a smile usually signaled happiness. Maybe showing his sister's image and talking about her would trigger the positive response in Azalyn.

Given everything she'd done to keep him from being raised a prince, it was the least he could do.

Chapter Five

Azalyn awoke at the sound of the door chime. The computer stated, "Kelzal Burrig."

"Allow entry," she answered with a yawn.

The door opened, and Azalyn admired the tall form of her son. It was still strange to think of him as such, but he was. At least something good had come out of her time with Keltor all those years ago.

Kelzal looked around the room before he spoke, "Where's the prince?"

"He sent his apologies and will be an hour late."

Pulling up a chair, Kelzal whispered, "Secure the room against any entry."

As her son tapped his fingers against his thigh and kept his gaze trained behind him, she didn't hesitate to say, "Computer, secure room. Only a level ten override can enter."

Level ten meant only the worst-case scenario—such as an invasion or palace takeover—and would allow anyone, even Prince Keltor, from opening the door.

"Understood." The computer paused a second before stating, "Room is secure."

Sitting up in her bed, Azalyn said, "Tell me what's wrong, Kelzal." He continued to drum his fingers, but didn't respond. She softened her voice, "Kelzal."

His green eyes finally met her own. "I want to tell you a secret."

Happiness bubbled inside her chest. While Kelzal wanting to confide in her was a small thing, it signaled he was starting to trust her. She might never be able to get back his childhood, but she wanted as much time with him as she could in the future. "I'm pretty good at keeping them, as you well know."

It was risky to joke about giving him up for adoption and hiding it from Keltor, but Azalyn wasn't going to hide who she was. She'd had more than enough years of doing that and was through with it.

Nodding, Kelzal whispered, "I know. But this is one you must keep from *him*. Can you do that?"

"I wish you'd give Keltor a chance."

"That is not what I wish to discuss. If you can't keep something from him, then I'll wait until you can. Because I have a feeling he will use this knowledge against you and hurt you once more."

Azalyn sat a little taller. "That's going too far, Kelzal. Keltor has dedicated his life to protecting Keldera, no matter the cost. We all make mistakes in life, and believe me I know that more than anyone else, but to judge someone solely on one mistake is wrong."

"I don't disagree."

She frowned. "You aren't making any sense."

"To judge only one party for a mistake that involves two is wrong. However, the prince was the one to cause you pain and hardship. There's a difference."

Not for the first time Azalyn wished she'd had a chance to talk with Keltor and have him answer some questions. "Not even I know the full story of what happened with Keltor. Until I do, I refuse to hate him. Because without the prince, I wouldn't have you."

At her words, Kelzal stood and paced the room. "Do you really see me as worth all the trouble you've experienced?"

"You're proof that my long-ago love was real. And in a strange way, I take comfort in that."

He stilled his movement and kept his gaze averted. "What if there was more proof?"

Scrutinizing his face, she looked for any clues as to what he was talking about, but didn't see anything. "Please just tell me the truth, Kelzal. I hate dancing around something. In that, your birth father and I are very different."

"Promise me that you can keep a secret first." He met her gaze. "It's important to me and not something I want to risk."

She could almost hear a touch of protectiveness in Kelzal's words. Considering he rarely had emotion in his voice, it told her that whatever secret he held, it truly meant a great deal to him. "I vowed honesty with the prince. However, as long as it doesn't affect his safety or ability to lead, let alone the security of the planet, then I suppose I can keep it from him until you think he should hear it."

Kelzal hesitated. Azalyn wasn't the sort of person to make false promises, so she waited. She wouldn't push him, no matter how much she desired a closer relationship with her child.

He finally spoke again. "I suppose that will have to be good enough." Kelzal took a small notescreen from his pocket and tapped the surface a few times. She was just about to prod for him to continue when he moved back to her bedside and flashed the screen at her.

The image was of a young female, probably about Kelzal's age. She smiled at the camera, her teeth white against her lavender skin. She also had golden hair, which was a genetic rarity on Keldera. Azalyn knew that well because her own mother had the same hair color and had often boasted about it during Azalyn's childhood.

"Who is she?" Azalyn asked.

"Her name is Toralyn."

A memory from decades ago, of Azalyn suggesting a male and female name for her child to her foster family, flashed into her mind. Kelzal had been her male name, but Toralyn had been her desired female name. Both had bits of hers and Keltor's name in them.

Brushing it off as a coincidence since names ending in -lyn had always been popular on Keldera and Toralyn could be seen as a tribute to King Kastor himself, Azalyn looked back up at her son. "I didn't think you had a bride."

"I don't. She's my sister. Twin sister, if I'm to be more specific."

Glancing back at the image of the young female, Azalyn started to notice bits of her and Keltor. The skin and hair color came from her family, but the shape of the eyes and smile were just like Keltor's. Even some of the symbols on the female's neck resembled some of the ones on Azalyn's own body.

Did she really have a daughter?

And yet the resemblance was clear to see. Keltor might need a blood test as proof, but Azalyn's gut said Kelzal was telling the truth. "I—I...how is this possible?"

"From what I know, the Sulanis kept her existence a secret from you. Since a female can't inherit the throne, she was deemed less of a threat and was adopted to one of the distant cousins. She works in a shop in Bakren. She found me shortly after our eighteenth birthday, when her family revealed my existence."

Azalyn couldn't tear her gaze away from the smiling female. She didn't care about genetic tests. The girl took after Keltor's family. On closer inspection, it wasn't so much

Keltor as his sister, Princess Kalahn.

Keltor. How could she keep from him that he had another child? Or, rather, that *they* had another child.

Glancing up at Kelzal, she murmured, "He should know."

"No. Toralyn already has fewer freedoms because she's female. To sentence her to a life as a princess would take even those few exceptions away."

Azalyn risked touching Kelzal's arm. He tensed a fraction but didn't move away. "Look at me, Kelzal." After several breaths, he finally did. "If I can secure an agreement with Keltor about his offspring and their future marriages, keeping it vague to protect Toralyn as well, will you let me tell Keltor about her? That way she won't be married off, as you put it. I may even be able to negotiate a few more freedoms."

He raised his brows. "I thought you didn't like dancing around issues, which you'd have to do to keep things vague and not give away my sister's identity."

"Normally, I hate it. But for the chance to meet my daughter and have both of my children in the same room, I'll do whatever it takes."

He searched her gaze. "Why are you so passionate about this? Toralyn and I are both fully grown. Fomenting any sort of relationship is going to be difficult, especially as her adopted parents are still alive."

Tightening her grip on Kelzal's arm, Azalyn didn't miss a beat in replying, "Because even if I didn't raise you, I gave birth to you and will do whatever it takes to protect you. I have no doubt that her identity will come to light eventually." Kelzal opened his mouth, but she beat him to it. "Not through me. However, once your identity is confirmed and your place in the succession solidified, many will either come forward claiming to have a royal child born outside of marriage, or go looking for any other potential heirs. However, if we act now, then Toralyn may have more rights to her own life in the future. But to do that, we need to act quickly. It's easier to put in place changes for a hypothetical situation than an existing one."

After considering her words, he murmured, "He will hate you when he finds out the truth."

"I can handle Keltor and any anger that comes my way if it means you and your sister may have a less daunting future ahead of you."

He nodded. "So, what's your plan?"

As Azalyn explained her idea, she only hoped she could pull it off. She'd learned a lot over the years about Kelderan law and royal traditions, in an effort to make up for her teenage naivety. She only hoped it was enough to convince Keltor to at least consider the changes when it came to marriages and forming alliances without a royal offspring's consent or input.

The difficult part would be in convincing the public of her ideas without causing the antimonarchy extremists to riot, or worse. Some wanted the complete dismantling of the institution. Laws or agreements that could secure the Kelderan royal family for generations to come would be deemed the utmost threat to their agenda.

But she'd never find out if it were possible to change things without trying. She wasn't about to sit back and give up any chance she had to meet her daughter. Even if the idea was deemed too much of a threat, she'd search for another way, and then another.

✹ ✹ ✹

Keltor stood around the corner from Azalyn's room and wished he could pace like a normal person. But with his guards following his every moment, it would be a tight squeeze for five grown males to walk and turn around in the narrow space.

He couldn't remember the last time he'd been so hesitant about a meeting. However, Keltor didn't think it was an everyday occurrence to inherit a grown family out of nowhere.

Stop being ridiculous. If he was to ever develop a relationship with Kelzal, then it would mean including Azalyn as well. It wasn't as if he'd be tempted to kiss her with the boy in the room.

Taking a deep breath, Keltor walked the remaining distance to the touchpad scanner. Once the door opened, he signaled for his guards to wait in the hall and he went inside.

While Azalyn still sat in her hospital bed, she'd twisted her dark hair up off her neck. He wanted to drink in the long, graceful curves, but forced himself to glance around the room before focusing on her profile. It was then he realized Kelzal wasn't in the room. "Where's the boy? If he's going to be a prince, he needs to learn how to follow orders."

Azalyn turned her head and raised her brows. "Kelzal isn't a boy. The sooner you realize that and treat him as the adult he is, the sooner you might have a chance at a relationship."

His first instinct was to make a diplomatic comment and avoid an argument. However, the way he acted now would forever dictate his future interactions with Azalyn. He may not be able to have her as a bride, but he wanted to see and talk with her from time to time. And not just concerning Kelzal.

Maybe he should be as forthright as she was.

Of course, that could give her the wrong impression.

Before he could decide how to proceed, Azalyn rolled

her eyes and sighed. "Keltor, just say what you want to say in front of me. Who am I going to tell about your lack of diplomacy?"

He must be letting his guard down if she could read his mind so clearly. He cleared his throat. "Maybe I just want to avoid angering you. I have a feeling your temper hasn't changed over the years, and I won't risk your health."

"And just what do you remember? Because if you think I'm going to rush over and jump you so that I can tackle you to the ground, then rest assured I can restrain myself."

His reply slipped out, "You'd lose, Aza."

She smiled, and Keltor felt as if someone had punched his gut. "Do you challenge females on a regular basis?"

His brows came together. "Of course not. I am an honorable male."

Snorting, she turned a little more toward him. "Hm, maybe your protestation means that it's your secret fantasy to be attacked by a female? That would be something new, as I don't remember that being a fantasy of yours before."

Grunting, he took a step toward her. "And it still isn't. My brother is the one who enjoys the warrior-like females, or I should say one particular female warrior. I prefer ones who battle with words and wit."

"And none of the females being proffered to you by their fathers fits that bill?"

"How do you—"

"Rumors spread before I left on the colony transport ship, and I'd assume you're still searching." She tilted her head. "Unless you've found a female that no one knows about?"

A thought rushed into his head—*I found you again.*

If Azalyn wasn't watching him so closely, he would've blinked. He'd barely spent any time with the female. He surely shouldn't want her.

And yet, as she looked at him with blatant curiosity, he felt more at ease with her than any other female in over twenty years.

No. To want Azalyn would be selfish. Keldera had to come first.

He decided to change the topic. "None of that is your concern. How about you tell me why Kelzal isn't here?"

She scrutinized his face a second before shrugging. "You two have enough trouble getting along without the awkwardness between you and me hanging in the air. We have much to discuss, Keltor. So, let's get started."

"First, I have something for you." Taking out a folded document from his pocket, he held it out to her. "Sign this and you'll have a private section of the palace, where even I will have to request permission for access."

As she took the synthetic sheet of paper, her fingers brushed against his. The brief whisper of warmth sent a tingle through his body.

He watched her unfold and read the declaration. Much like when she'd been younger, she occasionally bit her lower lip as she took in the information. Her bottom lip was plumper than the top one. But with a little nibbling, both would swell slightly from his attention.

Taking the opportunity, his gaze moved lower to her breasts. Even in the billowing hospital gown, he could see their plump outline. He wondered if the rest of her had also grown just as plump.

An image of her naked and writhing under his hands flashed into his mind. Blood rushed to his cock, but Keltor forced his thoughts to move to the dry agricultural reports from earlier in the day. When that wasn't enough of a distraction, he started to recite the Kelderan Royal Charter inside his head. Little by little, his body cooled.

The damn female did something to his libido; Keltor

was acting like a teenager all over again, constantly thinking of how and where to caress a certain lavender-skinned woman with green eyes and black hair.

A memory of Azalyn stroking his chest, down to his belly, and finally brushing the head of his cock flashed into his head. She'd had such soft fingers back then, and he wondered if they were slightly rougher with age or not.

Before his body could react once again to images of the woman, Azalyn finished reading and looked at his face. "This is a start, but before you officially acknowledge Kelzal as your heir, I want a few more things in writing."

Raising an eyebrow, he stated, "That guarantee in your hands is more than generous. You may be Kelzal's biological mother, but you have no say in political matters."

"So all of that talk when we were younger, about how you wanted to see more equality in the world, was just to get me naked. Good to know."

"That's not true."

"Then what's going on, Keltor? If you're worried about me seducing you to become the eventual queen at your side, don't worry, I have no interest in it. All I care about is my offspring."

He leaned down to try to intimidate her, but Azalyn didn't so much as move an inch away. "Do you want the complete truth, Azalyn? Because you're not going to like it."

Searching her gaze, he tried to read her thoughts, but failed. Was she truly indifferent to him now? Had her earlier kiss been merely a means to an end, in order to sway Keltor's mind?

Her voice was husky as she murmured, "Tell me the truth, Keltor. Always the truth."

He placed a hand on either side of her body. As her feminine scent filled his nose, any restraint or reason he'd once possessed regarding Azalyn was gone. He didn't hold back the truth. "If I let you into my world and we work together toward making changes to the status quo, or even plan the future of our son, I'm going to want more, Azalyn. Keeping my distance is the best way to protect both of us."

Her face moved a fraction closer to his. "How is this, right here, keeping your distance from me, your highness?"

He growled. "I'm not kissing you, am I? That's a giant chasm between us in my mind."

Azalyn's hot breath danced against his face, and Keltor wanted to close the distance and devour her sweetness.

"We shouldn't," she whispered.

He leaned over and nuzzled her cheek with his own. "No, we shouldn't."

Moving his lips to her neck, he kissed her warm skin. "And yet, I can't seem to push you away."

Lightly biting her neck, Keltor reveled in Azalyn's sigh. He soothed the same spot with his tongue before saying, "You must, or I might do something we both regret, Aza."

Running her hand down his cheek to his jaw, she forced Keltor to meet her gaze again. At the desire in her eyes, he wanted to growl and rip off her clothes.

But he focused on her words as she said, "Once I'm healed, I'll give myself to you, Keltor. All I ask in return are a few guarantees about Kelzal's future."

A chill replaced the heat in his body. Keltor stepped away as if he'd been slapped. "So you're offering your body as part of a deal?"

"Yes. No, that's not what I meant. Keltor, let me explain."

He moved to closer to the door. "You've said enough. You must be tired, so I'll leave."

Turning his back to her, Keltor exited the room and walked briskly down the hall, barely paying his guards any attention.

Out of everyone he'd ever known, Azalyn was the last person he would've expected to make deals with him. And for sex, no less.

It seemed that his boyhood dreams of a female who wanted him for himself were just that—dreams.

At least now he should be able to clear his head for his important meeting in the morning. The Azalyn he'd spent years yearning for was nothing more than a memory. Her actions were also a wake-up call.

Keltor's days would be nothing but political moves and diplomacy for the rest of his life.

And he'd start his new path in the morning, by greeting the latest candidate in his effort to find a queen. The sooner he took a bride, the sooner Azalyn would give up trying to sway his mind with her body.

Because if she kept it up, he might capitulate, and he couldn't afford for that to happen. Especially now that she knew his weakness for her. It looked like he'd have to keep his distance from her after all.

Chapter Six

A little over a week later, Azalyn was still cursing herself for screwing up. She had never intended to hurt Keltor. Her plan had been to convince the prince to change some traditions surrounding the royal family, using reason and facts.

But then he'd nuzzled her cheek and caressed her neck with his tongue, and her arguments had started to fade. She'd wanted both him and her changes. Before she could think about, the offer had slipped from her lips.

The flash of hurt in Keltor's eyes had been brief, but more than enough to wrench her heart. He may be a male in his forties with only weeks or maybe a few months before he became king, but all he wanted was the closeness average citizens took for granted.

He'd trusted her to act normal, as if he were just a male and not a prince, and she'd thrown it back in his face.

Placing her head in her hands, she took a deep breath. Keltor had yet to respond to any of her requests. She'd most likely ruined whatever type of civil relationship she would've had with the father of her child.

Or, rather, her children.

Raising her face, she lightly slapped her cheeks. Even if Keltor kept his distance and never forgave her, she would find a way to ensure Kelzal would avoid the same isolation. She didn't know how, but there had to be something she could do.

Before she could do more than think of maybe reaching out to Keltor's sister, Kalahn, for suggestions on how to handle her brother, the computer announced Kelzal's presence and he entered. Putting aside her distracting thoughts, she asked, "Is it time to go already?"

"It is the appointed time. Plus, I double-checked that the doctor cleared your health and our quarters are ready for us. I'm anxious to leave because once we're settled inside them, I have news for you."

"News about what?"

He shook his head. "Not here. It's not secure."

Mentioning security gave her an idea of what he wished to discuss. Since bringing up Toralyn a week ago, Kelzal had mentioned nothing about his sister. Maybe he'd have some information from her. And if not, she would find a way to coax some out of her son. After all, at the rate Azalyn was going with Keltor, she'd never have the chance to meet her daughter. Stories from Kelzal might be the best she could ever hope to have.

The news about having a second child was still sinking in. Toralyn's picture, though, was burned permanently into her brain. All those years she'd looked over Kelzal, she hadn't done the same with Toralyn. While it wasn't her fault since she hadn't known of the female's existence, Azalyn still felt guilty about it.

Later, Azalyn would reach out to the Sulanis and demand a full explanation. As much as she'd come to care for most of her adopted family, the leader of the Sulani merchants, Ulrick, never did something without a motive and detailed strategy behind it.

And if he planned to use her daughter against Keltor for

gain, she needed to know about it. While it may take a little digging, she had contacts of her own who could shed some light on her assumptions.

Kelzal grabbed her sole cargo case of belongings, and they headed out of the medical wing toward their quarters in the eastern half of the palace.

She'd grown comfortable with Kelzal's silences over the last week. Rather than try to engage in pleasantries he probably wouldn't respond to, she instead focused on her surroundings. While the composite walls were a light, nondescript cream color, after five minutes, they finally walked past a large window looking into a garden. The window material was transparent at the moment, but Azalyn could spot a dimmer screen. Merchants used them all the time for privacy in their shops.

"Computer, what is beyond this screen?" she asked.

"The East Garden. Access is currently open to everyone who has basic clearance to the palace."

Glancing at Kelzal, she asked, "Do you mind if we look inside for a few minutes? Between the hospital wing, the Kelderan transport ship, and our captivity with the Tallarians, I'd love nothing more than to be surrounded by nature."

He adjusted his grip on her cargo case. "I have work I need to do, so you go. When you're finished, come find me. We need to talk."

At the reminder of his news, Azalyn hesitated. But Kelzal vanished down the hall before she could do more than blink twice.

It was going to take years for her to adjust to his ways, but she would do it. Not for the first time, she appreciated the family who had not only adopted him, but by all accounts had loved him fiercely, quirks and all.

Entering the garden, Azalyn took in the multi-colored

flowers, the yellow and pale green leaves of the trees, and the yellow-colored grass wrestled into a wavy pattern by paths of black gravel.

Lightly tracing the petals of a deep purple flower, Azalyn smiled. She didn't think she'd ever see the flora of Keldera again. After all, according to her plans, she should be living in the Kelderan colony on the planet Jasvar by now. While some Kelderan plants would be introduced and cultivated on the planet, there was no telling how the light of a different sun and soil with a different chemical makeup would affect their coloring. With all the changes in her life recently, the familiarity of the flowers and trees comforted her.

Moving on from the flowers, she walked deeper into the garden and stopped at the entrance to a giant hedge maze. The pale blue foliage stood out against the green and yellow.

She should turn around and exit the garden. Some Kelderan mazes took tens of minutes or even an hour to complete.

And yet she needed to walk and build up her strength after her recent confinement, per the doctor's orders. Besides, she'd always been good at solving hedge mazes as a child, so it shouldn't take too long.

As Azalyn turned one corner and then another, she started to imagine a young child hanging on to each of her hands as they stomped in the imaginary puddles and urged her to take a dead end so they could see if there were any surprises waiting. When they walked into a water trap—which signaled that they were going the wrong way—a small spray of water would hit them, causing the boy and girl to squeal in delight.

For years, Azalyn had told herself that she could always have children again and experience motherhood. She was one of the strange females who wanted to both work and raise children, which rarely happened outside of merchant families. But the Sulanis would've embraced her desire, like many merchant brides before her.

However, she'd never found a male she wanted to claim as her own in the last twenty-odd years. There had been many who were kind, or loving, and more than a few had been attractive. In the end, none of them had stirred her heart the same way Keltor had done when they'd been younger. Maybe her expectations had been too high. After all, many Kelderan couples were partnerships with little in the way of passion and often without love.

And yet, after what she'd experience with Keltor, Azalyn had wanted passion and love again.

Turning another corner, the sound of the fountain in the center of the maze grew louder. She was close to finding the exit. While most mazes were designed to trick you into going toward the center, Azalyn went toward the edge. A few minutes later, she was rewarded with the sight of a four-tier fountain, the water cascading out of a giant feline's mouth at the top to rows below of carved fish and plant life.

She sat down at one of the benches to the side and stared at the water. The fountain was loud and drowned out everything else. No doubt it was by design to give royals and their families some privacy.

The solitude only made her think of the little boy and girl again, but this time they sat on the edge of the fountain's outer rim and hit the water to splash each other.

Placing a hand on her abdomen, tears prickled her eyes. Not only was she forty years old, which was an obstacle of its own with pregnancy, but the doctor also said it would be difficult for her to conceive again due to the damage caused by the Tallarians beating her.

In short, Azalyn had waited too long. She would never have children to raise as her own and to make memories with instead of mere fantasies. She couldn't even adopt thanks to her life as mother to the heir of Keldera's one-day king; King Kastor and Keltor would view the adoption as a possible security risk. If the biological parents ever came calling with demands, it could be disastrous.

While grateful to have Kelzal in her life, Azalyn mourned the loss of raising a child and all the experiences that came with it.

However, she couldn't ever allow Kelzal—and maybe one day Toralyn—to sense her grief. So in the solitude of the maze with the fountain to drown out her tears, Azalyn let go and sobbed for the children she'd never have.

✷ ✷ ✷

Keltor quickly ducked into the East Garden and made a beeline for the hedge maze. His latest bride candidate's father was determined to marry off his daughter to Keltor, and he needed a break from the constant chase.

While the latest candidate, Lakka, had a mild temperament and lovely blue hair, all she did was smile and nod. Even after a week spent with her at meals and various activities, Keltor couldn't recall the sound of the female's voice.

Some males would appreciate a bride who didn't chatter or offer an opinion. Keltor, on the other hand, had spent enough of his life surrounded by complacency. No doubt Lakka would merely smile as he pleasured her, too, and never reveal what she truly wanted.

Striding into the hedge maze for further privacy, he kicked some of the gravel rocks as hard as he could. He was aware that he'd have to do his duty and take a wife, but it couldn't be too much to ask for a bride who spoke more than "Yes, your highness," or "No, your highness."

Not that his councilors seemed to mind Lakka's bland

personality. All they were concerned about was putting Keltor out to stud so that he would hopefully produce a few more sons.

To distract himself from what awaited him outside the garden space, he walked into the maze.

The twist and turns were as familiar to him as breathing, and it wasn't long before he reached the center.

He stared at the cascading water for a few seconds before turning toward his favorite bench. That was when he spotted Azalyn off to the side, her head in her hands, her body shaking with what he assumed were sobs.

Her actions from the previous week still stung, but the sight of Azalyn in such pain erased his hurt a fraction. They may only be acquaintances who would discuss issues related to Kelzal and never be lovers again, but after everything his former female had been through, Keltor couldn't just walk away when she was in such distress. Especially if it had to do with interactions and treatment by others inside the palace; Azalyn was mother to the heir and Keltor wouldn't tolerate disrespect.

He approached slowly, careful to keep his footsteps light. Thanks to the sound of cascading water, she still hadn't noticed him when he was a foot away. Reaching out a hand, he stopped short of touching her shoulder. Instead, he clenched his fingers and said in a gentle voice, "What happened, Azalyn? If someone hurt or disrespected you inside the palace, tell me."

Her head jerked up. At Azalyn's red, puffy eyes and wet cheeks, he wanted to hug her close and soothe away her pain.

Since he couldn't do that if he was to maintain distance between them, he squatted in front of her.

After wiping away her tears, she murmured, "There's no need for concern. It's nothing."

He didn't like her lying to him. "Have you gone back on your vow of honesty? Because you're not okay, not even close."

A flicker of irritation flashed in Azalyn's gaze. "Honesty doesn't mean I have to reveal all my secrets. Besides, after last week, I'm surprised you care. After all, I'm only after you for your favors, apparently."

Sitting down on the bench next to her, Keltor stared at the fountain as he said, "I'm not a monster, Aza." He glanced at her. "You're still the mother of my child. Can't we at least be civil?"

At the word "child," Azalyn turned away from him. While quiet, he sensed she was crying again.

He had not the faintest idea why. And for some reason, that angered him.

Keltor spoke up again. "Even if you yell out that I'm a bastard during my coronation ceremony, I still won't send you away to the Barren, Aza. If that's your worry, then I'm not sure what else I can say to convince you of my words."

He strained to hear her reply over the water, "I wouldn't disrespect you that way, Keltor. I admire you far more than that."

With a week to cool his temper, Keltor wondered about Azalyn's former proposition. If she had been hell-bent on seducing him for favors, she probably would've pounced by now.

Few males could resist a female in tears.

Almost as if to read his mind and prove his conclusion, Azalyn stood and walked to the edge of the fountain, her back still to him. Her voice carried over the gurgling water, albeit scratchy from sobbing. "Have you ever thought about what you could've done with your life, but didn't? Not necessarily related to us, but just for the years that have gone by?"

He could say no. But against his better judgment, he replied, "All the time."

She bobbed her head. "That's all I was doing. I need to be strong for Kelzal's sake. So rather than bottle up my emotions, I just wanted to get everything out in private so that I can be the mother he needs me to be."

Hoping the distance would keep her talking, Keltor remained on the bench. "What were you thinking about? I hope it's not about you living here. I wish I could let you go and live your life on Jasvar, but you know I can't." He paused, but pushed on. "If you were killed, I'm not sure how I'd react. Now that I've found you again, I need to know you're safe, Aza."

She didn't reply for a few seconds, but Keltor waited. Sometimes people needed the silence to commit to something, be it a reply or a diplomatic decision.

Shaking her head, she turned to face him. "No, I understand that. Maybe one day the threats will ease, and I can go into space again. It's just..." Her voice died down, and she plucked at her skirts. Only when her gaze lowered did she continue. "I was thinking about my decision to give up Kelzal and all that I missed."

Keltor risked standing, but Azalyn didn't move away. "I wish you would've come to me back then once you knew you were pregnant, but with time to reflect, I understand why you didn't. To be blunt, my father still wouldn't have approved of you as my bride. By all accounts, he had a bastard child sometime after my mother died, but never offered to claim the mother of said child. I assume that to him, she wasn't queen material. It proves what he would've done with you, too."

Azalyn looked up at that. "What? You have another sibling?"

"It's possible. I've heard rumors for years, but I was

never close with my father before; we were two very different people. However, ever since he's been diagnosed with a terminal illness, he's been making an effort, and I've been trying to learn more from him before he passes. If I can get him to tell me about the rumored child, I want to make things right with my unknown sibling."

She took a step toward him. "Has your father really changed that much?"

He shrugged. "Death and realization of one's mortality have a way of changing people." Closing the distance between them, he put out a hand. "But enough talk of sadness and tears. I want to show you what's under the fountain."

Curiosity flashed in her eyes. "Under the fountain? I assumed there was an exit tunnel, but there's more?"

"Of course. While my brother, sister, and I were royalty with many restrictions, my mother wanted us to experience some childhood joys. What's underneath our feet is one of them."

She stared at his hand. He nearly reached out to take hers, but waited. If there was to be any trust between them for Kelzal's sake, he couldn't order Azalyn around or demand unequivocal obedience.

Finally placing her hand in his, she met his gaze again. "Don't make me regret this, Keltor. I'm coming with you out of curiosity and not because I'm trying to seduce you for favors. Accuse me of that again, and I won't give you another chance."

He squeezed her hand in his. "You won't regret it, Aza. What I'm about to show you not many people know about. That says volumes about what I think of you."

Never taking his gaze from hers, Keltor was more than aware of Azalyn's delicate fingers in his. He wanted to bring the soft skin of her fingertips to his lips.

In that moment, it was hard to remember why he'd been

so angry with her. Compared to the latest prospective bride thrown his way, Azalyn was the exact opposite. Maybe a little too stubborn at times, but unafraid to be herself. No father or family member would direct her what to do, even if it meant she refused a prince.

And that made her nearly perfect. If only he could find another female like her, one that could help ensure his people's safety and prevent war.

Not wanting to dwell on the impossible, Keltor tugged her behind him and down the stairs at the rear of the fountain. The steps led to a long corridor. Straight ahead was the exit to just outside the hedge maze, but to the left was a sealed door. He stopped at the locked entrance. As childish as it was to keep the area for his own as a place to remember his mother and childhood—and possibly for his own children to enjoy—Keltor had done so. He allowed the computer to scan his retina.

The door opened, and he walked a few feet inside. Azalyn gasped. "It's beautiful."

As the multicolored lights danced across her face, he wanted to say she was more beautiful. But instead, he merely murmured, "Welcome to the water maze."

✸ ✸ ✸

Azalyn had been trying her best to ignore Keltor's firm hand in hers when the door opened and she gasped.

Multicolored lights brightened the large area. A series of walkways zigged and zagged over a shallow pool of water. Statues of animals littered the planks of the walkway, along with brightly colored shapes made of some unknown composite material. But it was the centerpiece that stole her breath away.

A trio of children was carved out of stone. Each was

laughing at the carved water streams hitting their bodies. While she'd never seen them so young, Azalyn instinctively knew it was Keltor and his two siblings.

"It's beautiful."

"Welcome to the water maze."

Keltor's voice snapped her back to the present, and she met his gaze again. "What is this place? And don't just say it's a water maze. I'm not even sure what that is."

He nodded toward the inside of the area. "This is my mother's invention. She saw something similar as a child, when her parents took her to a vacation outpost in space."

Vacation outposts had been in fashion before the war with the Brevkan. Afterward, Kelderans had been banned from traveling to them because of safety concerns. "Your mother designed this?"

"Yes, although she hired a few people to work out the logistics. She also carved many of the statues. While it annoyed father to no end that she'd spend days locked inside a studio whenever inspiration hit, he indulged her. For all my father's faults, he loved my mother."

Glancing back to the trio of children, Azalyn replied, "It's clear to see she loved you."

Keltor cleared his throat. "I wouldn't say my siblings and I were that close, especially since Kalahn is sixteen years younger than me. As you can see, my mother took artistic license to make us look closer in age. The original statue was just Kason and me. The one with Kalahn came later, right before she died."

"I'm sorry about your mother, Keltor. I wish I could've met her. From what little I know of her, she was a special female."

"She was, and I think she would've liked you."

Her eyes darted to his. There was no anger or resentment. Keltor merely spoke the truth.

Keltor squeezed her hand and looked away first. "I don't have a lot of time, so come. I'll show you how this works."

Jumping on the distraction, she said, "Then explain it before I walk on the planks and who knows what happens to me. Just my luck the plank slides away and I get eaten by flesh-eating fish in the water."

The corner of Keltor's mouth ticked up. "I'm a royal prince about to be king. I'll be the ruler of your planet. And yet you think I'd simply feed you to some fish for amusement?"

She rolled her eyes. "After you tossed me into the lagoon near that waterfall when we were teenagers, no, I don't trust you around water."

He placed his free hand over his heart. "I had no choice. When I saw you in your swimming outfit, it took everything I had not to strip you down and take you. Tossing you into the cold water and me jumping in after you was a distraction."

Azalyn should leave the past where it lay, but she blurted out, "What? We'd barely known each other a few weeks at that point."

"Do you want honesty, Aza?"

At the heat in his eyes, she swallowed. Keltor's words would only remind her of their past and what could never be. But fool that she was, Azalyn bobbed her head.

Keltor lowered his voice. "You were the first female who constantly invaded my thoughts. And let's just say that teenage males do a lot of undressing inside their heads."

She caught his use of "first female." It was on the tip of her tongue to demand if there had ever been another.

Then one of the lights hit the thin, ceremonial circle around his forehead. The small piece of metal reminded her of the chasm between them. If she wasn't careful, they'd both do something they'd regret.

To help them both avoid scandal, Azalyn removed her hand from his and took a step back.

Decades may have passed, but Keltor could instantly tell when Azalyn decided to close herself off from him. For a few minutes, she'd acted as they had when they'd been younger, never holding back.

But as soon as her eyes fell on his ceremonial circlet, she'd grown reserved and pulled away from him.

He was more than convinced that his anger last week had been misplaced. She easily could've tried to kiss him or win favors since he'd discovered her in the center of the maze. And yet, she'd instead spent the time praising his mother.

Which meant she'd offered her body back in the hospital room simply because she'd wanted him. If only he could think of a way to woo her and still secure peace for his planet.

His timepiece buzzed inside the pocket of his trousers. In twenty minutes, he needed to attend a video conference with his brother. Since it was the first real-time video conference from Jasvar, Keltor couldn't blow it off.

If he were going to make Azalyn smile and laugh to forget her earlier tears, his curiosity and lingering questions would have to wait. Azalyn could put distance between them for the moment. However, he planned to have a much more thorough conversation with her later.

Taking a few steps toward the entrance to the maze, Keltor stated, "The water maze is like the hedge maze, albeit with a twist." He dared a look at Azalyn. She nodded. "You need to reach the center, but instead of shrubbery to confuse you, the planks themselves are deceptive. They all look the same, but if you step in the wrong direction, that plank depresses, and water begins spraying toward you. Like this."

Keltor went down two planks and turned left. Careful to only place one foot on the next plank and gently press it, a stream of water shot toward him. He darted back, and it stopped.

Azalyn came up behind him. "What if you step on it with all your weight?"

He raised an eyebrow. "Wouldn't you like to know. Try it."

She made to move around him, but instead, she shoved Keltor forward, and he stumbled onto the plank. Three jets of water hit him from different sides.

Dashing to the next safe plank, he turned to glare at Azalyn. However, as soon as he did, she laughed. The light sound made him forget everything but the crinkles at the side of her eyes and the dimple on one of her cheeks.

Yes, laughter suited her much better than tears.

However, Keltor wasn't one not to fight back. Before she could get away, he lunged forward, grabbed her arm, and dragged her onto the water-spraying plank. She shrieked as water hit her body. "Keltor! Let me go!"

Tightening his grip on her arm, he grinned. "Just another second more."

She opened her mouth to scold, but he quickly tugged her toward him.

Azalyn crashed into his chest and his arms instinctively wrapped around her waist to steady her. She tensed at the contact. An undefined sadness coursed through his body at her reaction. Maybe his anger the week before had cooled any desire she'd had for him. Or, more likely, she'd had time to reflect on how he'd ruined her life. No matter if the truth had been hidden from Keltor or not as a young man, he hadn't gone after her as he should have. If he wanted to see Azalyn happy, he needed to let her go.

He was about to step back when she slowly relaxed and rested her head against his chest.

Her comforting presence washed away his guilt. For what seemed like hours, they merely stood there. Keltor dared to close his eyes and lay his cheek on top of her head.

Memorizing her scent, the silkiness of her hair, and the softness of her body, he stored it away for the future. Because he had a feeling that to keep Keldera from war, he would have to sentence himself to a lifetime of loneliness and distance. No bride would compare to Azalyn. He'd been an idiot to think he could find another female like her.

So Keltor merely held the only female he had had ever loved and dreamed of the future they might've had. Because that was going to be the closest thing to happiness he would ever achieve. After this brief moment, he would force himself to keep his distance and allow Azalyn to find her own path in life.

Because to protect her, Azalyn's life had to be without his touch, his kisses, or his love.

All too soon his timekeeper vibrated again, denoting ten minutes until his meeting. If Keltor didn't change clothes, his brother Kason would ask too many questions.

In other words, it was time to release Azalyn and turn away.

Again.

Taking one deep breath to revel in her feminine scent, he finally stepped back. What he wouldn't give to banish the confusion in Azalyn's lovely green eyes. "Sorry, Aza, but I have a meeting I must attend. I can always bring you back here later, if you wish."

She cleared her throat. "Perhaps. I just need you to show me how to get out of here, and you can go about your business."

He didn't care for the flatness of her voice, but pretended not to notice it. "This way."

As he guided her to the exit and out of the tunnel, Keltor used the time to pack away his emotions. A ruler never showed desire, fear, or a multitude of other feelings, not even to his own brother. Transmissions may be secure, but a prince had to act as if someone were always listening. Weakness was akin to a death sentence for more than himself.

And with the Kelderan colony on Jasvar being so new, Keltor needed to focus on any problems or obstacles facing his people on the other planet. If the Brevkan ever discovered the Kelderan colony, it could start another war. After all, Jasvar was a low-tech colony and probably wouldn't stand a chance against the Brevkan warriors and their more advanced technology.

They reached the final exit point, which would lead to the main corridor. Keltor motioned toward a small side room. "You can dry off in there first, if you like. It's probably best if we're not seen coming out of here together, with both of us wet. That would raise too many questions."

Even though he'd known the words would create distance, he still didn't like the hardness of Azalyn's face. "As you wish, your highness."

Bobbing his head, Keltor left Azalyn to her own devices. His brief glimpse of happiness was over. It was time to become the heir to Keldera once more.

Chapter Seven

Azalyn barely paid attention to her surroundings as she walked toward her new living quarters. What she'd planned to be a private cleansing session of her thoughts—to mourn the truth and path of her life—had turned into in a fun session of teasing and joking around with Keltor.

Even though they were both older and slightly more mature, the minutes spent in the water maze room had reminded her of old times.

It also reminded her of why she'd fallen for Keltor as a teenager.

Beneath his royal facade was a warm, teasing male who loved nothing more than to hold his treasured female close. His cold, distant nature was by design, to fulfill the expectations held by Keldera about their one-day king. To spend most of his time behind the royal mask had to eat at him.

She wondered how any of Keltor's humor had remained intact.

Not that she could afford to care about such things. Yes, she'd enjoyed listening to Keltor's heartbeat as he held her in his arms. But the time inside the water maze room had been a fantasy. One that could never exist in public.

Lightly slapping her cheeks, Azalyn willed her mind to forget about Keltor and his warm, muscled chest. Kelzal was her life now, and she needed to remember that.

She finally reached the tall, wide door to her new quarters and pressed her hand to the scanning plate. A handprint scanner was more secure than a mere finger one. She'd have to thank Keltor later for his thoughtfulness.

The door slid open, and she waltzed into a small room, only to find another scanner. She repeated the process two more times before she finally made it to the entryway. The sight of the high ceiling, complete with view screens around the perimeter showing birds in flight, garnered her full attention.

Ever since she'd been a girl, Azalyn had loved to listen and watch the birds. Keltor must've remembered that.

Rather than dwell on that thought, she studied the movements of the birds as they pumped their wings. She itched to find a sketchpad and drawing utensil to capture their motion. Azalyn hadn't drawn anything since being kidnapped from the Kelderan colony ship a few weeks ago, and she was eager to do so again. Sure, she'd had a lot of free time during her medical confinement, but she'd lacked inspiration. Between the garden and the view screens, she now had it in spades.

But Kelzal was waiting for her, so Azalyn forced her gaze from the view screens and headed up the staircase. Kelzal's section, including his research lab, were on the second and third floors.

The upstairs corridor consisted of plain, pale blue composite material. What the walls lacked in decorations made up for it with small alcoves of electronic devices and components. She could just imagine Kelzal picking one up and working on it for a few minutes before switching it out with another one. She was going to have to make an effort to better understand his world. Azalyn lacked his knack for technology. Or, rather, the patience required. She'd much rather use the time to outline a new painting.

Reaching the door at the end of the hall, she pressed her finger to the scanner. After a few seconds, the doors opened.

Kelzal stood on the far side, next to a long table filled with hundreds of tiny things she couldn't identify. A large computer workspace was on his other side.

Since Kelzal rarely remembered to acknowledge anyone's presence when engrossed in his work, Azalyn walked up to him and said, "Hi, Kelzal. Any progress?"

He never looked away from the tiny processing board in front of him. "Wait forty-five seconds."

While tempted to count out loud to see if he was as accurate as usual, Azalyn restrained herself. The sooner he could pause in his work, the sooner she could ferret out the news he'd spoken about earlier.

Kelzal finally met her gaze. "I'm at a good stopping place. I'm hungry, so let's go to the kitchen, and I can share my news."

He didn't wait for confirmation. Azalyn merely followed him down the stairs and through a few doorways to the kitchen and eating area. Judging by the cooking surface and refrigeration unit, the place was designed for homemade cooking instead of just replicator fair. Azalyn had never had time to learn how to cook before because of her acquisitions position with the Sulani merchants. Maybe she could fill up her days that way.

Kelzal ordered a meal from the replicator. Once it was done, he moved to the table, sat down, and said, "Let me start by saying our section of the palace is secure. No known listening devices will penetrate my defenses."

Her son's news must be sensitive indeed. "What do you need to tell me?"

"I contacted Toralyn successfully."

At the mention of her daughter, Azalyn leaned forward.

"And?"

He took a bite before replying, "I didn't tell her about you. But she's safe and busy working at one of the Sulani merchant shops."

Not for the first time, Azalyn wondered if she'd ever ran into her daughter by mistake at one of the Sulani shops. "Is that all she talked about?"

He shrugged. "The only other important piece of information she shared was her thoughts about joining the next group of colonists to Jasvar, if given the chance. The pressure to find a lord is growing stronger and she doesn't want to procreate yet."

Since most Kelderan females had their first child by age twenty-five and Toralyn was twenty-two, society and her parents would expect her to make a serious effort to marry. "She has a few years. If Keltor has any say in the matter, there will be several more waves of colonists to Jasvar. And maybe if I can get Keltor to commit to some conditions regarding his offspring, then she won't have to leave at all."

"The prince avoided you for a week. Somehow, I think negotiations aren't going well."

She decided not to reveal her recent encounter with Keltor just yet. Considering it might've been a fluke, she didn't want to give Kelzal false hope.

Kelzal continued eating his food, so Azalyn prodded. "And what about your meetings with him? Maybe with his help you can put forth some conditions and change the laws."

"I'm not good at bargaining or persuading someone of something. It's why I hire people to do it for my company. Besides, he and I have nothing in common."

She raised an eyebrow. "Maybe you would find something in common if you'd stop avoiding him and canceling nearly all your scheduled meals together."

He shook his head. "I have no desire to do so. The male I knew as my father is dead, and I don't need a new one. Besides, I have a new plan."

She tried not to think about how Kelzal could say the same about his adopted mother. "Which is?"

Kelzal met her eyes. "If I help him find a bride and procreate again, then I can give up my place in the succession."

A surge of jealousy coursed through her body, but Azalyn put it aside. Keltor wasn't hers. "And how, exactly, do you plan to do that? Forgive me for being blunt, but you aren't very good at reading social cues and emotions. Finding a bride requires doing both of them."

"Emotions mean nothing in this instance. The prince merely needs a potential destined bride. Then he can easily procreate."

Azalyn frowned. "What are you talking about?"

Her son took another bite of food before replying, "The royal family suffers a genetic defect that makes it difficult for them to reproduce. Over the years, due to a slew of scientific experiments that enhanced their baser urges and instincts, there is an inner force that all royals have with regards to compatible mates. It makes it easier to keep the line alive and healthy."

Scrunching her nose, Azalyn asked, "Wait, what? How do you know this?"

"The one good thing about being confined to the palace and Keltor recognizing me as his son is that I've been given access to some confidential records. I have no desire to be king, but I was curious about my genetics. Potential destined brides was just one item I discovered."

"So this means I was..."

"You were one of his potential destined brides. Keltor's genetically altered biology means it's easy for you to conceive his offspring. If you didn't detest him so much, I would suggest you pair with him. You may be forty, but you have a few childbearing years left. However, from what I can deduce, you have no desire to do that. So I've begun a search on my own. Another son for Keltor equates my freedom."

Kelzal fell silent, meaning he had nothing else to add. Which was good, as Azalyn needed time to process his findings.

Keltor had never told her about destined brides, let alone how it meant she could conceive so easily. No doubt it was why she'd become pregnant with twins after one encounter.

If she hadn't experienced Keltor's tenderness earlier in the day, she might think he'd planned to get her pregnant so that she'd have to marry him. The younger version of Keltor had probably thought a pregnancy would've swayed his father, even though present-day Keltor had revealed earlier that it wouldn't have made a difference.

She sometimes wondered how anyone survived the naivety of youth.

But such deviousness warred with what she knew about Keltor. She had a hard time believing he'd use trickery to claim a bride.

However, being a potential destined bride had bigger implications. It meant Keltor was one of the few males who could probably still give her a child.

No. Azalyn wasn't about to use him for her own wants. But Keltor most definitely owed her a conversation and an explanation about why he'd kept such a big secret from her, especially when she offered her body to him all those years ago.

Moving to the computer terminal in the kitchen, she typed out a meeting request. Azalyn had many questions that only Keltor could answer. She only hoped she could keep her wits about her when she saw him. Unlike the future king, Azalyn wasn't as skilled in hiding her emotions or temper, especially when it came to a certain male.

✻ ✻ ✻

A green light blinked at the corner of Keltor's private comm unit, denoting a waiting call. Sitting taller in his chair, he said, "Computer, receive transmission."

The dark blue hair and golden-skinned face of his younger brother appeared on the screen. All of Kason's markings were a dark blue, denoting calmness, which was expected of a former general in the Kelderan Army.

Because Keltor outranked him, Kason waited for him to speak first.

So he did. "Kason, it seems the transmission towers project was completed successfully."

"There is only one tower completed for long-range use," his brother replied. "The others are still under construction as we find ways to use Jasvarian resources in place of Kelderan ones. However, the long-range tower is functioning, as you can see. But that's not why I wanted to talk with you. Is the line secure on your end?"

Keltor resisted leaning forward. "Yes. Is something wrong? Did Kalahn run off again?"

"No, our sister is behaving for the moment. We've found an antimonarchy sympathizer amongst the colonists."

Keltor resisted frowning. "I thought Ryven and Syzel had investigated all the colonists and rooted out the traitors."

Ryven and Syzel were both high-ranking Kelderan warriors. They had taken over command of the Kelderan colony transport ship when the original general, Thorin Jarrell, had left to rescue his eventual bride.

Kason grunted. "They did a thorough job. However, the female we found is a good actor."

He did frown at that. "Female? Since when do our enemies have female leaders and spies?"

"I don't know, Keltor. It's part of the reason I'm calling. Has father changed his strategy regarding the antimonarchy extremists and gathering information?"

"No, he still refuses to place informants among their ranks."

Kason growled, "Then change his mind or act on your own. Because if the use of female informants and troublemakers is widespread, then you could be in more danger than you know. Especially if this problem exists within the Barren citadels."

The Barren usually lived in isolation, away from populated areas, in complexes known as citadels.

Keltor could blame Kelderan ways on underestimating females, but that was merely an excuse. Given what his sister had done over the years, he knew firsthand that females could be as sneaky and clever as any male. "I will figure out a solution. I assume you're investigating all Kelderan female colonists now, as a precaution?"

"It's underway. If we find more, I'll contact you. The interrogation notes on our current captive should appear on your screen in a few moments."

He barely noted the confirmation of the files. "I know Kalahn will hate it, but keep her under guard and secluded for the time being. I can't risk someone kidnapping or murdering her."

"She's staying with the Jasvarians, in their innermost dwelling area. Few Kelderans are allowed entry. She'll be safe there."

The Jasvarians were human colonists, and for the most part, they lived in carved out rooms inside the mountains.

Kason's bride, Taryn, was their leader.

Keltor replied, "Only because I know what your bride is capable of am I going to trust her to guard our sister. Still, check on Kalahn daily to ensure she hasn't fooled her guards and escaped. Kalahn is more charming than she should be."

"You mean more rebellious than she should be."

"That, too. And one more thing—make sure to look after yourself, too, brother."

"Of course."

Silence stretched. As much as Keltor forgave his brother for chasing away Azalyn more than two decades ago—their father had been the main one responsible anyway—they had little in common. Kason had joined the Kelderan Army at sixteen, meaning he'd rarely lived in the palace after that. Keltor had spent the majority of his time with tutors and learning how to rule a planet.

And now Kason lived on an alien world. There was little hope of ever having closeness.

Just as Keltor was about to sign off, Kason spoke again. "I heard about your son and Azalyn from Thorin's bride. Are you handling it okay?"

Careful to keep his face expressionless, he said, "My feelings aren't important right now. I must devise a way to find and displace any female traitors on Keldera. I won't be seeing much of Kelzal or Azalyn until after the coronation. We will mostly have separate lives."

Kason grunted. "Tell yourself that you're too busy if you wish. But my bride is pregnant, and I'm going to be a father myself before too long. I hope you have the same vow as me—to not act as our father did during our childhood and to treasure the gift of a child instead of using them as a mere tool."

With that, Kason signed off and the screen went blank.

Rather than dwell on his brother's parting words, Keltor brought up the interrogation notes for the traitorous female. She hadn't revealed much, but she implied that she wasn't the only female working for the greater cause.

If only Keltor had time to screen potential female candidates, train them, and place them undercover. From his years exploring the main population centers in disguise, Keltor knew where most of the antimonarchy groups met and planned their attacks. It was just a matter of placing someone he trusted inside the enemy ranks. One person wouldn't be able to do it alone, but it would at least be a start while he put more permanent structures for intelligence gathering in place.

True, he did have one potential pool of fully trained candidates, but their skills were too valuable to waste on mere espionage. That was if his father even granted him the ability to use them in the first place.

A message flashed on his screen from Azalyn, asking for a meeting. At her name, it dawned on him that he had someone he trusted who had also spent decades living under the radar. Neither Kason nor Keltor had been able to locate her. And with some skin color covering and a makeover, no one would recognize her.

The only question was whether he risked Azalyn's life or not.

Of course, that was a king's way of thinking, to weigh risks and costs against results. However, Azalyn had been someone special to him, and he would never risk her life without her consent. He would talk and ask for her help. If she said no, he wouldn't force it. And if she said yes, Keltor would show her what he knew and how to navigate the extremists' ranks safely.

Not wanting to think of how it gave him an excuse to spend more time with her, he confirmed a meeting with her later in the day and made preparations in case she agreed to the assignment.

Chapter Eight

Azalyn sat outside Keltor's main conference room and tapped one of her feet. She was the type of person to arrive ten minutes early. Unfortunately, that meant more time to stress, worry, or fume over what was to come.

And considering Keltor had kept a big secret from her about what she was to him, back when they'd been much younger, Azalyn was impatient to find out the truth.

The door finally opened and three older males in long robes, which indicated that they were royal councilors, filed out. A few seconds later, Keltor appeared in the doorway. "Come in."

She stood and followed him inside. Keltor took a seat at the long, oval table and motioned to the spot next to him.

Azalyn sat at the opposite, far side of the table because if she sat next to him, Keltor might be able to distract her from the purpose of their meeting.

To his credit, Keltor didn't so much as blink an eye at her small act of defiance. He laid his hands on the table and asked, "What did you wish to speak to me about?"

Azalyn had never been diplomatic with anyone but a potential customer, so she spat out, "Why didn't you tell me I was one of your potential destined brides?"

His brows furrowed slightly. "How do you know about

that?"

"The how doesn't matter. Why didn't you tell me? If I'd known about how you could probably get me pregnant by staring at me, I would've been more careful."

Keltor's voice was calm as he said, "I hadn't intended to claim you until we married. What happened between us was unexpected."

She stood. Keltor was retreating behind his royal facade, and she wasn't having it. "That's all you have to say? That it was 'unexpected?'" She walked up to him and pointed her forefinger. "All these years, I've felt guilty for not telling you about Kelzal. For almost begging you to claim me the night I took you to those old ruins. And you knew what that could've brought. If you hadn't broken my heart already, this would do it all over again. Because despite knowing it was highly likely I carried your offspring, you didn't find me." Her voice lowered. "You abandoned me, regardless of consequences. Maybe you aren't the male I thought you were."

She moved to turn away, but Keltor was up and lightly grabbing her shoulders before she could do so. He gave her a gentle shake. "Look at me, Azalyn. I want you to see the truth in my eyes when I explain myself."

Since she wasn't a coward, Azalyn took a deep breath and met his gaze. If she'd expected to find emotion, it wasn't there.

And that only wrenched her heart further.

Keltor spoke again. "The real reason I didn't say any-thing is because I wanted you to love me for me. Not be-cause I was a prince with a palace, in need of offspring. Not because one day I would be king. And to my surprise, you did fall in love with me for me, Aza. I was going to tell you eventually, once we had a date for the official claiming ceremony. But then the special night with you happened, and you were gone. My brother and father said you were betrothed to another. Logically, I knew there was a chance you carried my offspring even though I was careful and spilled my seed on the ground. But when I couldn't locate you and the day of your supposed claiming ceremony came up, I decided either you hadn't conceived or you thought it was from your intended lord. I had no way of knowing until recently that my father lied about your intended." He leaned closer, and fierceness filled his gaze. "While I can't deflect all the blame—I should've told you the full truth—we were both pawns of my father when it came to his vision of the future. I'm sorry I never found you. I'm sorry I never told you about being a potential destined bride. And I'm sorry I wasn't strong enough to decline your offer to claim you. In everything else, I'm a rational and collected male. But with you, I can't seem to control myself." Keltor lowered to his knees. "I can't change the past, but forgive me, Azalyn. I was a young fool and I hurt you. On pain of death, I vow to never do it again."

At the sight of Keltor kneeling on the ground, begging for her forgiveness, tears prickled her eyes. Despite the pain and deception, she still wished they'd had a chance at spending the last twenty-three years together rather than apart.

Because with her, Keltor was a male and not a prince. He was merely himself, with all his faults on display.

And despite everything, she still cared for him. Maybe not love, but she definitely didn't want him begging on his knees.

Foolish as it may be, Azalyn kneeled as well. "I agree we can't change the past. But if there's anything else I should know, tell me now, Keltor. Because if I find out you're keeping more secrets concerning us—ones that aren't kept secret out of planetary security or some other such important reason—I will keep our relationship formal and distant. I won't have my heart broken again, which happens every time I learn of a new deception."

She was aware of how hypocritical she sounded, considering the secret of Toralyn, but she would tell him as soon as Kelzal allowed it. The circumstance may not be as vital as protecting the planet in the grand scheme of things, but if Keltor's son were to ever accept the responsibility of ascending the throne, trust would be required.

Cupping her cheek, Keltor murmured, "There is something else. I went looking for you. Once Kason told me the truth not that long ago, I donned a disguise and visited every Sulani merchant I could find. Every time I went in, pretending to have wares for sale, they'd fetch the acquisitions partner. My heart would thunder in my chest, only to be disappointed when someone other than you showed up. I had no idea you'd signed up for the new colony."

Her heart rate kicked up. "You went looking for me?"

He smiled. "Yes. I had expected to find you married with children. Still, I wanted to apologize for what happened all those years ago."

As Keltor strummed his thumb against her cheek, Azalyn simply gazed into his eyes. For him to don a disguise and go out alone was dangerous. Of all the things she could've said, she growled and whispered, "That was a stupid thing to do. You could've been killed and then where would Keldera be?"

Something she didn't often see—humor—danced in his eyes. "Kason would've been forced to come back. I expect his human bride would've brought her dagger-wielding female warriors and scandalized the planet."

She lightly hit his chest. "That's not funny."

He shrugged. "Finding you and apologizing was a priority because of how important you were to me once, Aza.

Although I must admit, I'm glad to still be alive. And not just to help steer change on my planet, but because it means I found you again."

Azalyn stopped breathing. Maybe she was reading too much into his tone of voice, but it almost sounded as if he... still cared about her. Maybe even wanted her.

The years melted away. It was as if she were still a teenager with her darling prince in front of her.

Her lips ached to take Keltor's. But Azalyn was older and not about to chance her heart without certainty.

Gripping Keltor's wrist, she removed his hand from her cheek. Confusion flashed in his eyes. Before he could stand and walk away, Azalyn spoke again. "There's much I want to say, but none of it matters. Even if we don't kill each other and find a way to rekindle what we once had, there's the matter of Keldera. You must take a worthy bride to secure peace, end of story."

His expression turned hungry. "You want to rekindle things between us?"

"Let's not play the what-if game, Keltor. It'll only cause more pain for the both of us."

Before she could do more than blink, he hauled her body up against his and leaned down to her ear. At his warm, muscled chest pressing against her, she had a hard time concentrating on his words. "There may be a way for you to become my bride, Aza. It even involves a little danger, which you love."

Careful to keep her hope bottled up, she asked, "What are you talking about?"

"If you become a spy and help to save Keldera, no one would question me taking you as my bride."

Despite decades of training and tutoring on what it meant to be the heir to the throne, as soon as Azalyn had hinted about maybe still wanting him, everything else fled his mind. For a chance to maybe get what he wanted, as well as to keep her from escaping before he could say what needed to be said, he hauled her up against his body.

And as soon as her soft body touched his, desire rushed straight to his cock. He could try pretending otherwise, but he wanted Azalyn. He always would.

Maybe, just maybe, he might be able to win her, too.

So when she asked her question, he murmured, "If you become a spy and help to save Keldera, no one would question me taking you as my bride."

"That is less than helpful, Keltor."

He smiled at her dry tone. Azalyn would never bow her head and acquiesce to his every whim.

And that was exactly what he wanted.

Focus, Keltor. It's time to fight for her. "I will explain in detail and answer your every question. But I won't be able to think properly until I do this."

Leaning down, he kissed her.

Without hesitation, Azalyn opened her mouth and accepted his tongue. Her encouragement stirred a baser urge, and Keltor devoured her mouth as he moved his hand to her plump rear.

At the movement, Azalyn hugged him closer and dug her nails into his back. Every time he tried to stroke and take control of her mouth, Azalyn fought back to do the same to him.

She wasn't afraid to take what she wanted.

And it was glorious.

He would've gladly coaxed her to the ground and taken her, but his blasted communicator beeped three times, signaling a call. Azalyn broke their kiss at the sound. "That might be important."

Nipping her bottom lip, he growled out, "It can wait. If it were important, it would beep five times."

The corner of her mouth kicked up. "What if it beeped eight times? Does that mean the world is ending?"

Without thinking, he lightly slapped her rear. "Don't be ridiculous. Six is enough. Those two extra beeps could spell disaster."

She laughed. Watching the crinkling of her eyes lightened his heart in a way he hadn't experience in years.

When she finished, Azalyn merely tilted her head and asked, "So care to tell me about this plan of yours? It'll help me decide what to do next."

At the playfulness in her gaze, he smiled. "I can't wait to see what that is."

Moving a hand to the nape of his neck, she lightly stroked his skin. At the soft touch, he wanted to bury his head in Azalyn's neck, pull her close, and never let go.

But in order to ever have a chance at that future, he needed Azalyn's help. "Computer, secure conference room. Level Ten."

The computer replied, "Conference room secured."

Azalyn raised her brows. "Now I'm intrigued."

He didn't want to let Azalyn go, but his knees were no longer that of a twenty-year-old and were protesting the hard floor. So he stood, careful to keep Azalyn with him, and moved them both to a chair. The second Azalyn sat on his lap, she wiggled her lower body. Keltor hissed and willed his cock to behave.

"Keltor." He met her green-eyed gaze, and she continued, "No more stalling. Just tell me what's going on. Because if there's a way I could kiss you again, I might just take it."

The long-buried urge to tease surfaced, but he pushed

passed it. "Kason found an antimonarchy spy amongst the Kelderan colonists on Jasvar. And not just any spy, but a female one. We suspect there are more female traitors on this planet."

She shrugged a shoulder. "That doesn't surprise me, really. What better way to get information than to tempt a male to bed. Once you have his cock in your hand, he'll say almost anything."

Anger flared in his belly. "You say that with such confidence."

She rolled her eyes. "Do I have a group of males following me around, begging to be with me? No. So just stop with the jealousy."

He grunted and ignored the truth she'd pointed out—he was jealous of the males she'd shared her body with in the past.

Bringing them back on topic, he continued, "At any rate, I need to know if the problem is widespread and if any of the antimonarchy leaders are female. My father has resisted placing informants amongst the enemy ranks, but I think it's vital we start doing so."

"Isn't this something a branch of the army should be in charge of?"

Keltor shook his head. "I don't know who to trust. Remember, not that long ago several previously trusted warriors mutinied against my brother. The few I do trust are now on Jasvar, helping with the new colony. Until they come back with the colony transport ship, this matter is completely up to me."

Searching his eyes, she said, "Don't take this the wrong way, but do you have any experience with this sort of thing?"

"Believe it or not, I do. And not just with searching for you. Before I ever knew the truth about Kason and my father chasing you away, I was using disguises to pinpoint hotspots of unrest." She opened her mouth, but he pushed on. "I know you're going to say that was unwise and dangerous, but I never attended meetings or went inside any establishments with antimonarchy-leaning sympathies. My purpose was to find them so I could send in others when I finally took over the throne."

She tilted her head. "I would think you'd be doing that already. Technically, your father is still king. But by all accounts, he's unwell. Or so I overheard when I was in the hospital."

He took a long piece of her hair between his fingers and rubbed the silky strands. "I was thinking of how to start placing operatives when a certain female and her son popped into my life."

"*Our* son, Keltor. If you don't start thinking of Kelzal that way, then you'll never have a relationship with him."

"We'll discuss Kelzal at a later time. For now, I need to know if you'd be willing to go out in disguise and be my spy."

Frowning, she said, "Will that even work? Putting aside the fact I've never done it before, I'm sure my picture will be circulating amongst the media soon enough."

"Your records were erased not long ago. I was puzzled about that at first, but now I think my father did it. Add in the fact I haven't announced anything yet, and I think you'll be safe enough. You've lived out amongst the people and can probably blend in far better than me. After all, Kason went looking for you shortly after you disappeared and couldn't find you. And even as a teenager, he was good at finding people."

Azalyn sighed. "That was a stroke of luck, more than anything. I was placed with an old Sulani auntie, who lived deep in the Dilsahn Forest. She was paranoid about everything, but the isolation made it easier to hide my pregnancy.

As much as I'd love to help you, I'm not sure I'd be the best fit." He opened his mouth to push for more details, but she beat him to it. "But before we discuss anything else, there is one thing I can do to help, Keltor. Vala Yarlen and I grew close during our captivity. If she knows someone within the Barren who can at least put an ear to the ground and pass on information that way, it would be a start. Too bad it'd take weeks to contact her and get a reply."

Vala Yarlen had been kidnapped by an alien race known as the Tallarians, along with Azalyn and Kelzal. She currently lived on Jasvar with her lord, Thorin Jarrell.

Keltor refused to let Azalyn's news about living with her aunt to deter him from finding a way to win her. "I can contact Vala much quicker than that. But before I do, just know that I'm determined to find a way for Keldera to accept you. Because if I can win your affections again, I'm never letting you go."

Azalyn wanted to take Keltor's words to heart and not question them, but she couldn't. "Why the change and willingness to fight, Keltor?"

"Some females would say I was being romantic and might even give me a kiss."

She raised her brows. "If you think I've changed that much, then there must be something wrong with you."

Smiling, Keltor murmured, "And that, right there, is one of the reasons I want to win you again, Aza. You have no idea how nice it is to hear the truth. My sister used to do so, but she's on Jasvar." He tucked a few strands of hair behind her ear. "But in full disclosure, I'm also addicted to your taste." He ran a finger down her cheek. "Your softness." His hand brushed lower, to just over her heart. "And your passion." Meeting her gaze, he whispered, "I just need to find a way to win you and protect Keldera at the same time."

While hearing Keltor's words caused her body to flush, Azalyn ignored it to focus on the bigger picture. "Is that even possible? Even if we root out most of the antimonarchy leaders, are you willing to risk taking an unemployed, forty-year-old female with an illegitimate child as your bride? It will shatter the millennia-long illusion of the monarchy as a higher-classed group of beings, ones that never display anything but the epitome of morality."

"You say that as if a change in perception is a bad thing. I've already helped coordinate a new colony to ease our overpopulation woes. If I can also reduce the likelihood of civil war, then maybe the masses will see me as much a politician as any of the commoners' representatives. If so, then they may start to believe I can effect change. Because if we don't start doing so, I imagine things will only get worse as news spreads of the freedoms granted to the Jasvarian colony."

She couldn't help but smile. "So, in other words, no big deal."

"Not if it means I have a chance with you again."

"Keltor."

"It's true. But maybe if I state I won't kiss you again until I've sorted this and proven my intentions, it will drive me to find a solution faster."

"And if it takes years? I don't like that scenario. So I have a better idea—you're going to let me help you."

"Let you?" Keltor echoed as he raised an eyebrow.

"Yes. You should feel quite honored, I might add. I was the best when it came to finding new products to sell. I even started a few trends. Finding a way to change Keldera for the better is exactly the kind of task I enjoy."

The laughter in Keltor's eyes made her heart sing.

"Then, oh wise one, I think the first step is contacting Vala and setting up an informant or two inside the citadels."

"You still haven't told me how you can reach her quicker."

He shrugged. "Kason just completed a long-range communications tower on Jasvar. He made the first call earlier, and they should still have enough power for another one. So, let's put in a request for Vala." He rubbed her back. "But to do that, you must disembark from my lap, my lady."

Snorting, Azalyn stood again. "I see the Keltor I once knew is starting to come back to life."

"He's always been there, but only seems to come out for a certain merchant's daughter."

Azalyn should merely enjoy Keltor teasing her and seeking her opinion. But Azalyn couldn't let the issue nibbling at the back of her mind to just sit there. "Is all of this because of me being your potential destined bride?"

"No," he answered as he stood, too. "My instinct only informs me that you can bear my children and that I should claim you as soon as possible. It has nothing to do with emotions or feelings."

She hesitated. The next answer could devastate her. And yet, she finally blurted out, "Is it still there? Because if you need more children to ensure peace, I may not be able to grant that."

He lightly placed a finger under her chin. "It only matters if you want children, Aza, because that doesn't matter to me. However, I have a feeling that's what you were crying about near the fountain. Correct?"

She wanted to hate him for being so clever, but she couldn't. "Yes. I just keep thinking about everything I missed. His first step, his first words, and even his first technological invention. I missed all of it. And yet, I don't want Kelzal to feel as if he's less to me if I had another child. It may have been from a distance, but I watched him grow up and treasured every single change and accomplishment."

"Kelzal is a grown male, whether you like it or not. I think he would understand."

"Maybe, maybe not. But I could be worrying for nothing after what the Tallarians did to me."

Keltor searched her eyes before finally replying, "Part of me wants to keep a secret from you, but I won't. Despite how much I've tried to ignore it, the instinct is still there. At least with me, there is still a chance for you to have a child, Aza, if that's what you wish."

❉ ❉ ❉

For a split second, Keltor had thought about keeping the constant, low hum of his instinct from Azalyn. He may be forty-two years old, but deep down Keltor was just a male who wanted to be accepted for who he was rather than what he was or what he could provide.

But the uncertainty in Azalyn's eyes had done him in, so he told her the truth.

Yes, he'd mostly been blocking the instinct ever since seeing her unconscious form in the hospital bed. At the time, he'd believed keeping his distance and burying himself in his work had been his only option for a future.

However, as soon as Azalyn had mentioned wanting another child, the image of a little girl running into his arms had flashed inside his head. Unlike his father who would've turned away and called one of the royal child caretakers, Keltor had embraced her, picked her up, and gently tossed her into the air. The imaginary girl's squeals still made him smile.

Keltor may be a prince, but Azalyn could give him the greatest gift of all—a child to love and cherish from day one.

Kelzal was his son, and he would work on the relationship, but Kelzal was a self-sufficient male who needed little help. Another child would rely on Keltor, and for once, he looked forward to being strong and providing for another person.

Much like he wanted to do for Azalyn.

Touching his cheek, Azalyn finally said, "It looks like I have a bigger reason to help you secure peace. And before you close yourself off to me and think I only want your seed, let me say this—I want more than your cock, Keltor. I want my best friend back, too. Please tell me he's still there, and I won't have to constantly battle to bring him out."

Staring into Azalyn's eyes, he murmured, "It will take some work and conditioning, but I'd like for him to at least come out without hesitation around you."

She finally looped her arms around his neck, and his heart rate kicked up at her heat so close to his skin.

He was starting to think Azalyn should always be naked when they were alone so he could make up for lost time.

Her voice garnered his attention. "Then kiss me to seal the deal." Moving his head, he kissed her jaw, and Azalyn growled. "That's not what I meant."

Keltor trailed kisses down her neck, to where it met her shoulder. Curious to see if the place still drove her wild, he lightly nibbled her skin.

Azalyn threaded the fingers of one hand through his hair and gently tugged.

He had his answer.

Keltor continued to nibble and lick the special spot, enjoying how Azalyn leaned more against him, and her breathing hitched several times.

Tempted as he was to kiss lower so he could take her nipple into his mouth, Keltor didn't want to rush things. If he wanted to prove to Azalyn he would fight this time, unlike his younger self, he would put off claiming her until their future was secure.

She chose that moment to rub her lower body against his trouser-clad cock. He groaned. "Don't tempt me, Aza. There's too much to do. And not just for Keldera, but for us as well."

Her movements stilled. Raising his head, Keltor nearly sighed in relief when he saw approval in Azalyn's eyes. She murmured, "I almost want to get my hopes up this time."

"But, you can't."

She shook her head. "No, my heart can't take it."

He kissed her lips gently before saying, "Then let's contact Jasvar and set things in motion. Maybe my brother will have some ideas on how to help us as well."

Azalyn pecked his mouth with a kiss. "I hope he does because if there is a possible future for us, I want to seize on it and start it sooner rather than later so we can erase the twenty years we were apart."

Keltor wished he had the ability to go back in time and watch Azalyn grow into the confident, clever female she'd become. "We'll see how it plays out. But I have to make one thing clear, Aza—in public and in front of others, I have to be distant. The last thing I need is for someone to recognize you as one of my weaknesses and use it against me."

She raised an eyebrow. "I hope that's not forever, because if—and that's a big if—we find a way to secure peace for Keldera even with me at your side, I want to make clear that you're off-limits to other females."

He smiled. "And now who's jealous of nameless females?"

"I learned as much as I could about the history of the Kelderan monarchy, and I know most kings took numerous mistresses. I won't tolerate that."

"As long as you don't seek out other males, I think we'll be just fine."

Her eyes turned heated. "Then just make sure I have no reason to wander."

Keltor should push Azalyn away and call his brother. But he deserved one kiss, so he took Azalyn's lips. Worrying the flesh of her lower lip with his teeth before thrusting his tongue inside her mouth, he stroked and tangled until Azalyn was breathing hard. Only then did he sever contact. "Consider that a preview of what's to come."

Finally mustering the strength, Keltor took a step back. He wanted to clutch Azalyn's hand and let the world know his intentions. However, he drew on decades of practiced self-control and motioned toward the rear of the conference room. "My secure comm unit is this way. Jasvar awaits us, my dear Azalyn."

"As gallant as you're trying to be in letting me walk ahead of you, I have no idea where I'm going. So, lead on, your highness." Azalyn lowered her voice. "If you take off your formal robes, it'll also give me the chance to see if your rear matches my memory."

Yes, Azalyn was definitely different from other females in his life, even more so than Kalahn. He refused to believe his sister asked males to disrobe so she could ogle them. "I would, but my guards will be waiting for us, and I don't want to draw attention. They will undoubtedly ask questions."

She snorted. "Their expressions would be worth it."

"Azalyn," he growled in warning.

Putting up her hand, Azalyn replied, "Okay, okay. I'll dutifully follow you and your flowing robes. Let's get a move on."

Not blinking at Azalyn's order, Keltor complied by disengaging security and exiting the conference room to the main corridor of his living quarters. If not for the guards stationed at fixed points, he would shrug off his robes and enjoy her attentions.

While he couldn't just yet, for the first time Keltor started to think that one day he could.

Chapter Nine

Azalyn smiled as soon as Vala's golden-skinned, white-haired head appeared on the screen. "It's good to see you, Vala. Although maybe someday, it will be merely to talk as friends instead of regarding urgent circumstances."

"I'm sure both of us are working to create a better future. Once it happens, we'll have plenty of time to talk," Vala replied.

Despite being an outcast her entire life and enduring a second-class citizenship, Vala's optimism never failed to amaze Azalyn. "Maybe you can send me a long-range transmission of what Jasvar is like? Even if I'm not joining you there now, I'm still curious."

"Of course." Vala tilted her head. "Although I wish you were here, I'm just glad you're okay. I've been told you had recovered, but it's not the same thing as talking with you."

Vala had been with Azalyn and Kelzal on board the Tallarian starship. But shortly after the rescue mission, Vala had been whisked away by her future lord to Jasvar, whereas Azalyn had been brought to the Kelderan palace.

Azalyn replied, "Same for me. Maybe one day you can come here to visit."

If the laws surrounding the Barren ever changed on Keldera was left unsaid.

Bobbing her head, Vala said, "I hope so. Now, what did you need to talk to me about? Thorin mentioned it was urgent."

After explaining the female spy in the Kelderan colony on Jasvar and how she and Keltor needed more information, she added, "Which comes to my favor. The Barren see and hear more than most people realize. Do you know of anyone within the citadels who can keep an ear open and report anything suspicious to us?"

"Thorin already explained about the spy here to me. Though why the males act so surprised, I have no idea." There was a grunt offscreen that Azalyn suspected was Vala's lord, Thorin Jarrell. Vala ignored the sound. "As for trusting someone in the citadels, my former Barren Mother will help, I know it. She's always been loyal to the king because of how many favors he granted her citadel. She will probably know of others who also favor the monarchy."

"Good. I can look up the details of your former citadel from here. Should I just mention your name?"

"My name is a start, but I would include the word 'guardian' in the subject. It will signify that a Barren endorses your request," Vala explained.

"Thanks, Vala."

"Of course. And one more thing—the human leader of Jasvar, Taryn, shared her female spy-training program with Thorin and Kason. The document also has hints of what to look for in how to identify one. I'm not sure if that will help, but I can send that to you, too, if you like."

Not for the first time, Azalyn was curious about the matriarchal power structure of the humans on Jasvar. "That would be great. I may read it myself before passing it on to Keltor."

At the casual use of the crown prince's name, a question flashed in Vala's eyes. However, before her friend could ask it, Azalyn added, "I should probably go. But before I do, I wanted to let you know that both Kelzal and I are safe. I'll send an update with more information when I can. Until next time, Vala."

Vala opened her mouth, but the light blue face of Thorin Jarrell—Vala's lord and former general in the Kelderan Army—came on screen. "Don't end the transmission just yet. I need to talk with Prince Keltor."

She glanced over her shoulder, to where Keltor was waiting outside the private comm unit. He was watching her through the clear window. She motioned for him to come inside. Once he complied, she said, "Thorin wants to talk to you."

Azalyn moved out of the way, and Keltor took her place. "What is it, Thorin?"

The warrior grunted. "I'm not sure you want Azalyn in the room for this."

Holding her breath, Azalyn waited to see what Keltor would do. By all rights, he should send her out of the comm unit space. She had no role in the government or even the prince's council.

But when he waved a hand in dismissal, she let out her breath, and he said, "She has my trust. Now, talk."

Since Thorin had spent most of his life in the army, he didn't question the order. "The head of the Sulani Merchants, Ulrick, has made repeated requests for an audience with you. He's petitioned not only your brother, but me and the other heads of the military command on Jasvar."

"Did he say about what?" Keltor asked.

"No, your highness. Just that it was important to the future of Keldera."

Keltor frowned. "And yet, he now resides on Jasvar."

"His son, Tyrick, comes every day and waits for an audience to be granted. He's sitting in the reception area of our military command structure as we speak. What do you wish to do about him?"

"How are the power levels? I know that a long-range transmission consumes a lot of energy."

Thorin grunted. "Enough for a brief meeting. If I may be forthright, your highness?" Keltor nodded once, and Thorin continued, "It would free up a considerable amount of resources if you would talk with him. The Sulanis would finally leave us alone and allow us to do our jobs instead of placating them at every turn."

"Then fetch him."

Thorin made a fist and pounded it over his chest in salute. The instant Thorin's face disappeared from the screen, Keltor put the comm unit on mute and glanced at Azalyn. "Do you have any idea what this is about?"

"No, I truly don't. As far as I know, the Sulanis avoid politics at any costs. The merchant business relies on selling to any and all customers, as Ulrick always says."

"And what about his son?"

She shrugged one shoulder. "I've met him a few times. Everyone says Tyrick is being groomed to take over the business."

"And considering the Sulanis are tied for first when it comes to the most powerful merchant organization on Keldera, that is quite a role."

She nodded. "Once this is over, I'll write up what I know and share it with you. The Sulanis may no longer open up to me because of my association with the palace, but I can try." Azalyn noticed the light teal face of Tyrick, who was only a few years older than herself. She motioned toward the screen. "Keltor, he's here."

As Keltor turned to face the comm unit and switched off the mute function, Azalyn strained her ears. When the second-in-command of the Sulani merchants had something important to say, one listened.

✷ ✷ ✷

Keltor assessed the dark eyes of Tyrick Sulani, but he didn't detect any emotion. The male might be a challenge.

Of course, Keltor had dealt with his fair share of challenges before, and he put as much steel into his voice as possible. "Speak, Tyrick Sulani. My time is limited."

Without missing a beat, Tyrick replied, "The Sulanis have a proposition."

So much for Azalyn's adopted family asking about her well-being.

The male also had yet to address him properly as prince. Tyrick Sulani was one to watch. "Then state it."

As if sensing his misstep, Tyrick bowed his head. "Of course, your highness." He met Keltor's gaze again. "While we've remained neutral during recent times, not outwardly supporting the pro- or antimonarchy factions, my father has laid plans to secure the future of our business. In order for it to thrive, he believes the monarchy is necessary."

As much as he wanted to make a dry comment, Keltor kept his voice firm and even. "Explain."

"Before I begin, let me say that all of this is conditional. Until a deal is reached, no help is being offered."

"Your license to practice business on Jasvar is conditional. You'd do well to remember that."

"Yes, your highness."

The words might be formal, but Tyrick's tone implied that it wasn't much of a concern.

Keltor was starting to think the Sulanis had more power than his councilors had realized. He would have to question Azalyn at length later on.

Even a few days ago, he might've suspected Azalyn had

been deliberately kidnapped, with the intention of him rescuing her. With her in the palace, she could then try to win his affections. But after everything, his gut said that wasn't the case. He would give Azalyn the benefit of the doubt.

He grunted, and Tyrick spoke again. "Over the past ten years, my father has trained and placed female merchant spies in every major settlement. They blend in with our competitors and pass on any information they find. As you can imagine, we know who is loyal to your highness in much of the business community and who isn't. That information would be useful."

Careful to keep any reaction from showing on his face, Keltor wondered just what the Sulanis had put into motion. "If verifiable, it would be useful. However, a skilled merchant would never give up such information for free. Provided it can be verified, what is it that you want?"

Tyrick spoke without hesitation. "If you take Azalyn as your bride, we will offer financial support and provide everything we know about your enemies."

Keltor wanted to look at Azalyn's face and see if she was surprised at the news. A flicker of doubt invaded his heart. Had she merely wanted to earn his good graces to advance her family's cause?

No. A good prince never made a decision without all the facts. He wouldn't risk losing her forever without hearing her side of the story first.

Keltor asked, "What do you gain from this?"

Azalyn's whisper filled the space. "Branding. They want the official royal endorsement."

At her tone, he did glance at her. Her lavender face was pale.

Before he could stop her, Azalyn was at his side and maneuvered her head into the camera space. "Did Ulrick plan all of this? Did he share my location to the Tallarians so that

I'd eventually end up in the palace? Did he risk my son's life so that he could try to increase his future profits?"

"That is not your concern, cousin," Tyrick stated.

"It is bloody well my concern, Ty. Did you know that I was *beaten* to within an inch of my life?"

"You wouldn't have died. That's all I can say."

With a growl, Azalyn turned and ran out the room. It took every bit of diplomacy and training Keltor possessed to say coolly, "I will contact you another time."

Switching off the screen, he ran after Azalyn, in the direction she'd headed. But once he reached the corridor, he didn't see her multi-colored dress anywhere. He looked to the guard and motioned toward Keltor's private library.

He dashed inside and found Azalyn pacing the length of the room. "Azalyn."

Her fierce gaze met his. "I had no idea, Keltor. I swear on Kelzal's life."

Not wanting to spook her, he took two steps forward and stopped. "I believe you."

She blinked and stilled. "What? Why?"

"You are many things, Azalyn, but a good actor isn't one of them. Your emotions are always close to the surface."

As she paced again, Azalyn growled, "I can't believe this. Ulrick was willing to risk my life in order to further his grand scheme. And Kelzal's...to think what might have happened."

Keltor closed the distance between them and took one of Azalyn's hands to keep her from pacing. He never broke his gaze as he answered, "But Kelzal is alive and well. And Ulrick is too skilled a merchant to allow a prized possession to be taken away so easily. I'm sure he had a backup plan."

"So now I'm a 'possession?'" She tugged her hand, but Keltor refused to let go. "And why are you so calm? They manipulated you as well, Keltor. I'm sure you see that."

"I will handle Ulrick and his son later. If they wish to have my good graces, then they have a lot to make up for."

She huffed. "After everything that's happened, you still want to work with that bastard?"

"Yes, because he has offered us a chance to be together."

She shook her head. "He used us, Keltor. You can't be thinking of taking him up on his offer. No doubt he probably has further plans for you and how to use it to his own advantage. You would be the first person to say a prince should never be in debt to anyone. Owing a favor will only lead to trouble later on."

He wrapped an arm around Azalyn's waist. When she didn't push him away, hope bubbled in his chest. "I will make it plain to them that there will be no lingering favors. And before you say the Sulanis are skilled negotiators, so am I." He ran a hand up her back to gently grip her neck. "I need you to believe in me. Because if you don't believe in me, then I'm not sure why anyone should, *zyla*."

✵ ✵ ✵

Azalyn's second chance at life had been a lie.

Learning of Toralyn's existence should've been the first warning. However, despite the Sulani family's problems and squabbles, they'd welcomed her with open arms, and she'd been willing to give them a chance to explain. Not only had they protected her and ensured the safety of her son, but they'd also allowed her to work in their business and had never pushed her to find a lord.

Well, except for her adopted brother in the lead up to and during her brief time aboard the Kelderan colony transport ship. But she had a feeling he'd done that without Ulrick Sulani's knowledge.

And yet, all of it had been part of Ulrick's plans. Her

stomach churned at the thought of what he'd done with Toralyn. For all she knew, they planned to marry her off to strengthen their political ties. A female bride with royal blood would attract the power-hungry like bugs to *jalak* nectar.

She'd just have to push Kelzal to allow her to share Toralyn's existence with Keltor as soon as she had the chance, because one way or another, she'd have to tell Keltor about their daughter or risk losing everything.

Then Keltor offered her a future and even called her *zyla*—a Kelderan term of endearment a male used for a female they cared about.

Ulrick may have pulled her strings over the years to get her to this point, but from now on, Azalyn would take charge of her own life. "I trust you." She paused and debated adding the male equivalent to *zyla*, which was *zylar*.

Keltor spoke before she could make up her mind. "Good." He leaned closer. "But I will not force you to be anyone's bride. The decision must be yours, *zyla*. What is your desire?"

With the heat of his breath against her cheek, it was hard to concentrate on anything else but Keltor's proximity. Tempting as it was to kiss him and merely say yes, there was too much at stake. "First I want your honest answer—will an endorsement from the Sulanis and their financial support be enough to prevent war? I have a feeling that not even Ulrick has the power to stop some antimonarchists from rioting or launching some sort of attack."

No frustration flashed in his eyes at her question, which was one of the reasons why she wanted him as her lord. "One of the council's potential bride candidates had been the granddaughter of the head of the Treslen merchant family. So I'd say yes, it probably will be."

The Treslens were tied with the Sulanis for the richest

merchants on Keldera. They had also been staunch monarchy supporters for decades.

"Do I even want to know how old the granddaughter is?"

He grimaced. "Twenty. Considering that makes me old enough to be her father, I declined." He searched her gaze. "One of the main reasons the Sulanis were overlooked was because of your ties with them. My father wanted nothing to remind me of you."

"I keep hearing about your father, but I've never met the man. I think it's time I did so."

"Is that a yes, to being my bride?"

"I want to jump into your arms, say yes, and think of a happy future. But until the Sulanis can deliver their promise of information—even a small piece as a sign of good faith before any agreement is signed—I'm not going to give you an answer. There's also something else I want from them as part of your deal."

Keltor raised his brows. "Care to elaborate?"

She didn't hesitate to answer, "As Tyrick mentioned, the Sulanis go against the norm and use females as merchant spies. I think one of the conditions Ulrick needs to meet is to allow you to place some of the trained female spies with the antimonarchy groups. At least for as long as we can keep our intentions secret. It'll become too dangerous for them if I do become your bride, so this is something we need to put into motion as soon as possible."

For a few beats, Keltor remained silent. Whether he knew it or not, this was a test. Because if he wanted her as a bride, then he needed to know she would be more than a mother to their children or a female to share his bed. Azalyn wanted to be his partner in all ways.

While it was a borderline treasonous thought, Azalyn believed it was high time for a female to influence the monarchy and their decisions. Females made up about half the population of Keldera and having that many people on your side would be a powerful thing.

Yes, there were many legal challenges they'd have to tackle to start any sort of change. But given what she knew of Keltor's actions regarding the Kelderan colony on Jasvar, he might be open to them.

He nodded. "I will require Ulrick to help us with infiltrating the antimonarchy groups."

She let out a breath. "I wasn't sure if you'd take my suggestion."

Gently squeezing her neck, he murmured, "I value your brain as much as your body, Azalyn. I may be older, but that preference hasn't changed."

For the second time in her life, Azalyn was starting to think things were too good to be true.

No. She wouldn't allow doubt to ruin whatever chance she had at seizing her future.

Still, she'd never been the best at accepting praise, so she maneuvered the conversation back on track. "When will you talk with Tyrick or his father?"

Keltor didn't so much as blink at the change in subject. "I'll request a video conference as soon as possible to construct the initial blueprint for our agreement. Placing the merchant spies will be one-half of their required signs of good faith. That way they can hopefully gather some information before any announcement is made concerning our marriage."

If Keltor went into the negotiations without knowledge about Toralyn's existence, it would put him at a disadvantage. "There's something else you need to know before talking with any of the Sulanis."

"Which is?"

"I can't tell you yet. I need to talk to Kelzal first."

He searched her gaze. "I must contact the Sulanis as

soon as possible if we're to have any hope of placing a few merchant spies among the antimonarchists in time."

"I know, but please trust me on this, Keltor. There's something you need to know before going into the negotiations."

He studied her face and she did her best not to fidget. As much as Keltor proclaimed to want her, he could still order her to tell him whatever she knew.

Moving his hand from her neck to her shoulder, he finally answered, "I believe you. But talk with Kelzal to garner his permission straight away. Meanwhile, I'll take care of a few matters, but call me as soon as you can, *zyla*. The sooner we put things in motion, the sooner I can make you mine."

Staring up at Keltor, the pessimistic barrier around her heart faded a little. Just knowing he believed her when she said something was important meant a great deal. "Thank you."

He gently kissed her. "Of course. There will always be secrets that must remain so for a short while between us. But I hope we can eventually share everything. I need honesty in my life, Aza. It's one of the few things that staves off loneliness."

"Oh, Keltor." She placed a hand on his cheek. "If everything goes to plan, you'll never be lonely again."

He smiled. "I'm going to take that as a conditional yes to being my bride."

At the tenderness and desire in Keltor's eyes, her heart skipped a beat. "I do want that future, *zylar*. But until we have a formal claiming ceremony, I can't accept that it'll come true."

He murmured, "You called me *zylar*." He kissed her jaw. "Say it again."

While she wasn't one to follow orders blindly, Azalyn

didn't mind this one time. *"Zylar."*

With a growl, Keltor took her lips and pulled her up against his body. She nibbled and licked back every chance she could.

And for the first time, she started to think she could have Keltor, Kelzal, and maybe even her daughter.

A family of her own.

Digging her nails into his back, she deepened the kiss. How she'd ever thought another male would suit, she didn't know.

All too soon Keltor pulled away. "If I don't stop, I'll be tempted to claim you."

Running a hand around to his chest, she murmured, "Such self-control. It makes me wonder what happens when it breaks."

His voice was husky as he said, "You'll find out when I have you naked and at my mercy."

At the heat in his eyes, she shivered. "As much as I liked Keltor the young man, I'm starting to think he aged well."

"Just don't call me old." He nipped her lower lip. "Now as much as I don't want to go back to reality, you need to talk with Kelzal. Because I don't know about you, but I want to get the meeting with Tyrick over with so that I can work at securing our future."

The determination in Keltor's eyes sparked wickedness inside her. "Before we do"—she ran her hand down between their bodies and lightly brushed the hardness of his trouser-clad cock—"you need to tame this."

Keltor hissed in a breath. "Keep that up and I'm going to spill my seed like an adolescent."

She grinned. "That's almost an invitation for me to try and make it happen."

After she stroked his hardness a few more time, Keltor grunted. "As much as I loved teenage Azalyn, I'm starting to like this older vixen more."

She should feel shame for her actions—a proper female would never tease her male in such a way—but with Keltor, it felt...right.

An image of her waking up Keltor by taking his cock into her mouth flashed in her mind. The prince moaned as he fisted her hair and urged her on. She had the power to make him squirm with nothing more than her mouth.

She licked her lips at the idea.

But Keltor's hand grabbed her wrist, and she snapped back to reality. His voice was gentle as he said, "I would be honored to have you bring me to orgasm, *zyla*, but there isn't time." His free hand cupped her breast. "But I assure you, as soon as we have some, I will show you a few of the fantasies I've built up over the years. And believe me, many of them are with you at my mercy and screaming my name."

"Keltor."

He released her and stepped away. As if to ease the sting of his distance, he took her hand in his. "Now, let's each go to our tasks." He glanced at her with amusement in his eyes. "And I assure you I'll be fully deflated before I reach my destination."

She snorted. "Not for the first time, I'm grateful that I can hide my desires by merely controlling the color of my markings. I would never want to be a male."

"I will forever be grateful you were born female." He squeezed her hand. "Now, let's work on securing our own future." He released her and motioned for her to exit ahead of him.

As she walked past, she touched Keltor's shoulder one last time for support. Convincing Kelzal that Azalyn had no choice but to share Toralyn's existence wasn't going to be easy. She only hoped she didn't lose what little trust she had from her son in the process.

Chapter Ten

Azalyn paced the length of her kitchen and back again. As much as she'd wanted to barge into Kelzal's workshop and get her conversation over with, she knew his brain had trouble quitting one task at the drop of a hat. So, she'd sent the urgent message to his computer terminal. A confirmation had come back, signaling he'd be down in fifteen minutes.

Fourteen minutes had passed, and Azalyn still didn't know what to say beyond laying out the facts and hoping Kelzal understood the necessity of sharing their secret with Keltor.

If that wasn't enough to make her heart race, the mere thought of seeing her daughter for the first time made her heart work even harder. Given how things had turned out in her past, Azalyn was leery of accepting a happy future. But maybe, just maybe, heartbreak was all behind her.

Footsteps on the stairs garnered her attention. That would be Kelzal.

When her son entered the kitchen, Azalyn sat down at the small table to one side. She motioned to the free seat across from her. "We need to talk."

Kelzal sat, remaining silent.

Azalyn had decided to ease into her request, so she

asked, "How much do you know about Ulrick Sulani?"

If he was curious about her topic, he didn't show it. "He's the head of the Sulani merchants. He's also a big investor in my research firm."

It seemed Ulrick had found a way into Kelzal's sphere, too. "Toralyn must work for him, too. Is that right?"

He shrugged. "She mentioned that she works in a Sulani shop. I never thought to ask for more details."

Azalyn had looked up Toralyn's public records earlier. "She's a shop assistant, but that's all I know."

Kelzal met her gaze. "Why is this important? You promised me that you wouldn't tell anyone about her. However, it almost sounds like you're trying to figure out where she lives and works."

Tapping her fingers against the table, Azalyn decided to be honest. "I found out earlier today that Ulrick Sulani used me to gain a connection to the prince."

He looked away. "Ulrick is supposed to be highly intelligent. Telling you that counters his reputation."

"It came from his heir, Tyrick."

"Ah. The male who tries hard but is never able to fulfill his father's expectations."

Frowning, she leaned forward a fraction. "How do you know that? I'll admit we haven't known each other long, but I wouldn't peg you as someone who frequents dinners and gatherings to listen to gossip."

"You're correct, I'm not. However, Tyrick started coming to my firm's investor meetings in his father's place. Since I like to know who I'm working for, I did my research. I have ways of finding information others can't." He stared at her shoulder. "Although discovering anything about you was impossible, which means someone didn't want you to be found."

Not wanting to be sidetracked, Azalyn pushed aside

the knowledge that Kelzal had looked for her. "Let's bring things back to your sister. I have no proof, but just a sense that Ulrick may have plans for her, too." Azalyn reached out a hand but stopped short of touching Kelzal's arm. "Keltor is about to negotiate a deal with the Sulanis, and he needs to know about Toralyn's existence before he does so, or he risks being disarmed. That, in turn, will weaken his bargaining power, which could end up hurting all of us." Her son said nothing. She resisted a sigh and pressed on. "Since I promised you I wouldn't say anything, I'm asking your permission to share the information now."

His eyes flicked to hers. "I told you that she deserves a better life than that of a princess to be married off."

"And I agree. I believe I can convince Keltor to give her some free rein. She doesn't even have to be acknowledged on Keldera. There are plenty of people on Jasvar who would look after her."

"Tell me how that is any better. All having a royal father is good for is to have your life decided for you."

She did touch his arm then. "Look, I know it's not the best situation. But would you rather have Toralyn safe, living a mostly free life on the new Kelderan colony? Or let her remain where she is on Keldera, and wonder every day if someone makes the connection, or worse, Ulrick exposes her connection and uses her for his own plans? At least in the former situation, Toralyn has some freedoms left to her."

"And what, exactly, are you asking me to do? I sense there is more than just my permission you want," Kelzal replied.

Even though Kelzal still hadn't given his permission, Azalyn decided to be forthright and hope that swayed him. "Well, I need to know how much Toralyn knows about your current situation."

"Nothing. Because once I mention it, she'll want to meet you and Keltor. Her life will change forever. And if you send her to Jasvar, I may never see her again."

Azalyn suddenly understood Kelzal's protectiveness. "Just because she'll know who her birth parents are and that she may end up with her aunt and uncle on Jasvar doesn't mean that she'll forget about you, Kelzal. She's known you as her twin brother for over four years. Meeting either me or Keltor, or even the distance between planets, won't take that relationship away from you."

"My adoptive parents are dead, and I have no family left on their side. I suspect that was part of the reason I was placed with them. You and Toralyn are my only family. If she is on Jasvar and you're sent away to the Barren, then I'm left with Keltor and a destiny I don't want."

Even though Kelzal rarely showed emotion, Azalyn heard the fear in his voice. Squeezing his arm gently, she said, "Keltor would never try to take you away from me, I promise you that. If all goes according to plan, I will become his queen and will have a say in what he does."

His brows furrowed slightly. "If it does become true, then how will you have a say in anything? Kelderan queens have no power."

"Let's just say that I'm going to change that." When Kelzal didn't say anything, she added, "Look at the facts—Prince Kason married a human, Princess Kalahn is living on Jasvar, and the Barren are treated equally on the foreign colony there. That's quite a change from the way things have been done in the past. Changing the role of princes and princesses will be difficult, but surely that isn't any harder than granting Barren females equal citizenship on Jasvar."

Kelzal tapped his fingers against the table, his gazed fixated on a spot on the floor. While patience wasn't her strong suit, she held her tongue.

Her son eventually stilled his fingers. "Fine, tell him." He met her eyes. "But if Keltor marries her off for political gain, then I will want nothing to do with either of you. If that means I will go to prison or be locked up for refusing my place in the line of succession, so be it. As it is, I'm hoping you'll have another son, and I can forget about all of this and go back to my life."

With that, Kelzal stood and left the room. Azalyn should be happy at the victory. After all, Kelzal had granted permission to share the secret, which meant Azalyn would soon see her daughter.

However, just because she was gaining a daughter didn't mean she would give up on her son.

There had to be a way for everyone to be happy, and Azalyn would figure it out. In the meantime, she retrieved her small notescreen from the pocket in her skirt and sent a message to Keltor, requesting a meeting.

She only hoped Keltor wouldn't hate her for keeping the secret of Toralyn's existence from him. She'd find out soon enough.

✸ ✸ ✸

The computer's voice boomed inside Keltor's private study, "Azalyn Sulani wishes to enter."

"Permission granted."

Keltor stood from his desk and rushed to the door. As soon as it opened, he reached for Azalyn and pulled her inside. He couldn't resist kissing her lips before finally saying, "Please tell me you have good news."

Even though she smiled, it didn't reach her eyes. "For the most part, yes."

With anyone else, Keltor would retreat behind a carefully constructed facade, and he'd conduct the meeting sans emotion.

However, he allowed concern to fill his voice. "Just tell me, *zyla*."

At the term of endearment, Azalyn looked away for a second but soon met his gaze again. "Kelzal gave me permission to share the secret. But I want you to promise me that you'll listen to everything I have to say before jumping to conclusions. You may be a prince, but when it comes to thinking the worst and pulling away, you are the king."

Dread pooled in his stomach, but Keltor kept his voice firm. "I promise."

She placed a hand on his cheek. "I want to preface this by saying I only found out about this secret recently. It's not something I've known for years and kept from you to use at some later point."

Covering her hand with his, he squeezed her fingers. "I'm patient most of the time, but now is not one of them. You can tell me anything, *zyla*."

"I hope so." She pushed gently against his chest. As soon as he released her, she took out her small notescreen, tapped it a few times and turned it toward him. "This is your daughter, Toralyn."

The smiling face of a young woman with lavender skin and blonde hair filled the screen. He barely noted the similarities and difference from his own face before blurting out, "I beg your pardon?"

"We had twins, Keltor. She was born the same day as Kelzal."

A million questions raced through his head. But for once, he didn't think through which might be the best. He simply demanded, "How did you not know about this until recently? And why didn't you tell me?"

She gripped one side of his robes. "Don't back away and close yourself off from me, Keltor. You promised to listen to my explanation."

Since Azalyn's proximity affected his ability to think logically, he shrugged out of his ceremonial robe and walked to the far side of the room. "How did you not know you had twins? Is this what you had to talk to Kelzal about?"

Azalyn squared her shoulders. "Yes. I was under anesthesia when I gave birth. When I woke up, they showed me Kelzal for a minute before taking him away. Until Kelzal showed me the same picture I just showed you and told me about her, I had no idea I'd carried two babies since I'd been denied all images and recordings of my womb. So before you think the worst of me, just know that it's been quite a shock to me, too. I wanted to tell you, but Kelzal made me promise not to." She kept the notescreen facing him and took a step forward. "She looks too much like me and you to be anyone else's daughter, Keltor. Please, just look."

At the pleading in Azalyn's voice, he stared at the picture. Her skin was the exact shade of Azalyn's, and some of her markings were similar to his female's as well. Not to mention Toralyn's eyes were the same shapes as his.

Even her smile reminded him of his sister, Kalahn.

Did he truly have a daughter?

As much as he wanted to scream yes and order her to the palace so that he could protect her, Keltor forced his mind on the bigger picture. "Why did I need to know this before negotiating with the Sulanis?"

Throwing her arms into the air, Azalyn closed the distance between them. "That's all the response I get?" She held the picture up again. "We have two children, Keltor. I don't know about you, but I'm scared more than ever before. That means there are two people who can be kidnapped or killed to get back at the palace. We need to bring her here and protect her."

The truth fell into place. "You haven't met her yet."

"No. The Sulani couple who adopted her are her family. Toralyn has no idea about who her birth parents are. She only knows that Kelzal is her twin brother because her Sulani parents shared his information on her eighteenth birthday. That's why I want to bring her here before the Sulanis know we know. Because Ulrick will use her against you, make no mistake." Her voice lowered. "And in that case, I may never see my daughter. It's bad enough I couldn't watch over her as a child. But to have her harmed now, when I have more resources than ever before...I'm not sure how I could recover from that."

By rights, he should be angry with Azalyn. She'd kept the secret of another child from him.

And yet, as he watched sadness fill her eyes and her shoulders stoop, he pulled her against his body and laid his head on top of hers. "We will protect our children, I promise you that."

"Our children?" she echoed.

"Yes, *our* children. Even if neither one ever acknowledges me as their birth father, I will always call them my children." He could leave it there. A prince should never show weakness or emotion. He'd been taught that since he could talk.

And yet, he didn't care. Azalyn was the one person he could simply be Keltor around. "And I'm happy to find out that I have more than one child. I want nothing more than to hug them and you in my arms. I've wanted a family for so long, but thought I'd never have one."

"But you do have one. Correction, we have one."

He smiled at the fierceness in her voice. "It seems so."

Azalyn melted against his chest. "I'm so sorry I didn't tell you sooner, Keltor. I just couldn't bring myself to violate Kelzal's newly formed trust in me."

"In a way, I understand that." He stroked her back a few

times before he asked, "Are there any other important secrets that you're keeping from me?"

When she didn't reply straight away, Keltor wondered if his dreams of a love- and laughter-filled future with Azalyn as his bride was pure fantasy.

Then her soft voice filled the room. "Just that I want to be your bride, Keltor." She raised her head. "If you still want me, that is."

His uncertainty vanished, replaced with a possessiveness he'd never experienced before. "Of course I want you. There's never been anyone else, Aza. Only you."

She swallowed. "Is that the truth?"

He lowered his head until his lips were a hairbreadth away from hers. "You will only ever get the truth from me, Azalyn. I vow that here and now."

Smiling, she whispered, "Good. I'm going to remind you of that many times in the future, I'm sure."

"Cheeky female." With a growl, he silenced her reply with a kiss. As soon as his lips touched hers, his every nerve came alive, registering her soft form against his bare chest. Simply tasting her lips wasn't enough, so he slid his tongue into her mouth, and he groaned at the sweetness of his soon-to-be bride.

Forgetting the outside world and taking a moment for them both, he slowly licked and explored her mouth. Without thinking, he moved a hand between them to cup her breast. As her hard nipples grazed the palm of his hand, blood rushed to his cock.

If he were a mere commoner, he would take his female right then and there. Once she'd called his name, he'd gather her in his arms and hold her close, content to listen to her beating heart and the sounds of sleep.

After a precious night with his female, he'd gather his family and quietly live out his life with them, savoring each argument, teasing, and even treasuring any resentment because the range of emotions all meant he was alive and no longer alone.

But Keltor wasn't a commoner with such freedom. If he didn't return to his duty soon and gain an ally in the Sulanis, too many would be hurt or even killed simply because he wanted a merchant's daughter as his future queen.

He drew out the bliss of Azalyn's taste for a few more seconds before he broke the kiss. The desire in Azalyn's eyes only made his cock pound harder with desire. What he wouldn't give for a night alone with her.

Growling, he said, "As soon as our daughter is safe and my initial negotiations with the Sulanis are completed, I'm going to claim you. Properly, this time, in a bed."

Her tongue darted to the corner of her mouth, tempting him to shuck his trousers and ask her to kneel in front of him. He could just imagine what she could do to him with that pink tongue.

Thankfully Azalyn spoke up before his desire took over his brain. "Only if I get to claim you as well."

Her straddling his hips, riding him as her breasts bounced, flashed into his mind. "How am I supposed to think straight after such a demand?"

Running her hand up his chest, she lightly brushed her fingers against the skin at the base of his neck. "You're Prince Keltor tro el Vallen, the heir to the Kelderan throne. You'll find a way."

"With you at my side, I will."

She smiled. "Well, we still need to make that happen. The first step in doing that is in finding our daughter and bringing her here. I'd do it myself, if I had the abilities, but I don't. Please tell me you have someone you trust who can locate and retrieve her because you're not going out to do it yourself."

"I could find her if I wished."

"It's not a matter of ability, *zylar*. It's a matter of discretion." She caressed his skin and added, "More than that, your skills are needed here."

Much like how he'd wanted to rush to save Azalyn from the Tallarians that awful night not long ago, he wanted to be the one to find his daughter. But Keltor rarely did what he wished. "I do have someone I can send. My long-time personal guard, Ervan. He often does things for me without my father's knowledge. I would also trust him with my life."

She raised an eyebrow. "Once everything settles down, you're going to have to share some of these assignments because I'm curious."

"I will tell you anything you wish, *zyla*. But let's bring our family together first."

Azalyn nodded. "I trust you, Keltor. Bring Toralyn to safety."

Chapter Eleven

Toralyn Sulani peeked around the corner of the building to check for anyone nearby. The daylight was nearly gone, which helped to hide her form, but what she was doing was too important to risk.

After carefully surveying the streets, windows, and even rooftops, she deemed the area safe. Clutching her wrapped parcel in her arms, she casually walked toward a three-story building made of a light green composite material. On the outside, it looked like dozens of other homes on the street, what with its flower bed and handful of shrubbery. There was even a decorative wreath carved out of wood on the front door. Looking at it, no one would guess what happened inside.

And that was the point.

The door opened to reveal an older female with white hair and magenta skin. She stepped aside, allowing Toralyn to walk past and down the corridor to a familiar door.

Turning the knob, she strode into a large recreation room with gray walls. While no program played at the moment, four other females were scattered around the room, going through a set of meditative poses, with an older female overlooking their actions.

The younger females were her Sulani cousins and fellow

merchant spies.

After quickly ripping open the parcel she carried and changing into a two-piece, tight-fitting outfit, Toralyn walked over to the four younger females and waited for them to finish. Once they did, the female with golden hair and golden skin overlooking them all, Dolvia, stated, "You're late."

Since Dolvia was not only their trainer but Toralyn's adopted mother, she knew better than to criticize during training sessions. Toralyn simply bowed her head. "Apologies, sir. My employer wouldn't let me go until I'd stacked the latest shipment to his satisfaction."

One of the other females, Ulvani, snorted. "Old Sorvel Rippak is a demanding bastard. I'm glad I wasn't assigned to one of his shops."

Toralyn looked to the light teal-skinned female with silver hair. "Better than working for a pervert such as the Treslen heir, who keeps touching your rear. I would most likely toss him across the room every time he tried."

Ulvani shrugged. "Because of me sharing some of the new Treslen design plans, the Sulanis adjusted their next jewelry line, and we're outselling the pervert two-to-one. I see that as a type of revenge."

"Enough," Toralyn's mother said. "We'll discuss all of your weekly reports and works situations later." She looked at Toralyn. "We held off formal meditation until your arrival." The trainer looked at each of them in turn. "Everyone sit down and begin."

Following her mother's order, Toralyn sat cross-legged on the floor and closed her eyes. She imagined a field of stars and zeroed in on one. As she slowly created an alien race with strengths and weakness, she devised maneuvers to defeat them or to at least create a situation where she could draw against them.

She had mentally taken one down when her mother's voice cut through the vision. "Time's up. Open your eyes and stand." Once all of them complied, the trainer continued, "Today will be the most important test of your stints as merchant spies. One of you will be selected for a special assignment. But old Ulrick only wants the best of the best of my warrior-trained females. So your sparring sessions today may well dictate your future."

Ulrick Sulani was the head of the Sulani merchant family and the original brain behind using females as merchant spies. "But Ulrick's currently on Jasvar. Does that mean the assignment takes place there?" Toralyn asked.

"Perhaps," her mother stated. "Triumph in the sparring sessions over the next few weeks and find out."

As a child, Toralyn had always hated her mother pushing her to be better, faster, and smarter than everyone else. But because of it, Toralyn had caught Ulrick Sulani's eye and won a place in merchant spy training program at age sixteen.

The only problem was that she was twenty-two and fast approaching the age when she should take a lord and give up work in the merchant shops. Well, unless she married a merchant herself, then she might still be able to work. But never again as a merchant spy.

Which meant giving up her hard-won freedom and training.

However, if Ulrick had an assignment on Jasvar, Toralyn might be able to escape the usual fate of Kelderan females and the restrictions put on their life choices. By all accounts, Jasvar's human leader was female. Not only that, but most of the female leader's warriors were also women.

If she won a place to Jasvar, Toralyn might never have to marry, which would suit her just fine.

Dolvia motioned for them to take their places. Toralyn stood opposite Ulvani and took her fighting stance. At Dolvia's whistle, she circled to the left and Ulvani mirrored her actions. She forgot about everything but her opponent, imagining her to be one of her competitors. Because if any of them ever found out the truth, it might come to sparring and escaping for her life.

Ulvani's weakness was a lack of patience, and she dashed forward. Toralyn feigned left before ducking and using her body weight to pin Ulvani to the ground. The other female grabbed her hair and tugged. Pain erupted on her scalp, but Toralyn pushed past it, rolling over and taking Ulvani with her.

Her opponent released her grip in the tumble and Toralyn took advantage but flipping Ulvani on her back. At the same time she dug her knee into Ulvani's lower back, she gripped each of the female's wrists and tugged her arms back to where she caused pain but didn't break any bones.

Although if it were a true enemy under her, the position would allow her to do so if need be.

Ulvani struggled, but Toralyn counted to ten, released her cousin, and stood. "I claim victory. Do you acknowledge?"

Rolling over, Ulvani rubbed one of her wrists. "I do, but how about not almost breaking my wrist next time?"

Grinning, Toralyn put out a hand, and Ulvani took it. Once her cousin stood, Toralyn answered, "I've done worse in the past. Remember when we were ten and visiting a distant relative at that farm?"

"Don't remind me. To this day, I swear you were trying to toss me out of that tree."

"You were the one who said you could climb better than anyone. I was out to win."

"I didn't expect you to play dirty," Ulvani muttered.

"Dirty is in the eye of the beholder," Toralyn said with a

shrug. "Until you embrace that fact, you'll never win against me, cousin."

As Ulvani shook her head, Dolvia approached. "Ulvani, as the defeated, take Toralyn's report and go to my office to begin filing the information."

Not willing to disrespect their trainer, Ulvani nodded and put out her hand. Toralyn took out a small digital file storage device from a hidden pocket and handed it to her cousin. Once Ulvani was out of earshot, Dolvia said, "I received a message that you're to go straight home."

She frowned. "What about the rest of the training? Or, the next set of sparring sessions?"

"I will entrust you to complete the training on your own, and I'll postpone them until next week. Now, go. The order comes from the top."

Toralyn had no idea what Ulrick or his son wanted with her, let alone why going home would be best, but she knew better than to question the order. "Yes, sir."

"Dismissed."

Toralyn raced to her clothes. Since undressing and re-dressing would take too much time, she tossed her dress over her training uniform and counted on avoiding any trouble on the way home.

Quickly exiting the room, she reached and paused at the front door and glanced at the security camera feed. However, the street was mostly deserted except for an occasional transport shuttle or pedestrian, which was usual for the time of day.

Stepping outside, she did her best to survey her surroundings and continued to do so as she went down one street and then another. As part of her cover, she lived near the main Rippak shop in the capital. But of course she never took the most direct route. She'd made a game of it, seeing how many different ways she could reach home without using the same pathway twice.

Not for the first time, Toralyn wondered what she would've done if she'd been born male. She might've liked to work as a spy for the royal family. Or, maybe as a warrior.

Too bad she was a female on Keldera, whose entire purpose was to marry and reproduce. She'd just have to find a way off the planet and possibly to Jasvar. She knew the new colony would have difficulties to overcome, the least of which would be missing her family, but the freedoms would more than make up for it.

When she was nearly home, the hairs on the back of her neck stood up. Someone was watching her.

Doing her best to observe from the corner of her eyes, she continued walking as if nothing were out of the ordinary. However, she made sure to avoid any alleyways or other obstacles someone could jump from.

She turned the final corner to her street and resisted a curse. The wide road was the only way to reach her building, but since it was one of the main shopping thoroughfares, dozens of streets shot off the main one. At least people still filled the sidewalks, and transport shuttles zoomed up and down the way, which should give her sufficient cover.

Taking a deep breath, Toralyn hoped being in a populated area would be enough.

She was about halfway down the street when the door to a vacant shop opened. Before she could do more than blink, a male tugged her inside at the same time something pricked her skin.

Toralyn barely had time to note the muscled, blue chest and the dark hair of a male before she fell into him and the world went dark.

Chapter Twelve

Azalyn pressed her thumb to the scanner and resisted the urge to shift her feet.

Ervan was back and had Toralyn in custody.

She was about to meet her daughter for the first time.

Her heart thudded in her chest. The doors opened, and Azalyn rushed inside to another set of doors. She repeated the process, but Ervan stood just inside the second door, his blue arms crossed over his chest. While Keltor hadn't made formal introductions, she'd seen him once or twice before and raised an eyebrow in question. When he didn't so much as move a muscle on his face, she sighed. "You know who I am. Why won't you move?"

"The prince didn't say you could enter without him."

Even though Ervan was nearly a foot taller than her, she didn't back down. "Look, if you don't let me in, I'm going to do something dishonorable."

Since the guard remained stoic, she lifted a knee and smashed it into his genitals.

Grunting, Ervan didn't move. His markings didn't so much as flicker from dark blue, either, meaning the bastard kept his cool.

Maybe kneeing him a few more times would do the trick. No one was going to stand in the way of her seeing her child.

Azalyn made to repeat her attack, but Kelzal's voice drifted from behind her. "As second in line to the throne, you must also heed my orders. Let my mother enter."

She glanced over her shoulder. "I could've found a way inside."

Kelzal lifted his brows in a gesture that reminded Azalyn so much of Keltor. "That is a pointless discussion." He closed the distance between them and Ervan bowed his head to allow Kelzal to enter. Azalyn followed her son, but the second she reached halfway inside the room, she stopped in her tracks. Her beautiful daughter lay on a bed toward the back of the room.

While she had memorized every feature from the photograph, to see her daughter in person made her heart skip a beat. Even laying down, Azalyn could tell her daughter was taller than her. Toralyn's hair was also longer, nearly to her backside, and fanned the bed to either side of her body.

Her gaze reached Toralyn's legs and she frowned at the tight-fitting trousers peeking out from under her skirt. That wasn't usual attire for a Kelderan. Just what had she been up to?

Kelzal sat on the bed next to his sister and took Toralyn's hand. At the sight of her two babies together, a sob choked her throat.

They were the family she should have had. The one she had given up. Partially because of circumstance, but mostly because of fear for both her children and herself.

Her son motioned forward. "Come, sit on the other side. She's stirring and should wake soon."

It was almost as if weights were tied around her ankles as she made it to the other side of the bed and sat down. Reaching out a hand, she gently brushed a few strands of hair off Toralyn's face—the jaw and cheekbones so much like Azalyn's own.

Toralyn's eyes fluttered open. They darted to Azalyn with confusion, but when she looked to Kelzal, she asked, "Where are we, Kel? Were you kidnapped too?" Her eyes darted over her brother's shoulder and looked to Ervan at the far side of the room. She sat up and pointed at him. "*You* were the one to drug me."

Toralyn made to jump off the bed, but Azalyn grabbed the girl's wrist. "He was just doing his job."

Her daughter's gaze shot to hers. The lack of recognition twisted Azalyn's heart. She pushed past the pain to focus on the girl's words as she demanded, "Who are you?" She glanced at Kelzal and back. "And how do you know Kel?"

Kelzal jumped in. "It's okay, Tora. She won't harm us."

At her two children calling each other nicknames, she smiled. "Or, at least, I won't ever again."

Toralyn's brows furrowed, but Kelzal beat his sister to the reply. "She is our birth mother, Tora. This is Azalyn."

Her daughter scrutinized her face methodically, displaying no emotion beyond distrust as she said, "Even if that's true, that still doesn't tell me why I'm here."

Keltor's deep voice boomed from the doorway. "Because I'm your birth father and your identity will soon be compromised, putting you at risk."

Azalyn's eyes shot to her male, but Keltor's focus was on Toralyn, his face calm and stern in what she deemed his "princely mask."

Toralyn's voice filled the room in disbelief. "Prince Keltor?"

Keltor strode to the bed, each step closer giving Azalyn strength she didn't know she'd needed.

Stopping a few feet away, he kept his attention on Toralyn. "Yes, that's me. Although you may simply call me Keltor. Welcome to the palace, Toralyn Sulani. This is your new home."

✵ ✵ ✵

As soon as Ervan had informed Keltor of Toralyn's arrival via a secure coded message, Keltor had wanted nothing more than to rush to where his daughter was being kept.

But his duty had forced him to instead negotiate with Tyrick first. As he'd expected, Tyrick hadn't yet received word about Toralyn's abduction. That had made the negotiations far easier.

The true test of their word would be once the Sulanis found out that Toralyn was inside the palace.

But he would worry about that soon enough. The second the view screen he'd used to conference with Tyrick went dark, he'd rushed to where Ervan had stowed his daughter and entered the room to find her awake. As soon as she said, "Even if that's true, that still doesn't tell me why I'm here," he barely prevented himself from smiling at her demanding tone.

Yes, his daughter took after her mother, that was for sure.

Or, maybe her Aunt Kalahn.

Given his luck, it'd be a bit of both.

Not that any amount of future trouble mattered in that second. He welcomed her to the palace and waited for her reply. Her silence for a few seconds made him proud; she was intelligent and weighed the options for the situation at hand before making a decision.

The girl looked at him and Azalyn before finally looking to her brother. "Is all of this true, Kel? Are these really our birth parents?"

Keltor held his breath and waited to see if Kelzal's former hatred would shine through. He could easily complicate matters to cause Keltor pain.

However, the boy merely stated, "Yes," and Keltor took that as his cue to move to Azalyn's side. Placing his hand on her shoulder, Azalyn raised a hand to cover his. Toralyn's gaze zeroed in on the action before meeting Keltor's eyes again. "Kelzal wouldn't lie to me, so you must be my biological parents. However, to my knowledge, the prince has been a bachelor his whole life, so I'm not sure how this is possible. Especially since I'm twenty-two and you would've had to have been rather young at the time of our conception."

His daughter was indeed clever. "I've never had a bride to date, that's correct."

Azalyn shook her head. "She's our *daughter*, Keltor. There's no need for formality." Azalyn reached out a free hand to Toralyn, but stopped short of touching the girl. "He and I were in love many years ago, resulting in the pair of you, but things happened to bring us to this point in time. My full name is Azalyn Rippak Sulani, which by the widening of your eyes, I know you understand that I've always been part of the merchant business and you might even have heard the rumors about me within the Sulanis. Let's just say that Keltor's father wasn't happy about the idea of his son being married to a shop assistant's daughter and found a way to drive us apart."

Toralyn looked at Keltor. "I want to talk to my brother." Her gaze shifted to Azalyn. "Alone."

Azalyn's shoulder tensed under his fingers. After giving her a reassuring squeeze, he gently took her arm and brought her to his side. "I will allow you some time with Kelzal. However, Ervan will stand guard. Tell him once you're done and we'll continue our conversation."

Toralyn raised her chin. "*He* can wait outside. Otherwise, I can't promise he'll remain unscathed if he stays in here."

At the determination in her voice, the corner of Keltor's mouth kicked up. "At the risk of my best warrior guard being murdered by my daughter, he can wait just outside the door." He looked to Ervan. While to everyone else the guard looked unaffected, Keltor's noticed the male's clenched jaw.

Keltor had a feeling that he would now have two females working to upset his palace, if not the whole of Keldera.

And while his father would detest such challenges, Keltor looked forward to them.

Toralyn continued to stare daggers at Ervan, so Keltor cleared his throat. And again.

Once she met his eyes again, he added, "We still need to talk once you're done with your brother. And if you think to escape, just know that's impossible. Ervan and his guards are not only the best trackers but also the best warriors still on Keldera. I will send Ervan personally to retrieve you, no matter where you go. And rest assured, he's good at his job."

Azalyn elbowed him in the side. "She's not a thing to be fetched, Keltor."

He gave a minute shake of his head, signaling they would talk in private.

Huffing, Azalyn moved from his side. "Take as much time as you need with Kelzal. I have more than a few thoughts to discuss with his *highness*, Prince Keltor."

She exited the room and he could do nothing but follow.

As soon as Keltor ensured Ervan was staged outside the door to Toralyn's room, he took Azalyn's wrist and guided her into a small side room. He waited for the door to lock before he said, "I know how much you want to hug her close and reclaim the lost years, Aza. But her allegiances are probably still with the Sulanis. The less she knows, the better."

"I can understand not giving away confidential information, but why are you being so distant with her? And treating her as a thing to be talked to instead of talked with? You said you hated your father being distant, so I'm just trying to understand why you're mimicking him."

He chose his words carefully, so as to not prod his female's temper further. "Right now, nothing is permanent. I've spent decades surrounded by people, and yet still isolated. If I allow myself to believe the isolation is over and it all comes crashing down, I won't be able to perform my duties as a Kelderan royal should. Therefore, I will keep my distance from both Kelzal and Toralyn for a while. It's safer for everyone that way."

Azalyn's eyes softened and placed a hand on his chest. "But not with me?"

Placing his hand on hers, he smiled. "No matter how hard I try, I can't seem to keep you at arm's length." He sobered. "But in reality, not even you staying at my side is settled. The Sulanis won't take her kidnapping well, and they could back down from their promises."

"But they agreed to some initial terms, did they not?"

"Yes. However, they would not be the first group to break their agreements. Remember, that is how the war with the Brevkan started."

The Brevkan war had been long and costly, in both lives and destruction. Keltor's mother had been one of the casualties.

Taking a step closer, Azalyn never looked away from his gaze. "Kelzal is close to his sister. And believe it or not, he takes after his father when it comes to fear of losing people he cares about." Keltor opened his mouth to protest, but Azalyn cut him off. "And you do care, even if you don't show it with hugs, words of love, or grand gestures. Ensuring safety and protecting others at the cost of your own happiness is just a form of caring. The teenage version of me was too immature to notice such things, but I see them now. However, don't be afraid to show a little of that caring to me, your siblings, or your children. You are more than merely a prince to us."

There were a myriad of reasons why Keltor should smile, nod, and change the subject. There was no guarantee Azalyn could be his. Kissing her and encouraging her could lead to more pain, especially if it came to choosing between her and war.

His father would say duty was all that mattered. But thanks to a passionate female unafraid to speak her mind, Keltor was beginning to see there was more to life than duty.

He wouldn't say it aloud, but he wanted love. And to do that, he needed Azalyn at his side.

However, if he didn't let her know how much he needed her, he might lose her.

For the first time since Azalyn had disappeared from his life twenty-three years ago, he decided duty could wait a few minutes.

Threading his fingers through her hair, he lowered his face to hers. As soon as his lips touched her soft ones, she opened and pulled him close. Each stroke or lick of his tongue was more than physical. What he could not say with words, he said with actions.

Licking, stroking, nipping—he let Azalyn know he cared. Maybe even more than cared, but he wasn't ready to confront that.

So instead, he ran a hand down her back until he gripped her bottom and squeezed. Azalyn moaned and proceeded to rub her hips against him. The delicious friction against his cock only made him want more. Much more.

He was deciding if Azalyn would hate him if he merely sat her on the table in the room, stepped between her thighs, and claimed her right then and there. Not gentle or slow, but rough and needy. Letting her know how much she had already come to mean to him.

How much he wanted her.

More than that, how much he needed her.

Before he could do more than walk them back toward the table, the computer chimed, meaning someone waited at the door.

Reality came crashing back down.

Keltor broke the kiss, but took a few seconds to stare into Azalyn's heavy-lidded gaze. He should say nothing. That would shield them both if the future turned sour again.

And yet he couldn't help but whispered, "I care. More than you know."

She smiled slowly, the action making his heart thud harder. She was so beautiful and free. And wild. Most definitely wild. Like many of the animals she liked to paint so much.

"I care, too." She lowered her voice to the point he had to strain to hear her. "And I hope to show you later, when we're alone, just how much."

He resisted a groan. Before he could reply to the innuendo, Azalyn spoke up, "Computer, who requests entry?"

"Kelzal Burrig."

Azalyn grinned up at him. "Leave it to the children to interrupt their parents just when things are about to turn steamy."

He snorted. "They do have a lot of interruptions to make up for."

She stroked his jaw. "And this is the male I hope they can see one day."

"Me, too, *zyla*. Me, too."

He turned Azalyn toward the door and stood behind her. "I need a shield for a minute. The trousers that royal males are expected to wear are already tight to begin with."

Turning her head over her shoulder, she winked. "Let's try not to traumatize our son." She faced the front again. "Computer, allow entry."

The door opened to Kelzal standing there, staring to the side. He glanced up and away again. "She wants to talk to you. But be careful, she's a tad upset."

Keltor decided to risk taking the first step with his son. "In other words, she wants to punch me in the jaw and knock me out cold."

Kelzal's eyes met his, full of surprise. "That's almost what she said, although it was somewhat less honorable."

Keltor snorted. "I believe it. You'll have to learn how to brush it off without so much as a blink, though, Kelzal. Both your mother and your aunt are that way, too. We males are going to have to stick together."

"I will...try."

That was a start. "If it's all right with you, Azalyn and I would like to talk with Toralyn alone."

Considering Kelzal still maintained eye contact, Keltor considered it a win. "Okay, although I promised to wait outside the door."

Azalyn snorted. "Probably to keep an eye on Ervan."

Kelzal glanced away, and they had their answer.

Keltor grunted. "She seems a bit obsessed with him. Maybe I should change her guard assignment."

"No, it's fine," Azalyn said as she waved her hand in dismissal. "If the tight trousers under her dress are any indication of what she's up to, I think she may do best to just spar with him and have it out."

"What are you talking about?" Keltor asked.

"She was all but ready to launch at him. I have a feeling

she knows how to bring a man down."

Kelzal frowned. "Kneeing him in the genitals is ineffective, as you found out, Mother."

Azalyn tensed in front of him. Keltor rubbed her arm but focused on the bigger picture. The distraction would help Azalyn regain her thoughts after being called "mother." Her actions said it was the first time he did so.

He leaned his head forward. "You did what to him?"

Her body relaxing, she turned her head with an unapologetic look in her eyes. "He was keeping me from my daughter. I had no choice."

Yes, his palace was most definitely being turned upside down.

Sighing, he stood tall again. "Just promise me not to do that in public. It will lead to many unkind words, and I'd be busy finding a way to deal with those who spoke ill of you."

Azalyn turned toward him, but Kelzal's voice filled the room. "You would defend her?"

"Of course. I lost her once and I'm not going to do it again."

"Keltor," Azalyn whispered.

Rubbing her back, he kept his gaze on Kelzal. He sensed this was a turning point with the boy.

When he finally looked at Keltor again, he kept a patient look on his face. His son finally said, "I will help you defend her, too."

He nodded. "Your help will always be welcome." Silence stretched, but he sensed that Kelzal was reaching his limit for social interaction. So with his trousers no longer tight, he hugged Azalyn to his side and moved toward the door. "We'll talk with your sister, then. Keep an eye on Ervan."

As they left the room and entered the next, Keltor steeled himself for what lay ahead.

But his problem wasn't ahead. No, as soon as the door closed behind them, someone launched at him from the side.

❈ ❈ ❈

Azalyn barely had time to bask in the glow of Kelzal calling her mother and Keltor declaring he would defend her when her prince in question was attacked by a twenty-two-year-old female.

Her daughter, to be precise.

Events played out in slow motion as Toralyn jumped and hooked an arm around Keltor's neck. In response, Keltor flipped her over until she lay on her back, on the ground. In another swift motion, he maneuvered Toralyn onto her stomach, pinned her to the ground with his knee, and held her arms behind her.

She had no idea when her mouth had dropped open, but she promptly closed it and said, "Don't hurt her."

Keltor didn't release his grip. "She must cede defeat first."

"Are you crazy?"

"No," Keltor stated.

She glanced between her prince and her daughter and back again. Just as she was wondering what to say or do, Toralyn grunted and muttered, "I cede."

Keltor instantly released his grip. "I've had more fighting and defense training than years you've been alive. Next time, I won't go easy on you."

Jumping to her feet, Toralyn brushed her skirts. "Next time, I won't be wearing a dress and can better defend myself."

Azalyn stepped between them. "How about we avoid any sort of fighting for at least a few minutes?"

Keltor and Toralyn stared at one another, but it was Toralyn who spoke first. "It wasn't fighting for the sake of fighting, but rather it was a test."

"And one I should've passed," Keltor said confidently.

"That's to be seen, your highness."

Her daughter hesitated as if debating to say more, so Azalyn jumped in. "Say whatever is on your mind, Toralyn. In this room, we're all just people."

She looked to Keltor, Azalyn, and back again. "Why aren't you appalled at my behavior?"

The corner of Keltor's mouth kicked up. "My brother married a dagger-wielding female warrior. I saw her pin a man to the ground, grab his genitals, and hold a knife to them. Any shock I may have once had is gone."

"You're talking about the Jasvarian leader, Taryn Demara," Toralyn whispered in awe.

Azalyn studied her daughter. Between the clothing, the attacks, and her awe at the human female warriors of Jasvar, Azalyn had a feeling Toralyn wished for something more than the usual Kelderan life of only marriage and children.

In that respect, they were alike.

Keltor nodded. "Maybe one day you can meet her. But for the present, you must settle for me and Azalyn."

Toralyn held her arms out. "Then tell me, why am I here? I'll admit that I was curious about my birth parents, but kidnapping me seems a bit extreme. Kel tried to say it was because I would become a target, but if he couldn't find you after years of searching, then I'm not sure how anyone else could link you to me at all."

At least it seemed Kelzal understood and maybe even accepted why he had to live in the palace now.

Pushing aside yet another thing to ponder later, Azalyn put her full attention on Toralyn. "Well, Keltor and I have reconnected recently. The news will spread soon, if not already, which means people may start putting information together and connecting the dots. After all, Kelzal looks incredibly like your birth father. Then all it would take is someone seeing Kelzal with you, calling him brother, and news of your relation would spread to all the wrong types of people."

Never taking her gaze from Azalyn, Toralyn said, "Don't take this the wrong way, but you're not my parents. Legally, you have no say or claim to me. And my mother will soon be wondering where I am."

She knew Toralyn's adopted mother was still alive. And Azalyn had indeed given up all rights to her daughter—even if it was somewhat unwillingly since she hadn't known of her existence—decades ago.

Even though that knowledge sat heavy on her heart, Azalyn wasn't going to let her emotions get the best of her. Toralyn's future was too important. For the moment, she needed to be like her cool, collected prince. "Keltor can contact her for you. However, it's too risky to let you wander the streets freely again."

"Because of the antimonarchists," Toralyn stated.

Keltor spoke up. "Yes."

"There's more you aren't telling me, Prince Keltor."

"There is," he answered.

Azalyn resisted rolling her eyes and decided to pounce. "I would expect you to know a lot about them, given that you're one of the Sulani merchant spies and you probably keep an ear on the street for who opposes or supports the monarchy."

To her credit, Toralyn kept her face free of surprise. "I don't know what you're talking about."

"Deny it if you wish, but I'm clever, Toralyn Sulani. Not many females can fight to begin with—on Keldera, at any rate—and the skintight trousers under your skirt, combined with your comment about them getting in the way, tells me you prefer not to wear dresses or skirts. On top of that, to reach your level of proficiency and skill with fighting, requires lots of training. And for what other role would that be? I don't think the royal palace or even the commoners' house of representatives hires female spies?"

Keltor shook his head. "Not yet."

"Right, so that means you're a merchant spy, Toralyn. But not even that training saved you from Ervan's grasp. Imagine if it were someone worse, much worse, who would do more than drug you? You're right in that I'm not your mother beyond genetics. However, I only discovered your existence recently, and I'll be damned if I let anyone harm you now that I know you're here."

Toralyn focused on her, which made sense since arguing with a crown prince would be intimidating to most Kelderans. "You haven't earned the truth from me, yet. Allow me to talk with my mother, Dolvia Sulani, and I will consider telling you more. But not before that."

Moving to the bed, Toralyn sat down and crossed her arms over her chest.

Azalyn couldn't help but notice that the slight lifting of her chin was something she did herself.

There was so much she wished to discuss with her long-lost daughter, but forcing a relationship wouldn't work. She needed to give the girl—no, woman—her space.

As if sensing her decision, Keltor placed a hand on her lower back and stated, "We'll return later. If you don't try to escape or kill my guard, then perhaps I will arrange a meeting with your mother. Until then, you have low-level clearance only. For many reasons, communications are prohibited."

Toralyn remained silent, unwavering from her demand

to talk with her mother.

While Azalyn could drink in the sight of her offspring for hours, she drew on every bit of strength she possessed and headed for the door. Keltor followed.

Once in the hall with Ervan and Kelzal, she spoke again. "Go to her, Kelzal. I think she needs a family member at the moment."

He met her gaze. "Give her time. I was angry at first, too, remember."

She nodded, afraid to speak or she might cry.

Keltor pulled her to his side, his heat helping to ease her pain a fraction. His deep, commanding voice filled the space. "Be careful, Ervan. I trust your abilities, but she is intelligent and will try anything to escape. Protect her at any cost."

Making a fist and pounding it over his heart, Ervan replied, "With my life, your highness."

"Good. If you need to reach me, I'll be in my private quarters. And Kelzal, you have my gratitude for helping Toralyn understand her situation."

Kelzal grunted, but didn't speak.

With everything settled, Keltor guided her out of the room and down the corridors to his quarters. Once inside and the security protocols engaged, she looped her arms around his neck. Rationally, she should talk with Keltor about their plans for Toralyn and strategies surrounding the Sulanis.

However, as she leaned against her male and his arms went around her waist, she wanted something to remind her of what she would be fighting for.

In other words, she needed her prince.

Standing on her tiptoes, she murmured, "I need you, Keltor. Claim me and make me forget about everything outside of this room."

Chapter Thirteen

At this time of day, Keltor would normally go over his daily reports and submit questions.

However, he had to admit that having Azalyn in his quarters, asking him to make her forget about everything else going on, was far more appealing.

But as much as he wanted her with each breath, he wasn't about to determine the future for her.

Lightly stroking her cheek, he murmured, "I want to, but I don't want to make the same mistake as when we were younger. There could be consequences, Aza. Even if age and injuries have reduced the chances, you could end up with child again. Abstinence or a fairly involved hormone treatment are the only forms of birth control that work with members of the royal family when it comes to potential destined brides, due to genetic modifications over the decades. Since you haven't had the hormone treatment, I can't guarantee you won't become pregnant."

She smiled. "So you have super sperm?"

"Aza," he growled.

"Okay, okay. But just know I'll tease you about it later." She tilted her head. "Well, I think the bigger question is if that's what you want?"

The simple fact she thought of his wants and didn't anger at his logical question made him want to kiss her and take her right then and there. "Despite the handful we've recently discovered, I still do."

As she pressed further against him, he groaned at her hard nipples against his chest. "Then I'm willing to risk it. Kiss me, Keltor. I've waited long enough."

At her pleading tone, he crushed her lips against his and placed a possessive hand on her backside.

While every fiber of his being screamed to be careful and take things slow, Keltor ignored them.

Azalyn was his chance at a future he wanted, not one forced upon him. It was time to let go.

He stroked the inside of her mouth as he caressed every inch of her rear, her back, and her side. But the material of her dress stood in the way of what he really wanted—to touch her skin.

Stepping back, he barely noticed Azalyn's swollen lips or flushed cheeks. Not even the flashing red of her markings—denoting desire—distracted him from his task. Gripping the front of her dress, he ripped it in two, tugged it off, and the material fell to the floor.

At the sight of her bare breasts, round belly, and shapely thighs, his cock pulsed in anticipation. "More beautiful than I remember."

Her hands instantly went to her lower stomach. Sensing the action important, he zeroed in on her hands and said, "Show me all of you, Aza. I hunger to memorize every inch of your skin."

She didn't move for a second, but then slowly let her hands fall away to reveal a long-healed scar and several stretch marks. Lightly tracing the scar, he met her gaze. "There is no reason to hide such badges of honor from me, *zyla*."

Her cheeks flushed. "Don't be ridiculous. It's just a scar."

Kneeling, he gently kissed the knitted line on her skin. "You sacrificed so much." He repeated the action over one of her stretch marks. "I am forever in your debt." He slowly traced another with his tongue. "I will work to deserve you."

Her breathing was ragged as she said, "Keltor tro el Vallen, if you really want to do that, then claim me. I'm still waiting to see the unrestrained side of you again."

Glancing up, he never broke eye contact as he took one of her breasts in hand and kneaded. "It will forever smash your image of the restrained prince."

"Good."

With a growl, he stood and took her lips again. He lifted her bottom, and she wrapped her legs around his waist. The feel of her heat through his trousers only made him deepen the kiss. Stroking, tasting, exploring as if this were the first time all over again.

Except this time, he took every sigh and groan and teased out more pleasure from his female.

As he stroked and battled for control, he somehow managed to maneuver them to the sofa without incident. Releasing her, he laid her down on the cushions and instantly pinned her wrists above her head with one hand as he undid the fastening of his trousers with another. The second his cock sprung free, he moved a hand between her legs. He groaned at how wet and swollen she was for him.

A noble male would resist the urge to take her, and instead would kiss slowly, driving his female wild before thrusting.

But an uncontrollable need—or maybe want—coursed through his body. Azalyn had always been where he'd belonged. And after so many years, he wanted her more than anything.

Hell, he'd gladly give up his crown and moved to a deserted outpost if it meant he could have Azalyn as his bride.

Because life without her was lonely and not worth living.

And now he had over two decades to make up for.

Positioning his cock, he murmured, "Forgive me."

"There is nothing to forgive," she stated firmly. "Here, right now, I'm yours, Keltor. Claim me."

With a growl, he entered Azalyn to the hilt. She arched her back, and he stilled. His impatience must've caused her pain.

Just as he began to retreat, Azalyn gripped his arm and dug in her nails. "Don't even think of stopping." She circled his hips. "Never hesitate with me, Keltor. All I want is you, unrestrained and free."

The words were a trigger, and he began a steady rhythm with his hips, changing his movements at Azalyn's little moans or sighs.

Each one urged him to find the best ways to bring her to orgasm.

And if he had anything to say about it, he would spend the rest of his life doing just that.

As much as he loved watching the emotions play out on her face, the tight points of her nipples called to him, as if to remind him that in order for Azalyn to find orgasm, he needed to pay attention to them.

Leaning down, he took one of her hard buds between his lips and suckled. Each gentle nip of his teeth, stroke of his tongue, or even slow breath on her wet flesh made his female squirm more beneath him.

He could lick every inch of her body for hours, and he'd never tire of her taste.

Moving from one breast to the other, he continued his attention. Never once did Azalyn try to free her hands and take the reins.

For a brief moment, Keltor was in complete control of his life. No duties or responsibilities beyond pleasuring his female.

And one day, his bride.

Desire pounded through his body. He needed to see Azalyn, and include her in this moment. Raising his head, he met her gaze. She smiled at him until he tweaked and gently twisted her hard buds with his fingers.

Biting her bottom lip, she moaned. "Just a little more, Keltor. I'm so close."

A memory of long ago, when he'd bitten her neck as he twisted her nipple and she came for him, filled his mind.

It had only been the one night, but his female had liked it a little rough. Time to see if she still did.

He played out the scene again, first licking her neck before sucking the flesh between his teeth. Azalyn's breathing quickened, and he knew she was about to come apart.

Timing another nibble with the pinching of her nipple, Azalyn screamed. As her core squeezed and released him, Keltor increased his pace, the sensations pushing him over the edge. He stilled as he called out Azalyn's name, the cry as much a claiming as his release inside her.

Once she'd wrung the last drop from him, he released her wrists and collapsed on top of her.

They lay that way, breathing but not speaking, for minutes. As much as Azalyn wanted him to not hold back, too many emotions threatened to burst through. It was almost as if decades of self-control were about to come crashing down, all thanks to the soft female under him.

Azalyn kissed his jaw and he finally met her gaze again.

Her smile made the world brighter. She murmured, "Not bad, prince."

✹ ✹ ✹

Azalyn wasn't one to hand over the reins and simply let

someone else take control.

But as soon as Keltor had pinned her wrists over her head, she'd sensed that he'd needed her at his mercy in that moment.

And so she'd let him.

Amazing didn't begin to describe the strong male above her, adjusting his movements to make the claiming better than she could've ever imagined.

However, as much as she loved the orgasm that had crashed over her, Keltor laying on her, as they breathed in unison, was a memory she wasn't likely to forget anytime soon.

The strong, formidable prince was clay in her arms, and she could sculpt him if she so chose. Azalyn may have had coworkers and an adopted family, but in a way, she'd been lonely, too. Pretending almost half your life had never existed wasn't an easy thing to accomplish.

Keltor, on the other hand, understood exactly what that meant, if not more so.

Even though she didn't want to break the spell of them lying in bliss, hearts pounding, confirming they had each other, she couldn't resist kissing his jaw, darting out her tongue, and tasting the saltiness of his skin.

Her prince rose his head, his hair disheveled from her fingers. The hunger and want in his eyes made her heart skip a beat.

If only she knew their future was certain.

Wanting to lighten the mood, she smiled and said, "Not bad, prince."

"Don't," he whispered as he cupped her face. "Don't push me away just yet."

She placed her hand over his. "I'm not, *zylar*. Teasing is a form of affection, and you'd better get used to it, because I can't help myself."

"I love your teasing. You're one of the few people who will do it around me. But, Aza..."

His words trailed off, and she placed a hand on his back, stroking to calm him. "You can tell me anything, Keltor. What is it?" He hesitated, so she narrowed her eyes. "Now who's holding back? Maybe I should try pinning you to the ground and demanding some answers."

Amusement danced in his eyes and Azalyn's heart melted a little. Keltor had so little joy in his life. She wanted to give it to him.

His voice snapped her out of her thoughts. "You can try later, though you won't be successful." His face sobered. "I just want to say I'm sorry, Azalyn. Claiming you again only reminded me of what I'd realized all those years ago—you are where I belong. I was a coward not to go after you before. But when I heard how you were betrothed to another, it almost reinforced the fact I was destined to be a monarch and nothing more. I convinced myself that it was the best path for everyone involved, to allow you to marry a commoner and not me."

At the sincerity of his tone, emotion choked her throat. She pushed past it to say, "Keltor."

"It's true, Aza. Even though we've only been reunited for a short time, the world melts away when I'm alone with you. So know this—no matter the odds or the obstacles, I'm going to find a future where we're together. Because going back to the isolated life, without your spirit and teasing, is unbearable and one I wouldn't wish on anybody."

Her heart rate kicked up at Keltor's words. Between him earlier kissing her scars and then him saying he would find a way for them to be together, Azalyn was falling for him again.

Reaching up, she pulled his face down to hers. "As long as you let me help make that future, *zylar*. No more facing tough times on your own." He nodded, and she rewarded him with a brief kiss. "But before we face reality again and start working toward that future, just hold me for a little while, Keltor. I think we both need it."

He didn't hesitate to roll onto his back and settle her on his chest. She listened to his heart under her ear as she traced the marking near his nipple. She'd been too consumed with lust and desire earlier to notice if his markings had changed color from their current dark blue.

She had no idea how long they lay there, simply taking strength and comfort from one another. But Keltor's voice finally broke the silence. "I want to stay with you here, forever."

"But you can't," she finished.

He sighed. "No. I need to ponder what to do with the Sulanis." He hugged her tighter against his chest. "Now more than ever, I don't want them to rescind their offer and take our chance of being together away from us."

Raising her head, she propped her chin on his chest. "Will you let me help you with them? I've spent a better part of my life negotiating prices with vendors, not to mention I know how the Sulanis operate."

His brows drew together. "If it were only me, I would happily take your help. But the problem is with my councilors."

Her heart fell at his statement. No matter what Keltor believed or how he may value her opinions, the outside world still viewed females as a nuisance to governing and politics.

Taking her chin between his fingers, Keltor said, "Don't have so little faith in me, *zyla*."

Scowling, she said, "I somehow can't imagine you tossing them all out on their rears and doing your own thing."

The corners of his mouth ticked up. "Not quite. I was

thinking more of replacing most, if not all, of them."

She blinked. "What?"

"While you're a part of why I want to do that, it's not the full reason. The councilors are my father's choices. I've been propping up his methods and ways, wanting to give him space. But as I will soon be king, and am already ruling in all but name, I think it's time I fill the council with my own choices, don't you?"

She tamped down the hope bubbling in her chest. "Can you do that even though you're not king yet?"

Keltor shrugged a shoulder. "Who will stop me?

Running a hand through his chest hair, she said, "How about we visit your father and talk with him? That may make overhauling the council easier, especially if he agrees to the plan."

"I somehow don't see him helping with the transition," he murmured.

"You never know. After all, you said he's changed since learning of his illness." Keltor frowned and Azalyn pushed. "Besides, I still have yet to meet this great king. Do we have enough time to do that without angering the Sulanis?"

"Perhaps. It is still night on Jasvar. In addition, Toralyn shouldn't be missed until work in the morning, I think."

"And Ervan would've contacted you if there was a problem with her, too. Let's visit King Kastor. I'm no longer afraid of him as I once was. Give me the opportunity, and maybe I can get you two to talk and agree on something."

He snorted. "Just like that?"

"Why not? I have quite a bit on the line, after all. A possible lord, and with time, maybe even a relationship with our twins."

And, if luck were on her side, another child.

Not wanting to get her hopes up, Azalyn raised her brows. "So? Shall we go?"

"Has anyone ever told you that you're determined and stubborn?"

She grinned. "All the time."

Chuckling, he caressed her cheek with his thumb. "Well, then let's save some of it for my father. However, I think a quick wash is in order, first."

Before she could do more than open her mouth, Keltor was up with her in his arms. "I can walk."

Grinning, he leaned down and whispered, "But this is more fun." He jostled her closer to his body. "Besides, I'm not ready to sever contact with your skin."

Playing with the stubble on his chin, she said, "Me, either."

He entered the cleansing room, and the spray engaged as soon as they were in the shower.

Not that Keltor paid much attention to it. He slid her slowly down his body, the friction of his hard muscles against her soft stomach and breasts making her pulse between the thighs once more.

Lightly caressing her back, he moved a hand over her hip and down her thigh. He gently lifted her leg and wrapped it around his waist. He kissed her slowly before saying, "A prince must always multitask. I see no reason to stop now."

Running a hand down his chest, she continued the path until she could lightly caress his hard cock. He hissed, and Azalyn took advantage of the moment to guide him to her entrance and arch her back.

She'd barely had a second of the wonderful fullness before Keltor kissed her again and moved his hips.

It wasn't long before she screamed his name again. And to his credit, the prince managed to also wash her before the daily allotted amount of cleansing solution ceased spraying.

Chapter Fourteen

Keltor wanted nothing more than to grin as he guided Azalyn down the secret corridors connecting his living quarters to his father's.

Not only had Azalyn shared her body with him, but he'd also finally realized it was time for him to make the future monarchy his own. And with a little good fortune, he might be able to add a family to that list.

Because now that he'd held Azalyn in his arms again, Keltor would do whatever it took to make her his queen.

He finally stopped in front of a door with both a retina scan and a handprint lock. Keltor leaned forward as he placed a hand on the identification plate. Once the double scan was complete, he glanced to Azalyn. "Let's break it to him gently."

Understanding his meaning, she released his hand. It took everything he had not to take it again.

Azalyn Sulani tested his self-control more than anything else ever had.

And that was a glorious thing because it allowed him to briefly put aside his duty and simply enjoy being alive.

With the door open, Keltor moved into his father's outer receiving room. Since his father hadn't been strong enough to move from his bed in over a week, Keltor went to the door at the rear of the area and pressed his finger to the scanner. The second door opened to reveal the wrinkled face and tattooed forehead of the Barren nurse that had been his father's main caretaker, named Jevla.

Jevla met his gaze. "I'm sorry, your highness, but the doctor will arrive any moment to begin his daily examination of his majesty."

King Kastor's weak voice came from behind the nurse. "Let him in, Jevla. The doctor can wait."

The nurse stepped aside. Even though Keltor visited his father every day, the pale face and fragile frame of his father lying in bed still made his heart twist. Despite a lifetime of arguments and battles of power, Kastor was still his father and one of the few remaining links to his deceased mother.

His father's gaze moved to over his shoulder. "Azalyn Sulani. I was wondering how long it would take you to find me."

Azalyn moved to Keltor's side and bowed her head. "Your majesty."

Keltor spoke up. "Jevla, you're temporarily relieved of duty. I'll let you know when we leave." The nurse curtsied and left the room. Keltor looked back to his father. "I think Azalyn has earned the right to be forthright with you, Father. I hope you agree."

After coughing a few times, his father replied, "I'm not sure why you bother to ask me that question. I signed the abdication papers. They're on my side table, awaiting your signature. Once you do, you'll officially be king."

Keltor glanced at the synthetic paper document on the table and frowned. "You know I can't sign them yet. One of the requirements is that I find a bride before taking the throne."

Kastor gestured weakly toward Azalyn. "And haven't you?"

Growling, Keltor took a step forward. "Don't force her into a decision, Father. You've done that once before, and I won't allow it to happen again."

"I have eyes and ears throughout the palace. I know you intend to take her."

"I suspected your loyal councilors would spy on me. Even after all this time, you still don't trust me."

"It's not a matter of trust, Keltor. My time is short, and I need information faster than you share it."

Keltor took another step toward his father's bed, but Azalyn placed a hand on his arm and cleared her throat. "If I may speak for myself?" she drawled.

His female's voice cut through his anger, and he met her gaze. "Maybe we should go and come back later, Aza."

"No. Because both of you are overlooking the one detail that could easily create a compromise." He grunted, but Azalyn continued before he could speak. "If the requirement about a bride is taken from the agreement, everything can go smoothly. After all, you have an heir, and no one needs the coronation ceremony to happen anytime soon, which would be the best time to present a bride. It'll give us enough time to see through our plans."

Kastor's voice filled the space. "She is correct. If you would merely take the time to read the document, you will see that finding a bride is no longer a requirement."

He looked to his father and blinked at the smile on the old male's face. "You find this amusing? This is my life we're talking about."

"I'm an old, dying man. If I can't provoke my own son for amusement while I still can, then I may as well pass today."

"Who are you and what have you done to my father?"

"Keltor, come closer."

He hesitated, but as his father motioned his bony hand

for him to follow the order, Keltor felt compelled to obey. Once he reached his father's bedside, Kastor spoke again. "Look at me. I have weeks left, at most. I want to ensure you are set up and that I can finally meet my only grandchild since Kason's child will be born after I'm gone. Sign the document and make your own plans for the future. But let me see Kelzal. He is proof that part of me will live on. If I have to make it my last order as king, I will do so. However, I hope you will grant it to me simply because I'm your father."

✵ ✵ ✵

Azalyn may have her own familial problems, but it was clear that Keltor and Kastor had a long history and plenty of animosity toward one another.

By all rights, she should hate the old king for what he'd forced her to do with her children. And yet, as he lay wasting away in a bed and asking to see his grandchild, her heart softened. She couldn't muster up her old hatred for a clearly dying man.

On top of that, she wanted to tell Kastor that he had two grandchildren. But there was no way she'd risk exposing that secret without conferring with Keltor, first.

Even though she could jump in and say she'd bring Kelzal around, she waited for Keltor to speak. If he was the male she believed him to be, she had nothing to worry about. He would do the honorable thing and bring Kelzal to see his grandfather.

Silence ticked by and Azalyn plucked the material of her skirt. When Keltor finally sighed, she knew he'd given in. "If what you say is true, about the changes to the abdication papers, I will see about bringing Kelzal to you. However, the boy will have the freedom to leave when he wishes."

"That is agreeable," Kastor replied. "Scan the document and sign it. While you do so, I will talk with Azalyn."

Keltor threw her a questioning glance, but she smiled to say she'd be fine.

Making her way to the king's bedside at the same time Keltor retrieved the document from the side table, she said, "If I may be blunt, your majesty—if you threaten my son in any way, I don't care if you're dying, I'll come here and scold you like you've never been scolded before. And since you are bedridden, you have nowhere to run."

Kastor smiled. "You would've gotten along well with my late wife. She protected the children at every turn, even from me."

She pounced on the chance to learn more about her children's grandmother. "Keltor showed me the water maze and her sculptures. I'm a painter myself, so I think there are many things Queen Solahn and I would've had in common."

The king raised his brows. "While we can dance around what you really wish to discuss—I love nothing more than to reminiscence about my late queen before I pass—I prefer that you just say it, Azalyn. Because if you wait too long, I may be dead and then you'll never have a chance to air your grievances. And before you say it's all right and you don't wish to upset a dying man, then let me speak my mind first—I wish to make amends before my passing. I wronged you greatly, and still wish to seek your forgiveness."

She felt Keltor's eyes on her, but this situation was something she needed to handle herself. "If you wish me to blindly forgive you, I'm afraid that won't happen. However, I don't hate you. Spending more than twenty years apart from Keltor, as well as giving up Kelzal, is something I will forever regret. And yet, at the same time, I wonder if Keltor and I are a better fit now than before. Kelzal was also al-lowed to become the male he wanted to be instead of having his future forced upon him. Some good came from the events of the past. The only thing I can't forgive yet is you lying to Keltor about me taking a betrothed and running away. Try your hardest to spend time with your son while you still can, as well as allow him and me to forge our own path. Do that, and I will find a way to forgive you."

The king searched her eyes, but Azalyn didn't look away or fidget. If she couldn't stand up to Kastor, then she wouldn't be a worthy bride for Keltor.

After about another minute, the king nodded. "I will try, Azalyn Rippak Sulani."

"Good." She turned to look at Keltor. "I think I need to leave you and your father alone for a while. Come find me once you're done. There's much for you, Kelzal, and me to discuss."

Not to mention Toralyn and handling the Sulanis. Kastor may have spies in the palace, but she wouldn't spill secrets he may not know yet.

Keltor reached out and took her hand. His warm fingers squeezed hers. "I will. Just try to be a little patient."

That was Keltor-speak for her not to tackle Toralyn by herself, let alone the Sulanis.

She nodded before moving her gaze to the king. "Your majesty, until next time."

He smiled in farewell. "See me again and I'll tell you a few secrets about the palace that not even Keltor knows about."

Bowing her head, she released Keltor's hand and headed out of the room.

While there was a lot of uncertainty about the future, she felt a little bit lighter. Seeing Kastor had cleared her head and revealed what was important to her. Not anger and retribution, but rather Keltor's happiness as well as hers and Kelzal's.

Now she just needed to focus on her adopted family. Maybe she'd be able to think of a weakness to use against the Sulanis that could secure the future she wanted.

✹ ✹ ✹

As soon as the door clicked closed after Azalyn, Keltor turned his full attention to his father. "I'm not sure what to make of what I just witnessed. Compromise has never been your method before."

"She is a worthy female, Keltor. She may have been young and naive as a youth, but she has become a mature, intelligent woman."

"I suppose you're going to claim credit for that as well? That by sending her away, you were forcing her to grow up?"

"Had I known she was pregnant, I would've handled things differently. The Sulanis managed to keep that secret well. In the present, all I can do is step back and allow you to do what you wish with her." His father looked to the document in Keltor's hands. "As you've seen, removing the bride requirement is the first step and proof that I mean what I say."

Curse his father for speaking the truth. Keltor much preferred the arrogant, aloof version of his father since he knew how to handle him better. "I've studied this document for weeks, and I can attest that removing the bride requirement is the only change you made." He placed it on the side table, picked up the slender laser pen, and burned his name into the document. He stood up. "There. I am officially king now."

"Best wishes for your reign, King Keltor."

As Keltor and his father stared at one another, he wished they could instantly become friendly and have an easy relationship.

But that would never happen. All he could do was take his father's hand and kiss the back of it. "I will keep Keldera peaceful, if it's the last thing I do. I vow it on the memory of my mother."

His father placed his free hand on top of Keltor's. "I know you will, Keltor." He released his grip. "Now, go. I may have been confined to this room, but I know there are many things you must attend to. Just make sure to see me when you have the chance and do everything you can to persuade Kelzal to visit."

"I will, but there's one more thing I wish to discuss."

"Oh?"

"I am king, yes, but I would much rather you convince your councilors to step down. That will provide them with an honorable exit."

His father raised his brows. "All of them?"

"I will keep Hinvel Mayta as an advisor, but not as a councilor. I sense great change coming to Keldera and a fresh council, unburdened by how things were done in the past, will help with that transition."

As his father studied him, Keltor kept his face calm and resisted tapping his fingers against his thigh. While he was making a request, the truth was that he was king, and it was time to see if his father would acknowledge it with actions in addition to his words.

Kastor finally nodded. "I will convene with them one last time to make the announcement, if you can hold off for a few hours with forming your new council?"

"That I can do, Father. Inform me when it's done." Keltor moved to the door. "I'll return when I can. And rest assured that I will stress the urgency of Kelzal coming to visit you."

As much as he wanted to tell his father about Toralyn,

there was too much at stake to risk it.

"Thank you, Keltor."

He took a second to memorize the moment when his father had finally accepted that Keltor could be a good leader and then went into the receiving chamber. He motioned for Jevla to attend to the king before heading out of his father's quarters.

He was nearly back to his private quarters when his communicator beeped. Taking it out, he noticed the symbol denoting a coded message. Typing in the keyword that would unlock the encryption, the symbols became words. It was from Ervan:

She has escaped.

Chapter Fifteen

Toralyn hated walking with her head bowed, murmuring apologies to anyone who bumped into her. But her flowing brown dress and temporary tattoo on her forehead meant nothing if she didn't act the part of a Barren, which meant living as if she were invisible.

Not to mention the fact that if she were caught impersonating a Barren, she'd face a prison sentence.

She reached the palace door used exclusively for the Barren to come and go. According to her brother, it was the only real weak point in the palace's security. As a guard barely looked at her and waved her onward, she agreed.

It also meant her biological parents didn't know she was gone yet.

Even though she'd only known her brother for four years, Kelzal hadn't hesitated in helping her escape. However, the promise she'd made to her brother echoed inside her head: *I promise to find out what I can about the anti-monarchists or any threats to the palace.*

While she still couldn't accept her father was a prince—making her a princess, of all things—Kelzal was determined to protect their birth mother, Azalyn.

The female had seemed interesting enough, but Toralyn had a mother, a life, and a purpose. A DNA test wasn't going to make her give it up.

Yes, the prince would send that bastard guard to look for her. But now that she knew about him, she would be more careful. Her first order of business would be changing her appearance.

The thought of cutting and dyeing her golden hair made her stomach flip, but Toralyn would get over it. Her freedom meant more than having pretty hair.

When she was at a safe enough distance from the palace, she ducked into a side street and began weaving her way toward one of the safe spaces she and her cousins used in case of emergencies. Not even her mother, let alone Ulrick Sulani, knew about the existence of said places.

She owed Ulrick much in life, but like many members of the Sulani family, she didn't fully trust him.

And the revelation from her brother about how Ulrick had deliberately taken her from Azalyn on the day of their birth, without telling her, still didn't settle well with Toralyn. Until he proved otherwise, Ulrick was on her "must watch" list.

She only hoped her adopted mother wasn't another one she'd have to add.

No. Dolvia Sulani had loved Toralyn every step of the way. There was no way she would hurt her daughter, even if Ulrick ordered it. She wouldn't allow doubt to cloud her judgment about every person she cared for.

Arriving at the abandoned house, she ducked behind a few tall shrubs and pressed herself against a wall. From her vantage point, she could just make out the sidewalk and the tops of the surrounding buildings. Unlike back on the main thoroughfare, she had no feeling of being watched.

Inching her way along the wall, she came to the hidden catch, pressed it, and a door opened a fraction inward. She slowly pushed it open, glad that the well-oiled hinges didn't make a sound, and entered the room.

With the door closed, the room was pitch-black. But after years of memorizing the layout, Toralyn moved to a wall and felt her way along to the small light. Pressing the round surface, a gentle glow illuminated the room.

Not wasting time, she went instantly to her emergency supply bag and riffled through it. Finding the black hair dye and a pair of scissors, she went to the small sink and mirror and went to work. She had a new mission to fulfill before reaching out to her mother—visiting some of the taverns reputed to be meeting places for the antimonarchists. Over the years she'd heard about them inside the merchant shops, but had stayed clear. She'd learned that they were usually filled with dangerous and backstabbing clientele. She would have to be more careful than ever before when scouting them out.

Especially as Prince Keltor had easily deflected her attack and pinned her to the floor. If nothing else, she admired his defense skills.

That settled it. When not visiting the taverns, she would increase her training practices tenfold. Even without a live trainer, she could mimic what she saw in training vids and possibly in a recreation room, if she could ever get the faulty one inside the safe house working again.

As she applied the dye to her hair, she ran through which location to visit first. After all, she couldn't start thinking of how to get to Jasvar until she fulfilled her promise to her brother. Even more than her promise, the prince would hunt for her as long as she remained on Keldera. Her only chance at a future of her making would be to leave everything she knew behind.

Her heart constricted at never seeing her cousins, mother, or brother again, but she pushed the feeling away. No matter what it took, she'd at least find a way to get her mother to Jasvar, too. Maybe even a few of her cousins could go someday as well. However, she wasn't as hopeful about Kelzal, but she would try her best. Their birth parents had given them up twenty-two years ago. As harsh as it may be, they needed to accept that. Neither she nor Kelzal were theirs to claim.

The tricky part would be in convincing her brother of that, too.

❁ ❁ ❁

Keltor reached the room where Toralyn had been held previously. Inside Azalyn was fussing over Ervan as Kelzal sat in a chair in the corner, playing with some kind of electrical device.

Since Ervan had been his guard for years, he didn't hesitate to demand, "What happened?"

Azalyn looked up from whatever she was doing to Ervan's head. "She's gone, Keltor. Yelling isn't going to help."

Keltor opened his mouth, but Kelzal's voice beat him to it. "I helped her escape."

He swung his head to Kelzal. "What? Why?"

His son finally stopped working on the device in his hands and met his gaze. "Because she asked me to."

"Do you not realize how dangerous it is for her, Kelzal?" Keltor took a step toward his son. "I understand wanting to protect your sister, but there are mercenaries for hire who will beat her, or worse, before bringing her in for their bounty. What happened to Azalyn could end up happening to our Toralyn."

Kelzal's voice was slightly less confident when he said, "Toralyn is more prepared and is aware she will be targeted."

Keltor somehow managed to keep from yelling. "If one

of my guards can find her, others will, too. She is ill prepared. Make no mistake, someone will discover her identity soon enough and will pay a hefty price to possess her."

Kelzal glanced back to his hands. "I didn't do it without a condition."

Azalyn's gentle voice cut in. "You promised to tell me the reason once Keltor got here. He's here, so tell us."

Shrugging one shoulder, Kelzal answered, "She is going to find out what she can about the antimonarchists and any threats to the palace. And before you yell some more, your highness, just know that she will do her best to fulfill that promise. It will also be one less thing you must rely on the Sulanis for."

"Kelzal," Azalyn began.

Their son shook his head. "It's the best option. Once she has information for you, then send her to Jasvar for her protection. That's what she wants, at any rate, to go to Jasvar and train with the warrior women there. Although I didn't mention how she would probably be under our aunt and uncle's care once she arrived on the other planet."

For the first time, Keltor started to see his son as an adult with potential and a knack for long-term planning instead of a reluctant young man out to defy his father. "While I respect your intentions and will concede the plan isn't horrible, there's still the matter of Toralyn's safety."

"She has her cousins to help her," Kelzal stated. "By all accounts, they're more like sisters than cousins. They won't share her location unless she wants it known."

"And when she reappears and contacts her adopted mother? What then?" Keltor prodded.

"By then I expect you to have things sorted with the Sulanis, your highness."

Keltor resisted the urge to demand more information. He would need Kelzal on his side in order to keep Toralyn safe. "Even if everything plays out as you expect, she will need extra protection." He glanced at Ervan. "Although I'm starting to wonder about my guards."

Ervan grunted, but Azalyn spoke first. "Kelzal drugged him. Not even you would've expected him to do that. It seems the pair of them hatched quite the plan."

Looking back to his son, Keltor took a few steps closer to him. "You seem to appreciate logic. If your sister has extra guards and backup, then there is less room for her to be taken. If you know where she went, then you need to let us know."

"And Jasvar? Will you allow her to go there?" Kelzal asked.

Keltor grunted. "We shall see. I can't make blanket promises right now, Kelzal. But even if it's for a short while, I will try to make it happen."

He could feel Azalyn's eyes on him, but Keltor focused on his son. As much as he wanted to have his two children and his female together, working on trying to be a family, it was an unlikely scenario. At least, for the foreseeable future. However, sending Toralyn to Jasvar would gain some of her trust, and maybe one day, she would consider coming back and getting to know them.

It would also allow his brother, Kason, to keep an eye on her. If there was one thing his brother did well, it was to follow through on an assignment.

Kelzal finally spoke again. "I will hold you to that. As for where she went, she should soon be on her way to Bakren."

Keltor cursed. Bakren was the main hotspot for the antimonarchists. More than that, the extremists mostly lived there.

Azalyn's voice garnered his attention. "What aren't you telling me about Bakren?"

Moving his gaze to his female, he answered, "It has the

highest concentration of extremists, which makes it dangerous. Many of them care little for lives lost or property destroyed. All that matters is their goal. While they've laid low for years, rumor has it that they're planning to strike in the next year, and in a big way."

Ervan, who rarely said anything, jumped in. "I know a few undercover law enforcers there. If you allow me and a team the honor of protecting your daughter, I can go there and most likely find a way into the thick of the dangerous areas."

He stared at his most loyal guard and decided to be blunt. "Can you handle this assignment? Because if you're distracted by my *daughter's* pretty face or form, then you should stay behind."

"I wish nothing more than to regain the trust and honor for my duties. I underestimated her for being female, just as I underestimated your son because of his personality. It will not happen again."

Part of him wanted to say no, and that Ervan had lost all trust.

And yet, Ervan had been protecting him for nearly ten years, since he was barely a soldier of twenty. Keltor had seen potential in the male, and still did.

He was also loyal to a fault, willing to die in the line of duty. He'd shown as much when Ervan had warded off a potential knife attack and had ended up being stabbed himself.

Keltor nodded. "I will give you a final chance to redeem yourself. You may go, but I want regular updates and for you to take Xerlig's sister with you."

Ervan blinked. "What?"

He moved his gaze to Azalyn. "I didn't lie before when I said we didn't have any trained spies. However, we do have a few trained female assassins who are only used for the most highly sensitive incidents."

Azalyn frowned. "Pardon?"

"I don't order assassinations for pleasure, *zyla*. But sometimes when it comes to war and protecting Keldera, we have need of one. The palace has long used females for the job."

"Because if they show a little skin and get someone alone, they can get the job done," she stated.

"Yes. But while I don't wish to assassinate anyone this time, she has the skills to infiltrate areas not even an undercover law enforcer could get into. I haven't suggested her before because once she does something so public, she will have to resign her position as assassin, which means her decades of training will be lost to the palace as a resource."

Even so, Keltor had plans for her forced retirement, but only once his family was safe.

When Ervan and Azalyn merely stared at him, he focused back on Ervan. "The question is—are you willing to work under the command of a female? Because she will be in charge of the mission."

To his credit, Ervan saluted and answered, "I am, your highness."

"Good. Then gather a handful of other guards you wish to take, have them sign the necessary paperwork, and Xerla will find you within the hour. Be ready to leave at a moment's notice."

Ervan deepened his bow and left.

Once the door locked and Keltor engaged the security protocols, he spoke again. "I think it's time we had a family meeting."

Azalyn had barely digested Keltor's news about female

assassins when Ervan left and he said he wanted a meeting.

Closing the distance between them, Azalyn asked, "What else don't I know about? I can't help you, Keltor, unless you start letting me know about all the tools at your disposal."

"I know, Aza. But what with everything going on, plus my vow to the king, I couldn't say everything I wanted."

She searched his eyes. "Then what changed?"

"I signed the document. I'm the king now." He looked to Kelzal. "And you're the crown prince."

Rubbing her forehead, she sighed. "So what does that mean? Everything is changing so fast."

Keltor placed a hand on her lower back and rubbed. She leaned into his caress as he murmured, "I know, *zyla*. But things are only going to happen faster. If all of this is too much for you, then you are under no obligation to stay by my side."

She instantly met his eyes with her own. "Don't even think of pushing me away, Keltor tro el Vallen. If you wish to protect me, then share information. That way I can help protect our family and our future."

He smiled. "Maybe I should make you part of my council."

She eyed him askance. "Are you being honest about the suggestion or are you merely trying to placate me?"

"I wouldn't belittle you by placating you. You are clever, with a deep understanding of the merchant class on Keldera. You would be a valuable asset to have."

"But Keltor, you know having a female council member simply isn't done. Not only that, if I do become queen, there are expectations."

He grunted. "I'm aware of expectations and standard practice. However, those practices drove my sister to stowaway on a ship, the love of my life to be ripped from my side, and our children to be separated from us. I was powerless to do much of anything under my father. But I am king now, Aza. And I think it's time to start changing how things are done."

Kelzal's voice drifted from the corner of the room. "I concur that change is necessary for survival. However, doing so may provoke war."

"Then we'll just have to ensure that doesn't happen." Keltor squeezed her side. "We must seal our deal with the Sulanis now. With their support, contacts, and financial assistance, the extremists will think twice about attacking. Especially if Xerla and Ervan infiltrate and manage to find some of the key players before things escalate."

"But that wasn't the assignment you gave them."

"I will send a message asking Xerla to bring any of the main leaders to me alive. Even if interrogation fails, taking away some of the heads of an operation usually leads to a quick demise. Just be aware that this will take time. Weeks, even months. And if Toralyn is in the thick of it, she will possibly need to remain so as to not draw unnecessary attention."

She placed a hand on Keltor's chest. "But can she handle it? We saw how easily you disarmed her."

"I know, *zyla*. But if it's necessary for Toralyn to remain in place, Xerla will find a way to protect her. You'll just have to trust my judgment on this."

"I do, but it doesn't mean I won't worry."

"Of course. But just know that I will do everything in my power to ensure her safety, even if it means utilizing what few other female assassins I have at my disposal."

Kelzal jumped in. "Unless another powerful enemy steps in."

Keltor glanced to their son. "That is a possibility. But I intend to place many trusted individuals undercover, on top of Xerla and Ervan. They should keep me informed of what is going on, with regard to threats to Toralyn and to the royal family in general."

Azalyn spoke up again. "All of that is fine and well, but if we don't have a successful public relations campaign, to convince the general population that having a monarchy is in their best interest, then all of your hard work and plans will mean nothing. Both need to work together."

Keltor frowned. "Public relations has never been one of my strengths."

"Then let me help with that. My main job with the Sulanis had been as acquisitions partner, but that also included strategies to advertise the new products I commissioned."

"Then what do you suggest?"

She tapped her chin. The average Kelderan citizen wouldn't care about diplomatic treaties or how the Kelderan king oversaw the military. No, they needed something they could relate to in their everyday lives.

An idea finally hit her. "We could use Jasvar."

Keltor's brows drew together. "I'm not sure I follow."

"Well, you and your brother were instrumental in securing the alliance. The first wave of colonists may have left already, but more will be expected to follow. Have the Jasvarian leader record a message that we can use and play on the public billboards. Almost everyone on the planet feels the strain of our ever-growing population. The promise of more relief via more colonists will stoke many a dream. Not only that, but if the message is clear that all negotiations must be made through the king and his staff, it will give many people pause. In their eyes, the monarchy will start to seem essential, if they want to achieve those dreams."

"And what about those who have no desire to leave the planet?" Keltor asked.

She waved a hand. "There's an angle for that as well. We mention how restrictions on resources will lessen as the population decreases. There may even be a chance for everyone to own property. Maybe not right now, but for their children or grandchildren. In other words, give everyone a reason to want to keep you in power. Some of your larger goals will have to wait a little while, though. We need to take one change at a time."

As she waited for Keltor's response, Azalyn resisted shifting her feet. She was all but asking Keltor to destroy the sacred image of the Kelderan monarchy, which had been around for hundreds of years, if not longer. Would he throw it all away to protect his newfound family?

He finally leaned down and gave her a gentle brush of his lips against hers. The contact made her sigh in relief.

Keltor's breath was hot against her lips as he said, "More than ever, I think you need to be a part of my council. I would be a fool to overlook such a clever female."

The corner of her mouth kicked up. "I hope you want more than my brain."

His eyes turned fierce. "I want all of you, *zyla*."

With those words, Azalyn fell in love with the king of Keldera for the second time.

Not that she could tell him just yet. Ensuring their daughter's safety and the future of the planet was far more important than one person's feelings. "Good, because I'm rather fond of all of you, too, *zylar*."

Keltor leaned in as to kiss her, but Kelzal's voice halted the action. "I would suggest giving Xerla her orders before you two waste time kissing."

She dared a glance at Kelzal. He wasn't looking directly at them, but he twirled an electrical component in his fingers. If he wasn't working on something, it usually meant he was upset.

Her son was about to lose his sister to Jasvar and probably also thought he'd lose her to Keltor and governing Keldera.

In other words, he needed her.

Patting Keltor's chest, she moved to stand in front of Kelzal and squatted to be more on his level. "Kelzal." He finally looked at her. "You're going to be vital in helping us, too."

He shook his head. "I don't want any of it. I only want to stay so I can get to know you better, Mother."

She dared to take his hand. When he didn't pull away or tense under her fingers, she squeezed gently. "We have plenty of time to think about the future. Until then, won't you help us in the present?"

He paused a few beats before replying, "I will help, but there's something you should know. It may help with the future." She raised her eyebrows in question, and he continued, "Toralyn is the elder sibling by a matter of minutes. She should be next in line."

Azalyn tucked away that piece of information for later. "As much as I think a queen can do just as good a job as a king, making Toralyn the next in line would require a lot of work with regard to changing the succession laws. Not to mention changing too much too quickly will throw Keldera into disarray."

Kelzal looked away again. "But you just said we had plenty of time. So at least consider it. She would be better suited to it than I."

She wasn't going to lie to her son, but she needed to placate him for a little while. "Perhaps. But for now, just work with us. We might need your help. You probably wish to keep Toralyn safer than any of us."

Silence stretched and Azalyn sent a silent thank you to Keltor for giving their son time to decide for himself.

There may be hope for them yet.

Nodding, Kelzal said, "For now. And I would start by

allowing me to improve the security of the palace."

Keltor spoke again. "Considering you helped Toralyn escape, I think that wise. You may go and begin on that, Kelzal. We will seek you out later to hear your suggestions."

Before her son could stand, Azalyn leaned forward and engulfed him in a hug.

At first, he merely sat there. But slowly he brought his arms up and hugged her back.

It'd taken decades, but she finally held her son in her arms.

Tears prickled her eyes, but Azalyn forced them back. Crying would only make Kelzal uncomfortable and possibly ruin the moment.

After a few more seconds, she released him and stood. "Go, Kelzal. We'll keep you updated on Toralyn's progress and whereabouts."

He nodded and moved toward the door. Right before he reached it, Keltor said, "Contact me at any time, Kelzal. I value your help and input."

Only a brief nod acknowledged he'd heard, and then Kelzal was gone.

With a sigh, Azalyn faced Keltor. "At some point, I hope things become easier."

Taking her hand, Keltor replied, "Me, too. Now, as much as I'd love nothing more than to hold you close and nibble the side of your neck, I must reach out to Xerla. While I do, you need to contact Jasvar."

She blinked. "Me? Shouldn't you do it?"

"As much as I've started to admire my brother's bride, I have a feeling she'd be more at ease discussing issues with the future queen of Keldera, especially since Kason and I have only begun to patch relations between us. Besides, it will be a good way to strengthen ties. After all, you will be in charge of the Jasvarian-related campaign. Taryn getting familiar with you will only make that easier."

If she hadn't already fallen in love with him, his faith in her and his unflinching belief she could handle things would've done it.

What she wouldn't give for an hour alone with her future lord.

Because, yes, she was going to find a way to keep him.

"I'll do it." She lowered her voice. "And keep including me and treating me as an equal, and I may just have to reward you, your majesty."

Smiling, he placed a possessive hand on her rear. "I look forward to it, your future majesty."

Tempting as it was to pull Keltor down for a kiss, she resisted. "Now, go. Because if you stay here much longer, it's going to be hard for me to concentrate on my tasks."

"As you wish, *zyla*."

Keltor exited the room, and Azalyn let out a huge sigh. If she ever wanted her male, she'd better get to work.

Chapter Sixteen

Stretching her arms over her head, Azalyn wondered if the leader of Jasvar would ever reply to her request.

Yes, the waiting had given Azalyn a chance to study as much as she could about Jasvar and its leader. The idea of a matriarchal society was difficult for her to believe, given her forty years spent on Keldera.

And while Azalyn would probably never have the chance to leave Keldera to see the strange culture on Jasvar, she had a feeling her daughter would enjoy the freedoms promised there.

The light finally blinked on Keltor's private comm unit and Azalyn took a deep breath before hitting Receive.

The brown-eyed, lightly tanned face of Taryn Demara appeared on screen, but so did the golden-skinned, blue-haired face of Prince Kason.

Before Azalyn could do more than open her mouth, Taryn said in accented Kelderan, "He translate only." She switched to the Common Earth Language—CEL—but Azalyn only knew a handful of words and couldn't follow along.

Once the human female stopped talking, Kason spoke up. "I'm only here to translate for my bride. She says that she's happy to finally meet you." Taryn elbowed Kason in the side, and he grunted. "Vala has said much about you and Taryn hopes Keltor is treating you well."

Azalyn studied the slightly younger version of Keltor. Given the way the human female prodded him along, he was nothing like the reputation she'd heard about in the various cities.

Gone was the calculating former general who never showed emotion and in his place was a male who didn't mind taking orders from a female.

If her influence on Prince Kason wasn't enough, Taryn's kind eyes and smile made Azalyn feel as if she could tell the female anything. Well, maybe if Kason weren't in the room.

Taryn said in Kelderan, "Keltor treat well?"

The question brought her back to the present, and she nodded. "Yes. More than well, actually." She glanced at Kason and back to Taryn. Since Azalyn had no idea if the line were secure, she kept her next statement vague. "We may even have some news soon."

Taryn grinned. "Good news, yes?"

"I thought you couldn't understand me?" Azalyn asked.

Kason chimed in. "She has a translating device in her ear, so she understands but is still working on her Kelderan. I still think she should take the translating device out. She'd learn quicker."

"Too busy." She said a few more sentences in CEL, and it gave Azalyn a chance to watch as Taryn said something with quite a bit of enthusiasm and Prince Kason smiled.

The comfort and familiarity they shared spoke volumes.

Azalyn cleared her throat and spoke up. "There isn't a lot of time. Many things are happening at the same time here, and I don't know how much power you have remaining for the long-range transmission tower."

Kason replied, "Enough for about ten more minutes. And before you ask, the line is secure and encrypted by our best technician. What did you need?"

She expected Taryn to frown and scold Kason for speaking up for her. But the female merely raised her eyebrows in question.

Taryn may be the leader of Jasvar, but the pair of them were a team and unafraid to lean on one another.

The interaction made her miss Keltor, and she wished he was at her side.

No. She was doing this to be with Keltor. Dividing up the tasks meant they could work quicker toward the future they wanted. If all went well, they would have decades to spend in each other's company.

Sitting up straighter, she said, "Well, Keltor is king, and—"

Taryn cut her off. "You be queen soon."

She bobbed her head and Kason swore. "That might bring war. I hope you have a plan."

Kason's tone washed away Azalyn's reluctance and hesitation. "That is why I'm calling. We were hoping that Taryn would make an official statement, saying that any approval for future colonists must be made through the monarchy." She explained her PR campaign and finished with, "Will you help us?"

Taryn studied her and said something in CEL. Kason interpreted, "What else have you got planned? Taryn senses that you're leaving something out."

"Keltor didn't give me clearance to share the other part of our plan, but we're doing something to handle the anti-monarchy extremists. Maybe not completely, but to a certain degree."

Taryn spoke again, followed by Kason's interpretation, "She respects your secrets, but hopes you'll share with us as soon as possible. My bride thinks you have more than one secret to share."

Azalyn moved her gaze back to the human female. She

tilted her head as if to say, "I'm right, aren't I?" And Azalyn responded, "Once everything is settled, I hope to speak with you again."

Taryn waved a hand. "No being formal." After Taryn said a few sentences, Kason spoke in a reluctant tone. "Remember this is Taryn. I would never say what I'm about to say—she is more than ready for a sister and hopes you'll talk many times in the future and maybe share princely stories." Taryn poked his arm and Kason murmured, "Because Kelderan royals are stubborn and a handful, and if a female doesn't have a chance to vent, she could explode."

Azalyn snorted. "I'll have to brush up my CEL, too. I think we'll have more fun without any males in the room."

"Kalahn speak CEL, but bad idea," Taryn said.

She smiled. "Yes, the sister shouldn't hear those kinds of stories about her brothers."

Kason shook his head. "Are we finished? The power is nearly depleted."

She resisted laughing at the warrior prince's discomfort. "I'll send a detailed text transmission, and if you could record a message as soon as possible, we would forever be grateful."

"Of course, sister," Taryn answered.

What Azalyn wouldn't give to meet Taryn Demara in person.

She signed off and ended the transmission.

At least she had one part of her grand plan in place.

Quickly checking her messages, she had one from Keltor: *Come to my conference room to meet the new council. We need you.*

So her male was following through on his promise to include her. She couldn't help but smile as she made her way toward the conference room. She only hoped that she would still be smiling once she entered. Because if it were empty apart from Keltor, it meant none would accept a female colleague.

No. She trusted Keltor's judgment. He would select the best people for the job.

Straightening her shoulder, Azalyn raised her chin and steeled herself for what was to come.

✹ ✹ ✹

Keltor stood at the head of the table inside his private conference room and surveyed the faces of the five males sitting around it. "Now that you know the truth that I'm king, there is one more piece of information you need to know before you decide whether you can accept or deny my request to be part of my council." He paused to take measure of each male before adding, "I wish to also add two females to it."

One of the males, a middle-aged one with magenta skin and black hair named Nyson, spoke up. "May I ask why, your highness? Females don't work in government, beyond secretarial duties. They have little to add in way of advice."

Keltor raised an eyebrow. "What of your bride? Does she have little to say when it comes to advice in your life?"

Nyson grunted. "That is a different matter."

"Regardless, I will have female councilors. So if any of you wish to decline my request, now is the time to leave."

Even though Keltor had carefully selected the five men in the room, Nyson stood and bowed his head. "I thank you for the honor, but I must refuse."

"I accept your refusal and trust you to honor the confidentiality agreement you signed regarding items discussed here."

As soon as Nyson exited the room, Keltor looked to each of the four remaining males. One of them, Farren, had a small smile on his lips. Keltor asked, "What is it that you find so amusing, Farren?"

"Do not be offended, your majesty. I was only thinking what if Nyson's wife found out what he'd said here. I suspect he'd get an earful and a half."

Nyson's bride had a reputation for being opinionated, regardless of who was listening. However, she was intelligent and correct most of the time. It was why Keltor had risked asking Nyson to join him. "Perhaps I should've asked her to be part of the council instead."

Farren grinned. "I wouldn't mind that. She's much livelier than Nyson."

More like Farren wanted to flirt with her; he was the only male councilor without a bride.

As much as Keltor enjoyed joking with another male, he steered the conversation back to what was important. "This is your last chance to refuse my offer before you sign the agreement which dictates you cannot leave the position for at least a year, on penalty of imprisonment."

The requirement was harsh, but if Keltor wanted any chance of stability despite the changes to how the council and monarchy functioned, he needed confidants who would stay the course.

Farren picked up the nearest laser pen and seared his name into the document. The other three males soon followed his lead.

Keltor had selected Farren because of his knowledge of trade relations—both on Keldera and with allies—and his former term as a commoners' representative. However, he was also a natural leader with an abundance of charm. Keltor would have to remember that.

Once everyone completed signing their names, Farren spoke up. "So, who are the females joining us?"

After collecting the signed documents, Keltor replied,

"One of them is Azalyn Rippak Sulani."

The oldest male still in the room, Rohvel, frowned. "Forgive me, your majesty, but isn't she the female you dallied with as a youth?"

The urge to castigate the man for dismissing his female coursed through his body, but Keltor drew on decades of restraint to reply calmly, "She has worked her whole life in the merchant business and will be a valuable asset." He paused, but decided that if he wanted to earn the respect and confidence of the new council members, it was better to be truthful. "She will also be your queen in the near future."

Murmurs broke out, but Farren's voice drowned out the rest. "I would assume you have a plan, your majesty. Otherwise, the extremists are bound to attack en mass at the announcement."

"Of course," Keltor answered. "As soon as Azalyn secures the necessary resources, she will join us and help me share our plan."

The youngest male in the room, Yorjan, who also was the quietest, asked, "Who is the other female? You mentioned there would be two."

"Two, yes. With Nyson gone, there may be a third." Yorjan merely tilted his head in question, and Keltor admired the male's ability to stick with a task. After all, Yorjan had been selected for his intelligence and analyzing skills and his broad swath of contacts. Keltor continued, "Once matters are finalized, I will introduce her, but not before. I'm certain you've never heard of her."

And for good reason. She was a former royal assassin forced into retirement because of a debilitating injury.

Keltor had debated adding her to his council, but Nalia had more knowledge of the dark side of Kelderan society than any male in the room. And her injury may restrict her abilities to fight, but her brain was as keen as ever; his father had often mentioned her as a resource.

The door chimed and the computer stated, "Azalyn Sulani wishes to enter."

"Permission granted," Keltor answers.

The door opened and Azalyn strode into the room, her head high and every bit the strong female he treasured.

To their credit, the males in the room remained silent. Once Azalyn was at his side, Keltor spoke again. "Meet your fellow council member, Azalyn Sulani." He made brief introductions, noting that Rohvel was the most hesitant, but Keltor trusted the male to come around. Otherwise, he never would've signed on for at least a year on his council. "Now, let's get to work."

As he and Azalyn explained not only their plans regarding the Jasvarian campaign, but also the truth about having a son and daughter, Keltor lost track of time. All that mattered was smoothing the way so that he could steal an hour or two with his female, to remind him of what he fought for.

Chapter Seventeen

Keltor and Azalyn had barely had time to take a fifteen-minute break for food and drinks after the end of the councilors meeting before the private comm unit attached to the conference room beeped with an incoming transmission.

He glanced at his female. "Feel free to listen, but I think it best if I handle this alone. As much as I admire your emotions, Ulrick or his son will no doubt see them as a weakness and pounce."

Azalyn sighed. "I know. It's hard, because he maneuvered my life even more than your father did, and I have a few words to say to him."

Rubbing her arm, he said, "Eventually he will get his comeuppance. Trust me, *zyla*."

"I do. You may want to enable the privacy screen and just broadcast the transmission to the conference room. That way I can yell as needed, without disrupting you."

He smiled. "As you wish. Just avoid throwing things, if you can help it."

Lightly smacking his shoulder, she frowned. "Just go before I do decide to throw something at *you*."

With a chuckle, he quickly kissed her and moved to the private comm unit.

As he engaged the privacy screen, Keltor took a few deep breaths to calm his mind and erase any lingering emotions. Because this was going to be one of the most important negotiations in his life.

Keltor clicked Receive. The light-blue skin and dark hair streaked with gray head of Ulrick Sulani appeared on screen. "Good to see you are leading these negotiations yourself, Ulrick."

Ulrick bowed his head a fraction before meeting Keltor's gaze again. "It is an honor to talk with you, your highness."

Judging by his address, Ulrick didn't know Keltor was king yet. It was better to keep him in the dark. "Let's talk about what you want in exchange for your support. Your son was overly vague about it earlier."

"A male who likes to get to the point. I admire that." Ulrick shifted his weight and continued, "However, you first need to tell me where Toralyn Sulani is located."

Keltor's suspicions that Ulrick had smuggled his own pirated technology to Jasvar, to maintain long-range communications, had all but been verified with that statement. "Am I supposed to know who that is?"

"Play the ignorant one if you like, your highness, but she wouldn't disappear without a trace. And seeing as your son has joined you, I imagine he's reached out to his sister."

Keltor forced a frown. "He doesn't have a sister."

"You are a skilled liar, Prince Keltor, but I am a better one. Shall we drop the pretense or would you prefer for me to withdraw my son's offer?"

He kept his tone casual. One of the first rules of negotiating was to never appear eager; an opponent would use it against you. "You may try, but coleaders of Jasvar would revoke your merchant's license if I even remotely believe you disloyal to Keldera."

Ulrick remained silent for a few beats and Keltor merely waited. If he allowed Toralyn to become part of the discussions, Ulrick may end up with a bigger advantage from which to make demands.

The older male finally spoke again. "As my son mentioned, we want your official endorsement on both Keldera and Jasvar. But one thing he forgot to add was that I want to prevent the Treslens from setting up shops on Jasvar for at least a year."

To get a leg up over their main merchant rival. "And in return? I need specifics this time, not vague promises."

"I shall divert 10 percent of my profits to supporting the monarchy by any means necessary, in addition to lending a few of my merchant...special operation members."

"You mean spies."

Ulrick shrugged. "Call them what you wish."

"What about the list of enemies? I've been able to verify the ten names your son sent earlier, as a sign of good faith. However, I expect to receive every one you know of."

"I will coordinate my special operation members to go where you wish and will make a public statement of support on the announcement of you selecting Azalyn as a bride. However, profits and further names will only take place after the claiming ceremony and your first public endorsement of the Sulani merchants."

Keltor considered the terms. Unlike many of the people he had negotiated with in the past, Ulrick had a clear goal in mind, with deadlines.

However, there was one final item he needed to make his future bride happy. "I think we're almost to a reasonable agreement. All that I would like to add is that I want every record related to Azalyn's pregnancy and subsequent labor and birth."

By the slight widening of Ulrick's eyes, Keltor could tell he'd surprised the older male. However, he quickly recovered. "I'm not sure they still exist."

"I believe they do. Find them, and once I receive and verify them, we shall have our agreement." He leaned forward a few inches. "And just know that if your records deviate from what little my father collected himself, then we will renegotiate and I guarantee the terms will shift."

"Careful, your highness. You need me more than I need you."

He raised his brows. "Are you sure about that? One message from me and you will not only lose your license on Jasvar to run your business, you will lose it on Keldera as well. You may recover through illicit channels, but the Treslens will quickly become the most powerful merchants on the planet. I suspect your pride won't allow that, especially considering the head of the family stole your female away from you all those years ago."

Ulrick studied him for a second before saying, "You are one of the few worthwhile negotiators I've encountered. Let me see what I can do. You'll hear from me shortly."

The screen turned dark and Keltor shook his head. Ulrick severing the connection first was yet another level in what he assumed would be years of power plays and struggles.

Typing in the disengagement sequence, the privacy screen receded, and he joined Azalyn in the conference room. She rushed to him. "Why did you ask for the birth records?"

He touched her cheek. "Because while I can't turn back the clock, I can at least give you more information on our children. Every small bit can help you form a bigger picture."

"Thank you."

"No need for gratitude." He kissed her. "Now comes the hardest part—the waiting."

"I'll freely admit that I'm not the most patient of people, but I will try."

He noticed the redness of Azalyn's eyes as well as the dark circles forming beneath them. His female was exhausted.

He could take her to his quarters and let her sleep. And yet, as he glanced at the timekeeper, he wanted to give her the surprise Veljan was helping put in place.

Azalyn's voice garnered his attention. "What are you debating?"

"You're getting too skilled at reading me."

Raising her brows, she said, "That's a good thing. But just tell me, Keltor."

"Well, you seem tired. I had wanted to take a small break with you and give you a surprise, but it might be best to wait until tomorrow."

Her eyes lit up. "A surprise? What surprise?"

"Are you sure you're up for it? I can't have you falling asleep partway through."

"I'm awake now."

"Okay. Then we need to stop by the East Garden on the way to my quarters."

"I surely hope you're not going to hold me hostage inside the water maze."

"No. But I won't tell you more than that." He took one of her hands. "Come. We need to hurry, or I won't have a choice but to wait."

As he guided her out the conference room, he checked the time again. They would indeed need to hurry, or Veljan would be otherwise occupied. "I could carry you."

"No carrying me. I can keep up." As if to prove her point, she increased her walking pace.

"Okay, but no complaining. I offered you an alternative and you declined."

"I won't complain. Now, let's hurry up, slowpoke."

Azalyn half-ran and he chuckled as he increased his strides.

She somehow managed to keep up the pace, even as he turned the last corner. He stopped them in front of the entrance to the East Garden. The doors opened, and he guided his female inside. After saying, "Computer, engage level ten security lock on the East Garden," the computer paused and stated, "King Keltor's voice pattern confirmed and protocols implemented. The East Garden is now secure."

Azalyn squeezed his hand. "Just what do you have planned?"

"You'll see."

He'd barely released Azalyn's hand, put an arm around her waist, and hauled her against his side before the lavender-skinned, silver-haired form of Veljan Ranna appeared from behind a set of bushes.

His friend gave a brief nod, signaling everything was ready for Keltor's surprise.

Keltor motioned toward his friend. "Azalyn Sulani, this is Veljan Ranna, the royal head gardener."

"And best friend." Keltor frowned, but Veljan bowed a fraction and continued before he could say anything. "A pleasure to meet you, Miss Sulani. I would take your hand, but mine are covered in dirt."

"As they should be, otherwise the garden would be a lot less beautiful," Azalyn said with a smile.

Veljan stood tall again. "A female who understands the work involved in bringing this place to life." He glanced at Keltor. "She has my approval."

Azalyn snorted. "While appreciated, I think my approval of Keltor is far more important."

Laughing, Veljan removed his gloves. "Yes, you are exactly what he needs."

His female glanced up at him with a question in her eyes, so Keltor explained, "Veljan has been my friend since we were boys. He likes to think he knows what's best for me."

"I used to think that. But now, it seems you've finally realized you need more than duty," Veljan said.

"Perhaps. However, would you rather discuss your advice over the years or show us your latest flower creation? Our free time is limited."

Shaking his head, Veljan said, "Sadly, my latest beauty isn't ready yet. But rest assured that once she blooms, I promise that Miss Sulani will be the first to see it."

Veljan winked and Azalyn chuckled. "Call me Azalyn. And maybe tone down the charm. Otherwise, Keltor may replace you out of jealousy."

Grinning, Veljan stood tall. "He wouldn't dare try to replace me. After all, I'm the best." He sobered. "Besides, I know how important you are to him. That means I'm just treating you as I would my own sister."

Keltor grunted. "Can you two stop discussing me as if I'm not here? I'm starting to rethink stopping by the garden."

Leaning her head against his side, Azalyn said, "No, the garden is the perfect spot to be. It's almost as if you leave your title at the door and the rest of the world doesn't exist when we're here. Well, almost."

He kissed the top of her head. "I know you're worried about Toralyn, but with the number of skilled warriors and others watching her—not to mention that all her records have been altered so that she is the biological child of Dolvia Sulani, to ward off people sniffing for her birth parents—she will be fine."

Sighing, she answered, "Deep down, I know that. But I still worry."

Squeezing her waist, he murmured, "It's only natural to worry. But hopefully my surprise will lift your spirits a fraction."

Glancing up, she stated, "Then you'd better hurry or someone else will snatch you away before I have a chance to figure out what you have in store."

As he stood with Azalyn at his side and his best friend watching them with a smile, something his father had said to him in recent months started to make sense: *Don't let the little moments pass you by, Keltor, because regret is forever.*

He'd assumed his father was trying to somewhat apologize for how he'd treated Keltor and his siblings when they were children. Perhaps that was part of it, but his father might also have been trying to tell Keltor to avoid his mistakes.

While he didn't have a lot of time before someone would require his presence, he had the moment.

It was time to make the most of it with Azalyn.

Releasing her, he looked to Veljan. "Guide Aza to the center of the maze as quickly as you can and deliver her to one of the benches. I'll meet you there."

Before either Veljan or Azalyn could do more than open their mouths, Keltor ran toward the maze.

He may not be able to erase the time he and his female had spent apart, but he intended to use something from their past to connect to the present. It was time to make new memories to replace the old.

✹ ✹ ✹

Azalyn watched Keltor dash away and wondered what he was up to.

However, Veljan's voice garnered her attention before

she could think long on it. "If I may have the honor of escorting you, Azalyn?"

Smiling, she met the male's magenta gaze. Even though she'd just met him, she felt at ease with Veljan. Once things calmed down, she'd make an effort to get to know him better. "Yes, but before we go, I want to say that I think you've been keeping Keltor sane all these years, haven't you?"

"Perhaps. But closer to the truth is that we kept each other sane. I may be a mere commoner, but no matter how much I don't care about it, the second I was made royal head gardener, I became famous on Keldera."

"Which means people look at you in awe, much like Keltor."

He inclined his head. "Exactly."

He proffered his arm, and Azalyn threaded hers through his. Once they were in motion, heading toward the maze, Azalyn said, "Thank you for being his friend. No doubt Keltor treasures the connection."

Snorting, Veljan maneuvered them through the first section of the maze. "If you can prove that Keltor ever used the phrase 'treasures the connection,' then I shall eat a bowl of dirt."

"I'll remember that. Give me a little time, and I might be able to coax it from him."

He looked at her askance. "You sound determined. Maybe I should retract my offer."

"Too late."

"Well, you can't blame a male for trying."

After she bobbed her head, they fell into silence. She took the chance to peek at the male who claimed to be Keltor's best friend.

The smile lines around his mouth told her volumes, as did the way Veljan carried himself with confidence and ease. And while not as handsome as Keltor, many a female would turn their head at his looks and bright smile.

Before she could think better of it, she blurted, "Do you have a bride?"

Something flashed in Veljan's eyes, but it was quickly replaced with a smile. "I'm flattered, my lady, but I'm not about to steal away Keltor's future queen."

She blinked before laughing. "You are a charmer."

"The best." He guided her into the maze. "But you may want to pay attention so that you can navigate the maze as quickly as Keltor next time, in case he challenges you."

Veljan clearly didn't want to discuss females, so Azalyn was more than willing to change the topic. "Did you design this maze?"

"There has always been a maze here, ever since Keltor's mother moved into the palace. However, I did change a few things to make it more interesting when I became head gardener." He lowered his voice. "There are some hidden surprises along the way, complete with tokens to find. Not even Keltor has found them all."

She barely noted the sound of the fountain growing louder. "I have a feeling we'll be spending quite a bit of what free time we can manage in this garden. Give me a few months. I'll find them all."

"A determined female. I like that."

Before she could question Veljan's unorthodox view of Kelderan females, they exited into the center, with the giant fountain in the middle. She couldn't help smiling at how much had changed since the last time she'd been here, when she'd cried about the children she'd never have.

That may still be the case, but even so, at least she'd always have Keltor. And maybe with time, she could earn both of her grown children's love.

Veljan stopped in front of a bench. "This one affords the best view of the fountain." He motioned for her to sit, and as soon as she did, Veljan bowed. "I would love to stay and talk further, but I must now depart."

She raised her brows. "Keltor didn't mention you needing to leave."

"Ah, but I know what his surprise is, as I helped put it together. Trust me, he wouldn't want me here."

For a second, jealousy flared at how well Veljan knew Keltor over her. But then she dismissed it as silly. She and Keltor had many years to discover everything about one another.

Not wanting Veljan to think her rude, she said, "Until next time, Veljan. Don't forget to summon me when your latest flower creation blooms."

"Of course, your majesty."

She opened her mouth to correct him, but Veljan disappeared into the maze.

Minutes passed, and Azalyn wondered where in the world Keltor could be. After all, they had so little alone time together. Why would he waste it?

Stretching her legs in front of her, she leaned back on the bench and braced her body with her hands. Closing her eyes, she listened to the soothing sounds of the fountain.

However, the peace didn't last long. Something heavy stepped on her foot and she cried out.

Opening her eyes, she found Keltor standing in front of her, dressed in a common artisan's outfit of brown synthetic material and a long cloak. He had also covered his skin with a temporary blue tint.

A memory from over twenty-three years ago flashed into her mind, when a much younger Keltor had worn something similar and had stepped on her foot inside the shop she was working at, causing her to drop some of her wares on the ground.

He was recreating how they met. And to Azalyn, it was

one of the most romantic gestures she'd ever received, throbbing foot and all.

Determined to play along, she recalled the words from their first encounter and repeated them, "Watch where you're going, sir."

"Forgive me, miss. I wasn't paying attention."

She stood. "Then you should because if you continue stepping on the feet of people working in this shop, you'll owe more than you can pay."

Amusement flared in his eyes, but his face mimicked the regret from their first meeting. "I shall try my best, miss. It shan't happen again."

She decided to deviate from the memory. "So does this mean you'll go away and come back several more times, purposefully bumping into me, before you ask me to go for a walk?"

He grinned. "I think we can fast forward that bit." Closing the distance between them, he hauled her up against him. "I much prefer reliving our first kiss."

Placing a hand on his chest, she said, "Before we do, I have a question. Why did you come back to the shop when all I did was scold you that first time? We had a whirlwind romance, and I always forget to ask you that question."

Rubbing a section of her hair between his fingers, he answered, "I could exalt your beauty and say I was smitten." She snorted and he added, "But the truth is that while you were—and still are—beautiful, I loved your honesty. Many shop workers would merely murmur an apology and scurry away. But not you." He tucked the section of hair behind her ear. "And then I thought maybe I could experience a few more instances of being a regular male and slice out a piece of normalcy while I still had the chance."

The corner of her mouth kicked up. "I'm not sure if it was exactly normal. By your third encounter and time of bumping into me, I strongly suggested that you should have your eyes checked."

He chuckled. "And as you recall, that's why I asked you to take a walk with me on your lunch break. I will never forget the confusion on your face when I asked."

She raised her brows. "Do you blame me? Here I thought I had a clumsy teenage male scouting out my store for who knew what. I'm still not sure why I said yes."

Keltor ran his finger down her cheek, leaving a trail of heat in his path. His voice was husky as he said, "Because as soon as I took your hand, right before I asked you to walk with me, your breath hitched. You felt the connection as much as I."

Searching his gaze, she asked quietly, "Did you know then, about me being a potential destined bride?"

"I had suspicions, but remember I was only nineteen. Kelderan males continue to grow until age twenty, and I put my attraction and desire to have you down to the hormones coursing through my body. Only later did I recognize the pull for what it was." Placing his hand over hers on his chest, he added, "But I know what you aren't asking me, Aza. I didn't come back because of some genetically enhanced ability to detect a female who could bear me children. You intrigued me with your wit and beauty. That's why I kept coming back."

His words sent a rush of warmth through her body. "And I'm glad you did, sore foot and all."

With a growl, Keltor closed the distance between their lips and she immediately accepted his tongue. As he licked, nipped, and suckled, the years faded away. It was almost as if they were kissing for the first time all over again, albeit they were both more skilled.

At that thought, she laughed. Keltor ended the kiss and grunted. "I hope you're not laughing at me."

"No, no. I was just thinking that this kiss is infinitely better than the first one." She looped her arms around his neck. "I like starting from right here, right now. We won't erase the past, of course, but no more regrets going forward. We have each other now, Keltor. And good fortune willing, for the rest of our very long lives."

He nipped her bottom lip. "So that makes this is our new first date?"

Raising her brows, she tilted her head. "Why say it in such a grumpy tone?"

"Because if it's our first date, it would be dishonorable to claim you on that bench behind you."

She brushed the warm skin at the back of Keltor's neck. "I won't tell anyone if you won't."

In the blink of an eye, Keltor lifted her by the waist and sat her on the bench. As his hand ran down her legs, she opened them without hesitation.

His fingers found the skin of her ankles. As he lightly strummed his fingers, Keltor's heated gaze met her own. She sucked in a breath.

Never looking away, he ran his hands up her calf, the inside of her thigh, and eventually stopped to caress the crease where her leg met her hip. His voice was husky as he said, "I never had the chance to taste you, *zyla*. I think it's time to change that."

He continued to caress her soft flesh, but otherwise didn't move. Azalyn finally growled. "What are you waiting for?"

"Tell me what you want, Aza."

Under any other circumstance, she would tease him about obeying a mere common female's orders.

However, each stroke of his fingers only sent more heat and wetness between her thighs. The idea of Keltor there, licking her secret place, made her squirm. "I want you to taste me."

"Where?"

Heat flushed her cheeks, but Azalyn slowly lifted her skirts until they bunched around her waist. She wasn't quite bold enough to touch herself in front of Keltor yet, so she gestured. "There."

Moving his hands to splay her thighs farther apart, he leaned down and teased her opening with his lips and tongue. Azalyn groaned at the strange, wet heat against her.

At the sound, Keltor thrust his tongue inside her and continued to lick, twirl, and explore. Not wanting him to stop, she threaded her fingers through his hair to keep him in place.

The action only made Keltor tease her harder. Any embarrassment she had, faded. Keltor would only treasure her body, never laugh at it.

He changed the wicked movements of his tongue and she groaned. She wondered what other things she'd always been embarrassed to try would be as glorious and as full of pleasure.

She had a feeling Keltor would try any and all of them. All she had to do was ask.

Soon lights danced in front of her eyes. She cried out his name as pleasure coursed through her body.

She was barely aware of Keltor kissing the inside of each of her thighs before he kissed her dress-covered abdomen, between her breasts, the side of her neck, and eventually took her lips in a gentle kiss.

Keltor pulled away and smiled at her with satisfaction in his eyes. She should make a witty remark, or simply ask Keltor to claim her.

But between reliving the memory, the way he stared at her with adoration, and the haze of her orgasm, she murmured, "I love you."

With a growl, he took her lips again, and after a bit of fumbling, Keltor thrust his cock inside her. It was only later, after he made her scream in pleasure again, that she realized he'd never commented on her declaration.

Chapter Eighteen

It had taken almost a month, but as a tall, thin male led Toralyn into one of the private rooms at the back of the Twin Moons Tavern, excitement thrummed through her body. She was finally attending her first official antimonarchist meeting.

The initiation test—to donate funds, pass a skills test, and to deface one of the public billboards currently running campaigns about Jasvar without being caught—had been easy enough. However, the next step would be infinitely harder since she needed to keep her cool and act the part of a disgruntled Kelderan citizen. She'd had some practice at keeping secrets, but never as something so contrary to her own beliefs. Even before finding out her birth father was a prince-but-now-king, she'd never had an ill opinion about the monarchy. Most merchants preferred the stability of the status quo over the unknown.

There were many times she could've backed out and merely passed on what information she had gathered so far to her brother. But as she'd learned one fact after another, she'd decided that only once she was truly undercover and considered one of them could she give her brother the best information. And so, she'd stayed the course, even though it meant delaying her chances at going to Jasvar.

What surprised her most, though, was the fact that her birth father's guards hadn't found her yet.

However, before she could think on that yet again, the thin male stopped in front of a door and pressed his hand to a palm scanner. Once the light turned green on the device, the door opened and he motioned her inside.

Steeling herself for what was to come, she strode in and surveyed the area.

About twenty people sat in the rows of chairs facing the front, where a podium and large view screen were situated. The light cream walls were of a low-cost composite material and strangely bare. The minimalist style was probably to avoid giving away what went on in this room; the Twin Moons Tavern had a reputation of being able to keep secrets as well as bribe off law enforcers. As a result, everyone from antimonarchists to space pirates met in the infamous back rooms.

Toralyn moved toward the chairs. Just as she was about to slide into one at the back, a female in her thirties with black hair, golden skin, and dark eyes looked right at her.

She'd never seen the female before, but something about her gaze and the way she perched on her seat as if she were ready to jump up and attack at any moment screamed dangerous. The scar on her chin and dark clothing only enhanced the image.

Not willing to be intimidated since that might get her tossed out of the meeting, Toralyn nodded at the female and sat down.

A male in his late forties walked to the podium, garnering Toralyn's attention. Even with her eyes on the podium, she could still feel the other female staring at her.

If the dangerous-looking female was common for the antimonarchists, then they may be a bigger threat than Toralyn had given them credit for.

The male at the podium spoke. "You are all new recruits to the cause. While I admire your generous donations and acts of vandalism to show your contempt of the king and his wastrels, I'm sure you understand that there are still a series of tests and trials before you will be allowed into the most inner circles of our movement. If this sounds like too much work, feel free to leave now while you still can. Because after this meeting, you will be watched and at the first sign of defection, we will hunt you down and keep you in captivity until such time you embrace death or are willing to prove yourself to the cause. Make your choice now."

For a few seconds, no one moved. But then a couple toward the front stood and scurried out of the room.

The male leader looked at every person in turn before continuing, "The loyal remain. Good. Now, let's begin." The view screen switched on, displaying around one hundred circles, grouped in various clusters across the rectangular space. "Every recruit is grouped according to their skills and talents." He flashed a light on a circle near the top right corner, grouped with a few others, but the group itself was spaced far apart from the other clusters. "This is where you are, in the cluster of those with highly desirable skill sets. Everyone here will play an important role in the liberation of Keldera."

A male in the crowd shouted, "When can we start making the bastards pay? They live off our earnings, doing nothing in return. They shouldn't be allowed to continue in such luxury while my neighbor struggles to pay his monthly expenses."

Toralyn bit her tongue to keep from correcting the male. The monarchy lived off its own investments. Kelderans were only expected to pay in times of war, when the palace might have to hire mercenaries to defend the planet. Tax revenue went to the budget maintained by the house of the commoners' representatives.

The male leader replied, "I agree that it's time to end their leeching, but small acts will accomplish nothing. Patience, my friend, and we will bring them down."

So, it seemed that the antimonarchists like to play off misinformation and anger. Keeping herself in character and not betraying her true thoughts was going to be tougher than Toralyn had imagined.

The male at the front of the room paused and finally spoke again. "And that is where you all come in. The faster you train, the faster we can implement one of our most daring strategies. Don't ask what as not even I know what it is.

"Each circle has their own orders, with a select few sharing the grander plan with those who earn the leaders' trust. As long as you continue to show your support and advance up the ranks, one day it will end in victory." A few people nodded. "So let us begin and get closer to our ultimate goal. You will be paired off with someone who, after your earlier interviews and demonstrations, is deemed to be your best fit. When I call your name, stand up, connect with your partner, and wait for further instructions."

As he went through his list, Toralyn had to admit that whoever was leading the antimonarchists was being smart about it. Keeping orders and plans localized to certain ranks ensured that there were fewer leaks.

The male at the front of the room continued calling names until the pool of potential partners dwindled to the point that four were left—Toralyn, the dangerous-looking female, and two short, but muscled males.

"Toralyn Sulani."

She perked up at her name and stood. The male announced her partner, "Xerla Cyntah."

The female from before stood. Her surname denoted her as also being from a merchant family, although the Cyntahs were fourth in overall revenue on Keldera.

Xerla stood and raised an eyebrow at Toralyn. She expected her to come.

Even though it went against every cell in her being, Toralyn capitulated and walked to Xerla. She couldn't afford a petty fight. After all, partnering with the female was her best chance at advancing and getting information to protect her brother.

Once she stopped about a foot from the female, they merely eyed each other while the leader announced the final pairing.

Since they hadn't been told to introduce or talk with one another, Toralyn remained silent.

The leader clapped his hands once, and all eyes went to him. "I applaud you for not speaking and merely waiting for further instruction. It shows me that you are in the right place. Now, the person paired with you will be your partner for as long as we continue fighting for victory. You weren't paired to be friends. You were paired to keep each other alive. And for the next few weeks, you're going to be completing a series of tests to prove that you can do so. Those who fail will probably end up as ash, to be scattered by your closest relative as they weep for your death."

The words were meant to scare, but Toralyn refused to cower.

"Now," he said, "it's time to assign your first series of tests. The pair who gets closest to the final objective will advance to the next tier. There you will receive more secrets. It is our hope that all of you will eventually get there."

As Toralyn listened to the task, she willed her face to remain neutral.

The truth was, she could easily complete it because of certain knowledge she possessed. But if she did, it may end up hurting someone she knew.

When the male finished explaining, Xerla spoke for the first time. "You had better be in this to win because I don't accept failure."

Bobbing her head, she answered, "Of course."

"Good. Then let's move to one of the private areas and begin devising our plan."

She walked, and Toralyn didn't have a choice but to follow the older female. As Xerla stepped into a small room off the bigger one, Toralyn stood tall and resisted swallowing. Being alone with someone who probably didn't think twice about killing a person wasn't the best of situations.

Xerla took something out of her pocket, a small tube of some sort, and clicked the top. After five seconds, she spoke again. "No one will be able to eavesdrop on our conversation. So listen closely, Toralyn Sulani, because I have a plan and you're going to do what I say."

It was now or never for holding her ground. She crossed her arms over her chest. "I'll decide that for myself, actually. I'm not your lackey to order around. We're partners."

Raising an eyebrow, Xerla studied her for a second. "You're young and out to prove yourself, I get that. But if we're to both succeed on our individual missions, then you need to follow my lead."

She frowned. "What are you talking about? We have the same mission."

"I'm not talking about our most recently assigned mission."

It hit her then—Xerla knew she wasn't a diehard out to bring down the monarchy. "So you plan to blackmail me to cooperate?"

The corner of the female's mouth ticked up. "Be grateful that's all I'm doing."

"But why? If that device truly shields this room from eavesdroppers, you can at least tell me the reason."

"Why? Your choices are to work with me or be discovered by the vile male out there. I know how to escape from just about any prison, but can you?"

Her curiosity won out over her pride. "Who are you?"

"Xerla Cyntah. You need to work on your memory retention."

She resisted huffing. "I know your name, but who do you work for?"

"Myself. But there's only one male I take orders from—your father."

Before she could stop herself, Toralyn spat out, "My father is dead."

Xerla shrugged. "You can play dumb if you like. But the male who sent me here is very much alive."

Keltor. "Damn him and not trusting me."

"It's not personal. I'm more skilled than you in every way. That's a fact. Him sending me here tells me you're valuable and he prefers you alive. And before you go on about trust, I don't care about your feelings. Keeping you alive and getting information is all that matters. Unfortunately, it now means relying on you. So spare us a lot of back and forth and tell me—are you ready to take orders and rise through the ranks?"

This was a tipping point. If Toralyn capitulated easily, Xerla would never consider her suggestions and advice. And while the female claimed to be better at everything, everyone had weaknesses. Even an intimidating-looking female who could probably snap her in half.

And considering Keltor had sent the female to watch over her, Xerla wouldn't kill her for voicing her opinion.

Uncrossing her arms, Toralyn answered, "I will take orders that make sense and don't cross a line."

Surprise flashed in Xerla's eyes, but vanished before she could blink. "Which is?"

"I won't kill anyone."

"Good thing I'm trained to do just that. So if there's nothing else, let's finalize our strategy."

Xerla's response intrigued her. Apparently her birth father had a female assassin.

Before meeting her, Toralyn would've dismissed the idea of any female trained to kill as ridiculous. After all, Kelderan tradition dictated females lived to marry and reproduce.

However, she was beginning to realize that the palace had many secrets. Part of her wanted to find out as many as she could, while the other part of her just wanted to complete her task to safeguard her brother and leave Keldera forever.

For the time being, she nodded. "Let's get started."

Chapter Nineteen

Azalyn finished her last stroke and placed her paintbrush in a cup of cleaning solution.

She'd always preferred animals over people as subjects, but she'd tackled the challenge in order to capture her son's image.

Painting a straightforward portrait wasn't her style, so there were strokes of color used strategically throughout Kelzal's face, neck, and shoulders to make the image stand out. Even with the unusual hints of colors, no one would mistake it for anyone but her son.

Stepping back and turning toward the sink to wash her hands, Azalyn tried not to think of what she wanted to paint next. Since nearly a month has passed since last seeing Toralyn, she'd hoped to see her daughter again by now and convince her to at least allow Azalyn to sketch out a preliminary image. Only once she had a portrait of both their children would she present them to Keltor as a gift.

Even with her daughter still participating in some undercover work—or, so Xerla and Ervan's reports said—Azalyn had nothing to complain about. Keltor had formally announced Kelzal's line in the succession as well as broadcast his new role as king, both with only minimal resistance. Well, at least for the time being. She had no idea what the future held.

Things had also settled down inside the palace and she now spent most of her time in Keltor's quarters, allowing her to spend time with her male and to give Kelzal his space. And when not there, her duties with the Jasvarian campaign and council meetings occupied most of her time.

But every once in a while, Kelzal would immerse himself in research and Keltor would have kingly duties he needed to perform, which left Azalyn with an occasional chance to paint.

Turning back to Kelzal's portrait, she didn't realize how much she'd needed to reclaim the part of herself that had emerged during her years apart from Keltor. In a way, painting her children and giving it to him would bridge the two lives together.

The computer system chimed, followed by, "Kelzal Burrig."

Wiping her hands on a towel, she quickly headed toward the main foyer.

Even though Kelzal was free to wander Keltor's quarters, he stood near a side table that had a few of her older paintings in frames. He ran his finger around each frame at a steady pace before tapping the table in a rhythm she'd heard many times before.

"What's wrong, Kelzal?"

He didn't look away from the table. "Will Keltor remain busy with his duties for at least an hour?"

What Azalyn wouldn't give to have her son refer to Keltor as his father. But she would never force the issue. "According to his schedule and the update he sent me, yes. Why?"

He moved his gaze to hers. "I want you to take me to see King Kastor."

Azalyn resisted widening her eyes. "Are you sure?"

Nodding, he looked back to the table. "I am. They say his health is declining further and I believe I should meet him at least once to get answers for some questions. I want you to come with me."

"Kastor is not the formidable male he once was; you would do fine talking with him alone."

"I understand that. But in case I miss a social cue or implied emotion, I want you there to help me because what I have to ask is important."

Pushing aside her curiosity, she took a step toward Kelzal and placed a hand on his shoulder. Her son needed her. "I will go, if you like." He nodded. "I should change clothes first."

"Why?" His eyes flicked to the blue, green, and yellow splotches on her skirt. "I like the paint. It adds more color to your clothes."

She snorted. "As much as I agree with you, I'm not sure the former king would approve."

"Does it matter? In a matter of weeks you will be queen, with or without his approval."

She did her best not to smile at Kelzal's protective tone. "More importantly, I suppose he is family now." She held out her multicolored skirt and half-twirled. "Besides, I always look for ways to surprise the royal guards. I'm sure my appearance will do the trick."

Kelzal grunted. "I don't like the guards. They are always in the way, not to mention inefficient. No one will attack me while walking down a secret hallway."

Not wanting to rehash the argument they'd had many times before, she squeezed Kelzal's shoulder and took a step toward the door. "Come, let's go. If we hurry, we can catch Kastor before his afternoon medication is dispensed and he'll be more alert."

Without another word, Azalyn headed out the door and

down the secret corridor to Kastor's quarters. Kelzal followed on her heels.

While Kelzal wanting to meet his paternal grandfather was a big step, she was glad he'd asked her along for her own reasons, too. The meeting would allow Azalyn the opportunity to ask Kastor something without Keltor present.

Namely, if Keltor had a half sibling or not.

Father and son had no trouble discussing policy or royal history, but anything personal was silently agreed upon to be off-limits. Not to mention that any time Azalyn brought up the subject, Keltor kissed or teased her on purpose, putting off her curiosity.

So it was up to her to find out the truth.

Soon they reached Kastor's quarters, and Kelzal passed both sets of palm and retina scanners. Kastor's Barren nurse, Jevla, greeted them. "I did not expect you."

Azalyn spoke up since Kelzal detested formalities. "We decided to visit unexpectedly. I believe Kastor asked for Kelzal to come when he was able."

"I shall check if his majesty is receiving visitors." The nurse went to a side room. She and Kelzal waited silently until she returned. "He will see you."

The nurse guided them to Kastor's room. Azalyn braced herself for the worst, but upon entering, blinked at Kastor sitting in a large, stuffed chair instead of laying on his bed.

Kastor noted her confusion and smiled. "Without any real duties to perform, I find myself more refreshed and not quite ready to die yet."

"I should hope not," Azalyn stated without missing a beat. "After all, you vowed to hang on until you met both your grandchildren."

Keltor and Azalyn had decided to share Toralyn's existence with the former king; he'd had no idea of a second grandchild.

She gently pushed Kelzal forward. Her son took another step toward Kastor's chair, but Kelzal merely stood in silence with his eyes averted.

Kastor's voice filled the room. "Thank you for coming to see me, Kelzal. I have a feeling you blame me for your parents being apart and your eventual adoption. As such, I am honored to be in your presence."

Her son's gaze met the former king's. "I've had a good life and am glad for it. However, you are the cause of my mother's pain."

"You are correct," the older male said without apology.

Azalyn held her breath to see what would happen. She'd intervene as a last resort, but Kelzal was a grown male and needed to test out Kastor's boundaries on his own.

✵ ✵ ✵

Kelzal Burrig frowned at his paternal grandfather. "I didn't expect for you to be so forthright."

"I am no longer king and finally have the freedom to say what I wish, at least to my own family. Part of me regrets my actions in the past, but part of me knows it was the right thing to do. Being a monarch isn't always easy."

The old male didn't say anything Kelzal didn't already know.

However, his decision to visit Kastor hadn't been made lightly. Kelzal had come with a purpose. "I hear enough about that from Keltor. I came here to ask you a historical legal question."

Kastor's brows raised. "Then by all means, go ahead."

Kelzal looked to the side of the room and focused on one of the light fixtures. Imagining the internal wiring and construction helped him to focus and recall a passage he'd read earlier in the week. "One hundred and thirty-five years ago there was a crisis in the line of succession. The event required the courts to put in place a temporary exception, allowing a female to assume the throne until a distant male cousin of hers could be located and brought to rule."

"You mean Queen Laranna," Kastor answered.

"Yes. Since there is a legal precedent for a female ruler, even if only temporarily, would it be possible for it to happen again? I am not as adept at understanding Kelderan law as you since it has never interested me until recently."

Kastor grunted. Eight seconds passed before he finally spoke again. "Queen Laranna was a mere placeholder, not a long-reigning monarch. However, a legal case could be made that a female has ruled in the past and should be allowed to do so again in the future. To change the law would require the assistance of the commoners' representatives. And that would be a long shot, at best, Kelzal. Especially given your sister's activities over the years. A female ruler would cause enough talk and outrage, but for one that has been trained in defense and espionage is nearly impossible. She would be viewed as a threat to Kelderan tradition and way of life."

"I understand the odds against it," Kelzal said. "However, Toralyn would be more appropriate for the role."

"And why is that?" Kastor inquired.

As always, Kelzal spoke the truth. "I'm not skilled in discerning lies from truth, at least until I have the research to disprove something. Nor do I understand the need for saying one thing when I mean another. Keltor always says that a monarch must realize his strengths and weaknesses. I am merely stating mine—I would be too easily manipulated. That is dangerous for Keldera."

His mother spoke up from behind him. "I think you're selling yourself short, Kelzal. With practice and trusted councilors, you would do well."

Glancing at his mother, he said, "I appreciate your support. However, it is one clouded by emotion. Toralyn would be a better choice not just for Keldera, but also for ensuring your safety."

After weeks of studying his mother, he recognized the flash of concern. She was trying her best to support him. And while he appreciated it since it was her way of showing affection, Kelzal lived by facts and truth.

And he sensed Kastor did as well.

Moving his gaze back to the older male, he added, "You know I am correct."

"Perhaps. But for the moment, you are the heir, Kelzal. Until you can find a solution and enact it, you must acknowledge that fact."

"I still don't understand how an accident of birth makes me the most suitable candidate."

Kastor barked out a laugh. "I've asked myself the same question many times. But our society functions with both a house of commoners' representatives and a monarchy. Too big of a shift from the status quo might renege our treaties with nearby planets and risk war."

"And yet we risk war with my mother marrying Keltor."

Shrugging, Kastor stated, "That is something we can at least attempt to contain."

Why did no one understand how poor a choice he'd be for a ruler? He wasn't being selfish. He'd laid out his case and admitted some of his worst faults.

And still they wanted to force him into a situation that would end badly for all.

Turning away, Kelzal focused on the painting of a female he'd seen only in digital pictures before—the late Queen Solahn, his paternal grandmother.

He shared a few of the same genetic traits, but he would never smile as freely as the female in the picture. He was the only one in his family who seemed to be different.

Not wanting more reminders of that fact, he murmured, "I must return to my research."

He made to exit the room when Kastor's voice rang out, "If you have other questions, return at any time."

Nodding, Kelzal briefly met his mother's eyes before exiting the room. He wasn't done finding a way for his sister to assume the throne. All Kelzal wished was to protect his mother and sister. Being left alone with his research would also be ideal.

Tapping his fingers against his thighs, he exited Kastor's quarters and picked up his pace, doing his best to ignore the royal guards who escorted him.

He would find a way for his sister to be next in line to keep Keldera at peace, if nothing else. And he'd do whatever it took to ensure his plans became reality, even if it meant changing the law.

The first step would be studying every case related to a female assuming ownership of key positions. Only then could he devise the best strategy.

✲ ✲ ✲

Azalyn watched her son leave and did her best to hide her emotions.

Kelzal might be slightly different from most people, but she had a feeling he viewed it as worse than it really was, possibly even as a defect.

And that broke her heart.

Kastor's voice interrupted her thoughts. "I know you are his mother, Azalyn, but the boy has a point. I also think his sister would be a better ruler."

She swiveled around to face Kastor once again. "Since when are you open to changing the status quo? Especially when you did nothing for Keltor and me, nor, if the rumors are true, your illegitimate children."

He quirked a brow. "You, of all people, know that rumors aren't always true."

This was it, her chance to find out the truth. "So are you denying them?"

"No," he whispered softly, to the point Azalyn doubted she'd heard him correctly.

"Pardon?"

Kastor looked over at the portrait of Queen Solahn. "I didn't expect to find a female for more than a few nights of pleasure once Solahn died. Our children may think I didn't care for her because of how much time I spent away, ruling the planet. But I loved her." He smiled. "She was much like you are with my son, in that she forced me to stop and enjoy life every once in a while. But then she died during the Brevkan wars and I had no one to prevent me from working nonstop. Even seeing our children was too painful; they only reminded me of her."

Azalyn remained quiet, afraid that a question might break Kastor's memories and she'd never find out the truth.

Nearly a minute passed, but the older male continued, "A few years after Solahn's death, I went to the small city of Cillaren to meet with one of our now foreign allies to negotiate trade agreements. The meetings took place in an upscale retreat complex, on the outskirts of the city. Jalarra was one of the servers for our meals. At first glance, my instinct kicked in and I knew she was one of my potential destined brides. Her being a commoner meant that I needed to keep away from her."

"And somehow you didn't."

"No. At that time, she worked many jobs at the retreat facility, and I stumbled upon her cleaning my rooms. She scowled and told me to wait until she was done, otherwise she wouldn't be paid if the job wasn't completed. Her boldness surprised me, and I realized how much I missed it; few had acted that way with me since my bride's death. I soon found myself searching her out. Even once the negotiations completed, I devised excuses to visit the area to see her. After some time, she found herself with child."

Kastor met her gaze again. "I met her for the first time over twenty years ago, before you and Keltor, back when Keldera was still trying to rebuild after the devastating war with the Brevkan. Jalarra convinced me not to acknowledge her or test tradition for fear of what might happen. Her requests only became more fervent once our first child was born. I could not say no to her, and so our assignations and love remained secret."

Understanding dawned on Azalyn. "When Keltor and I were together back then, and you discovered it, the situation must've seemed clear—any monarch taking a commoner as bride would be too disruptive."

He nodded. "It doesn't excuse my meddling—believe me, if I had known about your children, I would've tried a different tact—but I believed that if I had to hide away and publicly not claim Jalarra to protect Keldera, then Keltor should do the same."

"Where is Jalarra now? Is she still alive?"

"Yes, she still lives in Cillaren, with our youngest daughter, Kasarra. Our eldest daughter, Kajala, joined the colony on Jasvar. And then there is our only son, Korjal."

Azalyn would wrap her head around the existence of Keltor's three half siblings later. For the moment, she pushed for more information. "Why do you sound irritated when mentioning your son?"

Kastor sighed. "Because he is a young fool, and he's embroiled himself with the antimonarchists."

She blinked. "How is that possible?"

"By all accounts, he hasn't revealed his parentage. The people in Cillaren believe him and his sisters to be the children of one or more of the retreats' patrons. None suspect me, however. Jalarra and I were careful in that respect."

Azalyn wasn't quite as confident of that fact since no doubt at least some of the staff knew the secret. "But Korjal knows you are his father?"

"Eventually, yes, they all found out. However, as Korjal grew older, he demanded to be acknowledged. No amount of discussion from me or his mother changed his mind. And one day, he left a note and vanished. Later one of my guards learned of him joining up with the antimonarchists."

Taking a seat in the chair next to Kastor, Azalyn touched his arm. "And you've been carrying around all these secrets over the years, haven't you? Because Keltor doesn't know about this."

"No, nor do Kason and Kalahn. Keltor had enough reason to hate me. Him discovering I had a female commoner I loved and had children with would only intensify the hatred. For the sake of succession, I kept the secret."

"Then why tell me?"

He smiled. "If anyone can break the news to Keltor and make him listen, it's you. I only hope he'll continue to ensure their well-being. While I bought the retreat complex as a gift and bestowed it on Jalarra so that she has a source of income, if anyone finds out the connection between me and them, their lives could be in danger. Promise me that you'll convince Keltor to look after them."

For the first time, Azalyn believed the old king approved of her. "I promise. But out of curiosity, when was the last time you saw them?"

"Not since I became severely ill months ago."

She squeezed his arm at the sadness in his voice. "Then I will reveal this information to Keltor and find a way to bring Jalarra and your children here, if you so wish. Or, at least your children still on Keldera."

"Whether they come or not should be Jalarra's decision; she may not wish to see me since our last visit ended in an argument. But if she does, and if Keltor knows and vows his duty to protect them, then I would love to see them one last time. Although I'm not so sure Korjal would be open to leaving the antimonarchists to join his mother and sister."

"I'm sure we can work on that, too." Azalyn stood. "I'll break the news to Keltor as soon as I'm able. The more family he has, the better."

Kastor reached up and took her wrist, preventing her from leaving. "I allowed my own circumstances and unhappiness to cloud my judgment about you, Azalyn. For that, I'm sorry."

"You've made an effort, Kastor, and for that, I commend you." She tugged lightly, and he released his grip. "Now, rest. With any luck, it won't be long until you see the rest of your family again."

He nodded, and it was then that Azalyn noted the dark circles under his eyes and the yellow-tinge to his normally golden skin. Kastor may be refreshed for the moment, but she wasn't sure how many more weeks he could hold on.

Exiting the room, she signaled to the nurse that it was time for her to return to her duties.

As she turned a corner, Azalyn started to think of how to break the news to Keltor. Because if she didn't act soon, Kastor's other children might never have the chance to say goodbye to their father. Despite everything that had happened to her because of Kastor, he deserved to say his farewells to as many of his children as possible.

Since it'd still be hours before Keltor came home, it gave her some time to research what she could on Jalarra and the three children. The more information she had, the less time it would take to convince Keltor to risk bringing Jalarra and her daughter to the palace.

Chapter Twenty

Approving the last document for the day, Keltor stood and rotated his shoulders. It was time to go home to his female.

Even though the act had become routine, he still smiled as he made his way to his quarters. Or, rather, what was fast becoming their quarters.

He had been a fool to think living alone and remaining isolated had been the best approach to being a monarch. Yes, Azalyn, Kelzal, and Toralyn had all become possible weaknesses for enemies to use against him, but having them in his life ensured that he worked harder for the best future he could make.

And since the Jasvarian campaign was doing well and public opinion was turning more for the monarchy than against it, he was toying with announcing his intended marriage to Azalyn. Especially since Ulrick Sulani had so far kept up his end of their agreement.

Granted, he still needed to ask her formally. But he had a feeling she'd say yes, especially once he told her his true feelings.

Keeping them secret had been out of necessity. Keltor would never offer a future he couldn't guarantee. And when he told Azalyn he loved her again, it would be forever.

Not wanting to think about how his brother would call him a lovesick fool, Keltor picked up his pace and his guards matched him. After clearing the security scanners, he entered his quarters alone. The guards would only come in if invited or if there was a perceived threat.

Because of the time, he went to the kitchen area first. And sure enough, Azalyn stood over the cooker, stirring something in a pan. It would be barely edible, but he'd choke it down simply because she'd cooked it for him.

"What are you making?" he asked as he walked toward her.

She turned her head as soon as he came behind and wrapped his arms around her waist. She smiled, but it didn't reach her eyes. "A simple stew."

Usually Azalyn leaned back against his chest and lifted her head for a kiss when he pulled her close as she cooked. Instead, all she did was turn back to the pot, and he knew something was wrong. "What's going on?"

Sighing, she moved the pot from the heat source, turned off the cooker, and turned in his arms to face him. "I went with Kelzal to visit your father today."

He tensed. "What did he do?"

She shook her head. "Nothing bad." Meeting his gaze, she continued, "But we have a potential problem."

"Just tell me, *zyla*."

"Well, Kelzal should tell you his plans, but what I can tell you is that I asked your father about any half siblings and he said they exist."

He blinked. "They? Just how many are there?"

"Three, and all with the same female. I guess he fell in love again after your mother's death, but didn't think he could ever marry her. She's a commoner."

He frowned. "How did I not know about this?"

"Kastor was king. I'm sure he had his methods."

Growling, he looked off to the side. "The old fool. I can't protect someone if I don't know of their existence."

She touched his cheek, guiding his face to look back at her. "I know this is another level of deception between you and him. However, you should focus on the more important fact—you have two more sisters and a brother."

Azalyn was correct, of course. "I will, of course, seek them out and ensure they are provided for."

"I know you will, Keltor. But while one sister lives with her mother and helps runs a high-end retreat, and another sister is part of the colony on Jasvar, your half brother is the potential issue." He raised his brows and she added, "He works with the antimonarchists. By all accounts, he hates the monarchy because Kastor never publicly acknowledged him or his mother."

He cursed. "Does the fool not see that if he is public about his parentage, the antimonarchists will use him and possibly kill him in the end, to ensure that he can never claim the throne?"

"As far as Kastor knows, your brother—Korjal—hasn't revealed the identity of his father."

"Then he has a modicum of intelligence."

Azalyn sighed. "He is young, Keltor. Barely nineteen. I'm sure you remember what it was like to be that age, what with hormones raging through your body as you reached the final stage of adulthood."

Kelderans reached full maturity at age twenty.

Keltor had indeed rebelled during those years, and not just with his secret relationship with Azalyn. "I won't apologize for that, but me wearing a disguise and venturing outside the palace walls is not the same as working to bring down the monarchy because of a grudge against Father."

"Regardless, we need to tread carefully with this. Forcing Korjal's hand may only make matters worse."

The fact Azalyn considered it their problem instead of his only made him love her all the more. "My first instinct is to locate him and bring him to the palace. However, I'm open to hearing your suggestions."

She tilted her head. "You aren't going to like it, but here goes—I think we need to legitimize them in a public statement. Not straight away, but as soon as we can without disrupting our current plans. Guards can secretly watch over your half sister and her mother on Keldera, and I'm sure Kason will do the same with your half sister on Jasvar. The announcement will probably convince Korjal to at least reconsider his life choices."

One of the good things to come out of all this would be the shock on Kason's face when Keltor told him the news of their half siblings.

"Perhaps." He sighed. "And here I thought I would come home and enjoy a quiet evening with my female."

"I'm not going anywhere, *zylar*. And I know what I signed up for when it came to loving a prince who became king."

At the steel in her tone, Keltor decided to briefly put aside everything else and focus on his female. Raising a hand to her cheek, he murmured, "I love you, too. I hope you know that."

Smiling, she replied, "I do, but it's nice to hear it. I suspect you had reasons for not voicing your feelings."

He lightly ran his fingers down her cheek. "You know me too well, *zyla*."

She arched a brow. "Care to tell me your logic? That way I can debunk it and hope to avoid you using it again in the future."

"You almost make it sound as if I'm a computer to be deprogrammed."

Shrugging, she said, "In a way, you are. Duty has been

your sole reason for living for decades. I won't ever try to lessen how important duty is to you, but it's okay to have other priorities at the same time. Even if you're male, I'm sure you can multitask."

He nipped her lower lip. "Cheeky female."

Her grin stole his breath away. "Of course." She kissed him slowly and pulled away far too soon. "Has there been any news of Toralyn?"

Rubbing her lower back, he said, "Not since yesterday. By all accounts, she'll be undercover for months to come."

"I'm not sure I like that."

"Look at it this way—she has a purpose, and maybe the activities will tame the last of her rebellious spirit."

"Considering she's my daughter, I doubt her spirit will ever be fully tamed, nor would I want it to be."

"Well, I've been thinking about how we could convince Toralyn to stay on Keldera."

Hope bloomed in Azalyn's eyes. "I'm listening."

What he wouldn't give to be able to grant her desire to have their children home and part of their family. "I'm thinking of adding some female guards to the palace. If she trained with them, not only would she be better able to protect herself, she might start to believe I won't marry her off to form an alliance. I want her to stay here, and be part of our family."

Azalyn looked away and bit her lip. Just as he was about to press her on the reaction, the walls shook a second before the red alert alarm sounded.

Without thinking, he asked, "Computer, status report."

"Voice print recognized and clearance granted. A section of the palace had been damaged."

Right as the computer finished, his communicator beeped furiously. Clicking Receive, the chief of palace security's voice came over the line, "For your safety, remain in your quarters, your majesty. The disturbance was a bomb, which detonated in the hospital wing. No further explosive materials have been detected at this time."

"Casualties?"

"Ten so far, although many more are injured."

Keltor resisted a growl. "Alert me immediately once you find out more."

"I will contact you at regular intervals. End transmission."

✵ ✵ ✵

An hour later, Azalyn wondered how she hadn't worn a pathway on the floor in Keltor's office, located inside his quarters. She understood that Keltor's quarters were some of the most defended and guarded areas of the palace, but she was anxious to see her son with her own eyes and confirm he was okay.

After telling Keltor as many details of his half siblings as she could, and doing what little research she could concentrate upon, she'd resorted to pacing so as to leave Keltor to his work.

Her male sat at his desk, studying his view screen. Never looking up, he said, "Security has sent an update."

She moved to stand at his side. "Well?"

"The recorded surveillance shows a Barren female heading into a room, and within minutes, there was an explosion from the same room. She was the first casualty."

An uneasiness settled in her stomach. "Why do I get the feeling the explosion wasn't an accident?"

He met her gaze. "Because it wasn't. The sensors recorded the individual chemicals being exposed in the room, as well as the change when mixed. We are almost positive she mixed them on purpose, to create the bomb-like explosion."

She leaned against Keltor, and an arm went around her waist. "What else aren't you telling me?"

"There was an electronic message delivered a few minutes afterward." He motioned toward the screen. "Here, have a look."

Azalyn leaned down to read the text on the screen:
This is just the beginning.

"That's rather vague," she murmured.

"Yes and no. I suspect she may be one of many Barren who've teamed up with the antimonarchists."

"While I understand their possible hatred after better knowing what Barren go through because of my friendship with Vala, surely they would see that the antimonarchists care little for the Barren, let alone granting them greater freedom."

"That depends. A charming, charismatic individual could do a lot of harm." He squeezed her hip. "I need you to reach out to the Barren Mother Vala recommended but we've put off contacting. She may have information which could help the security team. I would do it myself, but I sense she will be more at ease with you, since you're female."

"Of course—"

Azalyn was prevented from saying more because a giant box appeared on the view screen, flashing an urgent message in red, before a transmission appeared.

A male concealed by a black face mask spoke. "Citizens of Keldera, you may or may not have heard that an explosion went off inside the royal palace. They are vulnerable at the moment, with security members scrambling. Now is the time to attack and release your anger at the wastefulness of the king. We need your help to end our subjugation once and for all. I repeat, now is the time to attack. Don't let fear hold you back, as there is strength in numbers. Let us combine forces and be victorious."

The transmission switched to an overhead view of the palace, smoke rising from the hole created by the explosion. Words soon flashed on the screen: *We can destroy it together.*

Keltor was on his feet and dragging Azalyn to a secret door at the rear of his office. "You need to go to the underground shelter."

"No, I don't want to leave you, Keltor."

"I know, *zyla*, but you can better help me from the emergency bunker. Contact the Barren Mother and find out what you can."

"What about you?"

"I need to oversee emergency protocols, ones that can't be done from a bunker. Besides, if I cower now, it will only fuel hatred and feed into their propaganda. I must ensure everyone is safely evacuated from the palace before seeking cover myself."

Time slowed as she stared at Keltor's face and struggled to make a decision. Logically, she should go into the bunker and do as he asked. And yet, the thought of leaving Keltor behind made her stomach drop. She'd only just gotten him back. And now, there was a chance she could lose him forever if the masked male carried out his threat.

He cupped her cheek. "I will join you shortly, *zyla*. I not only need your help, but you need to protect Kelzal and look after my father. They should be following protocol as we speak, and will most likely already be waiting in the shelter."

A loud bang sounded overhead, vibrating the room to such a degree Azalyn stumbled into Keltor's chest. His arms immediately went around her as he shielded her head and upper body with his own.

A section of the ceiling crashed to the ground a few feet away. Dust filled the room and she choked.

Once the debris settle and she'd stopped coughing, she asked, "Are you all right?"

"Fine. But I need you safe so I can focus."

"I will go to the bunker, but promise me you'll join me as soon as you can, Keltor."

"I vow it, Aza. Now, go."

He maneuvered her into the doorway of the stairway to the bunker, kissed her quickly, and shut the door.

For a second she stood in the darkness until the lights whirred to life.

Shaking her shoulders, she turned and dashed down the stairs.

Chapter Twenty-One

Keltor dodged the bits of ceiling on the floor and made it to his doorway. He had to manually disengage the lock via a side panel and slid the door open by hand. He came face-to-face with his guard Xerlig.

His guard growled. "You must go to the bunker, your majesty."

"Not until the others are safe. Have you received the latest status report?"

Thankfully Xerlig didn't waste time trying to change his mind and nodded. "Some larger shuttles are coming up on the radar, and some individuals are gathering around the perimeter."

"It's too quick to be coincidence or for the average person heeding the call of the transmission. This was planned."

Xerlig motioned, and they headed down the corridor toward the tunnel to the security headquarters. "I suspect some will heed the call, but it will take time. However, the army is sending reinforcements. Once they arrive, there is no way for them to triumph."

"I agree, but I suspect it is more for rallying others to their cause. Show the palace is weak, and soon everyone will think they can overthrow me."

"If I may speak freely, your majesty?" Keltor motioned

for him to continue, and Xerlig complied. "Their reasons for overthrowing you are based on lies. Surely there is a way to counter that?"

"Perhaps. I think everyone has underestimated how far the antimonarchists have woven themselves into our society. No more. As soon as the palace is protected and the imminent threat neutralized, I think it's time we start seeking out and capturing the heads of the operation. Take away the leadership, as well as the main sources of revenue, and they will be much easier to dismantle."

"I will help in any way that I can, your majesty."

"You already are, Xerlig."

Thanks to Xerlig's sister and his role in communicating between her and Keltor. But he left it unsaid. The current state of security was unknown, and he wouldn't risk someone overhearing sensitive information.

They turned the final corner to the reinforced door of the security headquarters inside the palace. Keltor pressed his palm to the scanner at the same time it scanned this retina. For the final phase, he said, "King Keltor tro el Vallen requesting clearance. Water Garden"

When he passed voice recognition and the current password, the light above the door flashed green and slid open.

Inside security headquarters, males raced around the room while various men manned their computer stations. Keltor went immediately to the General in charge, Morvel Ripna. "Status report, General."

"We've begun teleporting individuals from the palace to the nearest army base. About half have been evacuated so far. It will take another twenty or thirty minutes to clear the rest," Morvel replied.

Keltor glanced at the schematics of the palace displayed on the side of the room. One area was red, with a few other sections a light pink. "And the structural integrity of the palace?"

"So far, it is still sound except for the room where the initial explosion took place. However, if you wish to remain in the capital city once this insurgency has been subdued, a list of upgrades and changes will need to be addressed. Your son's security suggestions are a start, but I have a few more."

Even though the general was giving him options, Keltor sensed the male didn't wish for him or his family to remain in the capital city. "I will review and probably heed every suggestion. I do not wish to make your task more difficult, but I'm afraid running away is not the monarchy's prerogative."

"Of course, your majesty. Although it may be wise to remove yourself from the premises for a short time so that we can secure the palace without worrying about your safety."

Keltor had an idea. "I will discuss that once this situation is handled. I believe I have a location in mind."

If the general thought it odd the king came up with a safe location so quickly, he said nothing.

One of the males at a computer station bellowed, "Unknown starship entering Keldera's atmosphere without permission, sir."

Keltor frowned, but the general beat him to the question. "Describe."

"Sensors indicate a foreign vessel, although the origin is unknown."

General Morvel stated, "Follow the established protocols. If they refuse to heed the summons to return back to space, detain them. However, if at all possible, refrain from destroying the ship. I want whoever is inside alive."

"Yes, sir."

The male went to work and the general faced Keltor. "The situation is growing dangerous. If the unknown starship refuses to turn back, I will invoke my right to order you to the bunker to ensure your safety."

Keltor nodded and moved to the general's computer panel, typed in the required codes, and brought up the sensor's image of the foreign vessel, along with its specifications.

After scanning the information, he silently sighed in relief that it wasn't any known Brevkan vessel. Dealing with the antimonarchists was bad enough, but add in Keldera's greatest enemy, and the situation would quickly become catastrophic.

However, the green starship emblazoned with gold lettering was unfamiliar. He typed in a command for the computer to translate, and the reply appeared on screen: *Language unknown.*

He wondered if the antimonarchists had found a way to hire mercenaries from an unknown alien planet.

Glancing at the general, he stated, "Keep me apprised of the situation. I want to know immediately once all but the most essential security personnel have been evacuated."

Morvel gave a curt nod. "Yes, your majesty."

Assured that the general had things in hand, Keltor moved toward a private room off the main floor, motioning for Xerlig to follow. Once the door closed, Keltor made a clicking motion with his hands. Xerlig removed a tube and obliged.

The temporary privacy shelter might be enabled, but Keltor was still going to keep things as vague as possible, just in case. He didn't want to give away Toralyn's identity and current mission. "You need to reach out and ensure they're both okay. For all we know, part of their assignments requires attacking the palace."

And if so, they should've reported the attack. But he left that unsaid.

Xerlig grunted in agreement. "I had thought the same, your majesty. But it would be a grave dishonor to leave the palace at this time."

"I understand your desire to stand guard, but protecting the person in question is more important, especially given their value." He paused and added, "I will order you if need be, Xerlig. But I would hope after so many years, you'd do it as a favor to me."

The male stood taller. "No need to order me, your majesty. But if the person is in danger?"

"Then abort the mission and order them to safety. However, if the person isn't compromised, continue to observe from a distance. I trust you to act as you see fit. I will contact you via our regular methods, once things have calmed down."

Another shock reverberated through the palace and Keltor crashed into a wall. The alert sirens blared.

Xerlig disengaged the privacy shield and the pair of them rushed into the adjoining room.

Debris had crushed the computer terminals on one side of the room, but the remaining men were typing, shouting, and doing everything they could to contain the situation.

General Morvel rushed to Keltor. "You must retreat, your majesty. The spaceship has opened fire on us."

Another explosion rocked the building, but nothing beyond dust rained down on the room.

Keltor found his footing. "I'm on my way. Remember to follow protocol yourself, General." He looked to Xerlig. "You have your orders."

Without another word, Keltor exited the room and ran toward the nearest secret entrance to the bunker, which was in the secure conference room two doors down from the security command center.

He'd just managed to manually open the door and reach

the far wall when another explosion sounded. Just as he heard a creak, the world went black.

✷ ✷ ✷

Toralyn watched another bomb drop on the palace and clenched her fingers until they turned white. She may not have wanted to reconcile with her birth parents, but she certainly didn't want to kill them.

Not to mention her brother could be fighting for his life as well.

However, if she followed her current set of instructions, she would only help along either cause.

Xerla spoke quietly. "We'll be strategic, to appear we're following orders but will avoid any real damage. However, we must do this, or we're out."

Not caring that the female could probably kill her with her bare hands, Toralyn glared at her companion. "I don't care about staying in. I'm only doing this for my brother and I've more than fulfilled what was expected of me."

"So you're willing to risk everything you've already done for him and give up the information we could compile to better protect him?"

She growled. "There are other ways to protect him."

Xerla looked at her with disgust. "Then you are silly, weak, and not as loyal as I thought you to be. Because keeping our cover is the best way to protect him. Few can make it as far as we have."

Trusting that their location on the roof of a building, behind a temperature control unit, would shield them from view, she tackled Xerla to the ground. For a brief second, she pinned the older female. But in the next instant, Xerla had her on the ground with a knife to Toralyn's throat. "Until you take duty seriously, you will never defeat me."

Anger surged through Toralyn. With a roar, she knocked the knife from Xerla's hand, wrapped her legs around her neck, and flipped her over.

With the female on her back, she wrapped an arm around her neck and restricted her airway. "There are more important things than duty." She tightened her grip a fraction. "I love my brother, and if you attempt to go through this exercise and hurt him, then I will be forced to detain you by any means necessary."

Xerla gave a strangled laugh and went limp in Toralyn's arms. Her split-second confusion was enough for Xerla to once again pin her to the ground, but this time with her arms wrenched behind her back and her knee grinding in her spine. Pain radiated through her shoulders, but she forced herself not to cry out. Xerla finally said, "There is more fire in you than I had originally thought. Love can sometimes give you an advantage, but it also provides a weakness."

The deep voice of Xerlig—one of her biological father's guards that she'd been introduced to during previous clandestine report meetings as Xerla's brother—filled the air. "Enough. Let her go."

The pain vanished as Xerla released her. She jumped to her feet, readying her stance for another attack. However, Xerla merely said to her brother, "You and Ervan weren't supposed to meet us here for another two hours."

"Things have changed. Per my orders, I am authorized to have her abort the mission."

"On what grounds?" Xerla barked.

"Threats to her safety. From you."

Xerla shook her head in disgust. "And this is why you are a mere guard, brother. All of this was part of her training."

Toralyn frowned, but Xerlig spoke before she could.

"That does not matter. For all we know, she could be the only surviving member of the royal family still on Keldera. You are relieved of protecting her, sister. She is my charge now. Per the king's orders, you are to return to the safe house and await further instructions."

Xerla tossed her one last look. "Since the king would be displeased if you were killed, remember to change your appearance and name. Otherwise, the antimonarchists will find you."

Before Toralyn could say anything in reply, Xerla vanished into the doorway and down the stairs.

Xerlig motioned with a hand. "Come, your highness. I must get you to safety."

"My name is Toralyn. And before I go anywhere, I want to know about my brother. Is he safe?"

"He was when I left the palace. Now, come voluntarily or I will take you forcibly."

A part of her wanted to scowl and ask why everyone kept ordering her around. But until she knew Kelzal was alive and safe, she had no choice but to obey Xerlig's orders. "Then lead on, *your highness*," she drawled.

She swore she saw the corner of Xerlig's mouth tick up, but if so, it was instantly replaced with his usual stoic expression.

He went to the door, checked inside, and motioned for her to follow.

As she made her way down the stairs, out the building, and maneuvered through a series of streets, she counted every blast or explosion along the way. What she'd thought had been an exercise for low-level inductees had turned into an all-out attack.

She only hoped everyone was okay. The anger she'd had at meeting the mother and father who had given her up had morphed into a solid knot of fear in her stomach. She'd lashed out, assuming she'd have the chance to know them later. But now, she might've given up her only chance to ask the questions she'd had since learning of her adoption at age eighteen.

One thing was for certain, if she were reunited with Kelzal and her birth parents, she would at least remain in their company long enough to get some answers to her questions, and maybe better know herself. The Brevkan war had ended before her birth, but at the rate, things were going, Keldera might face another war. And if the history of the previous one had taught the world anything, it was that one shouldn't take friends and family for granted. Toralyn would just have to find a way to balance her adopted mother, birth parents, brother, and cousins. Because in a way, they had all helped shape her into the female she had become.

It was time to grow up, embrace that fact, and seize what opportunities she could.

❋ ❋ ❋

Azalyn had just ended the transmission with the Barren Mother when another incoming call flashed on the screen. While it could be for Keltor, she decided to hit Receive. The stern face of General Morvel appeared on the screen. He said without preamble, "Has King Keltor reached the shelter?"

She glanced at another screen in the small room, showing the security footage for the underground set of rooms. Kastor, his nurse, Kelzal, and a few essential staff members were all she saw. Looking back to the general, she shook her head. "Not yet. Should he be?"

"Yes. He stated he was going to the bunker twenty minutes ago. That's more than enough time for him to have arrived. I checked the computer's sensors, but they're too damaged to find out where he is."

Dread pooled in Azalyn's stomach. "Have you sent anyone to look for him?"

The general barked an order to someone off-screen and then met her gaze again. "I wanted to ensure he wasn't in the shelter. Until the army arrives, my resources are limited."

"I can help look—"

"No. It is best for you to stay with the former king and the crown prince. Once the king is found, he will join you."

The screen turned dark and Azalyn cursed. Keltor had better be alive. Otherwise, she'd have to find a way to bring him back so she could kill him herself.

Yes, anger was easier than the alternative. She didn't care if it were selfish or not, but she wanted more than a matter of weeks with her male after being decades apart.

Especially since she was fairly certain she carried a good secret, but hadn't wanted to share with Keltor until she'd been positive.

Taking a few deep breaths, she willed her nerves to settle. Kelzal was an astute observer, and she didn't need to worry him unnecessarily.

She exited the private comm unit and headed to the main living area, where Kelzal waited. Kastor had retired to take his medications. She only hoped the attack and evacuation didn't end up killing him.

She found Kelzal watching a small notescreen in his hands. "Did you find a way to access the public transmission channels?"

"Yes. I'm watching one of the live feeds."

Since her son didn't elaborate, she moved to stand at his side and peered at the video.

A sphere-like spaceship darted to and fro above the palace, dodging anti-aircraft lasers. The dark green hull of the ship was a foreign-looking color, as was the strange symbol emblazoned in gold on the side. Azalyn had never been good with foreign languages; yet again she longed to have Keltor with them. He would probably understand what was painted on the side of the ship, or at least be able to identify the branch of languages it belonged to.

The dark green ship dropped a blazing ball of light, which exploded upon impact. She expected to feel the shock, but the shelter was deep enough underground that she didn't detect the faintest vibration.

The ship ascended higher into the sky before it exploded. Frowning, she asked, "Did I miss something? I didn't see any missiles or lasers hitting it."

"No. I believe the ship self-destructed."

Red-hot shards scatted over the palace, with the largest remaining chunk of the spaceship crashing just outside the walls of the compound.

The reddish-brown shapes of Kelderan Army fighter ships rushed into view, forming a protective circle around the palace and surrounding property.

However, before they could do more than settle into position, the main elevator to the bunker chimed. A second later, the doors opened.

Two soldiers carried something between them. Azalyn rushed to them and saw Keltor's pale, blood-streaked face above a blanket.

For a split second, she feared the worst—that after so many years apart, he'd been ripped from her side for eternity. But then she noticed the rise of his chest, and the fear lessened a degree. He was still alive.

And if she had any say in the matter, she'd make sure he stayed that way. She croaked, "What happened?"

The doctor who had helped Azalyn weeks ago, plus two

familiar nurses, rushed out behind the soldiers. The doctor spoke. "The king was injured. He's alive, but I must get him into emergency surgery."

She opened her mouth, but Kelzal appeared at her side and placed a hand on her shoulder. "Let them work."

Following the soldiers carrying Keltor, it was only when they had disappeared into the medical wing of the shelter that she looked to her son.

Kelzal took her hand and squeezed. "That particular doctor and his nurses have been vetted more than any other medical professional on the planet. They will do everything they can to help Father."

Tears prickled her eyes. "You choose now to start calling him your father."

"He has proven a worthy male, who wishes to protect everyone but himself. A bit foolish, but honorable in a way. He has also allowed Toralyn to do things I never thought he would. Not to mention you care for him. It all merits that I try to accept him. Although I'm still determined to give the crown to my sister."

"I do more than care for your father, Kelzal. I love him, just as I love you and your sister."

Her son shifted his feet. When he didn't say anything, she softened her voice. "And no, I'm not expecting you to profess your feelings about your new family. I just want to make sure you know that I love you, Kelzal. Especially since today has only reinforced how much we should treasure what time we do have together."

The warriors who had carried Keltor into the medical wing reappeared and headed toward the elevator. Azalyn spoke up. "Can you give me an update on what's happening?"

One of the warriors, who couldn't be much older than Kelzal, answered, "The army is securing the premises. The general will contact you once the task is complete."

Kelzal spoke up. "Will we be moved from this location?"

"I don't know, your highness. Until the traitors are contained and the danger has passed, it is best for you to remain here."

The warrior bowed his head, made a fist, and pounded it over his heart.

Within seconds, Azalyn was once again alone with her son.

"Come, Mother. You're part of Father's council and I need your help."

"With what?"

"While most likely unnecessary, I want to ensure I have a speech prepared, in case the planet needs reassurance."

She resisted praising Kelzal's foresight, especially considering how much he detested public speaking. "Of course. I will help you in any way that I can."

As they sat down and went to work on crafting a speech, Azalyn forced her mind to focus on her son. Because if she started thinking about Keltor's blood-streaked face, she might start crying.

No. Keldera needed all of them right now. It was time for her to follow Keltor's example and fulfill her duty to Keldera as their future queen. After all, her stubborn male would pull through. He just had to.

Chapter Twenty-Two

Afew days later, Azalyn sat next to Keltor's unconscious body and outlined the shape of the markings on his arm closest to her. He'd pulled through the surgery and all signs pointed to recovery, but the stubborn male had yet to wake up.

Not even the move to a remote, secure location had jostled him from his unconsciousness.

The door slid open, and she looked up to see Kelzal. She opened her mouth to ask what he needed, but he moved aside to reveal Toralyn's lavender-skinned, golden-haired—albeit a different shade than before and only chin-length—form in the doorway, and she forgot what she was going to say.

Toralyn raised her brows. "Hello to you, too."

Her daughter's dry tone snapped her brain into action. "We didn't expect you."

Toralyn glanced to Keltor's form on the bed. "Since Xerlig and Ervan refused to tell me the exact location of our destination, I didn't know where here was until a few minutes ago."

Kelzal walked up to her. "The two guards thought it would be easier to protect her by bringing her here."

Inclining her head, Azalyn said, "I agree. Although the

bigger question is whether Toralyn will stay or try to sneak off."

Her daughter squared her shoulders and stood taller. "When they asked me to come, I did so without protest. If all you're going to do is accuse me of dishonorable acts, then maybe I should rethink my decision."

Azalyn stood. "No, don't. But my concerns are well founded. After all, you said you didn't ask for any of this."

Her daughter looked to the side. "I did say that, but I changed my mind and decided to stay. Just for a short while, mind you. I have no desire to be a princess. It's bad enough people keep saying 'your highness' to me."

She smiled. "Better than them trying to figure out exactly what to call me. Keltor and I haven't married yet, after all." Silence fell. Given all that had happened recently, she decided to ask what she was thinking. "Why did you agree to come here, Toralyn?"

Toralyn shrugged. "Like most children who find out that they are adopted, I have questions. I figured I should ask them while I have the chance."

Because I don't want to stay on Keldera, was left unsaid.

Azalyn would take what time she could with her daughter. "Then ask me whatever you wish."

From the corner of her eye, she saw Kelzal sit in the corner, take out a device, and fiddle with it.

However, when Toralyn took a few steps closer to Keltor's bed, Azalyn zeroed in her attention on her daughter.

Waiting for her to speak, Azalyn took the time to memorize the curve of Toralyn's nose, the slight wave of her golden hair, and the placement of her daughter's markings. If she never agreed to sit for a portrait, then this could be the only chance Azalyn had to study the daughter she'd never known as a child.

She had no idea how much time had passed, but eventually, Toralyn spoke while never moving her gaze from Keltor. "Kelzal said you didn't know of my existence. Is that true?"

"Yes. I was unconscious during the birth and didn't know I carried twins. Kelzal is all they showed to me when I woke up."

What she wouldn't give to go back and hold both babies in her arms. Even if it had only been the once, it would've made the world of difference to Azalyn and might help alleviate some of the hurt and betrayal at the midwife's actions. No, make that Ulrick Sulani's actions; she had undoubtedly worked under his orders.

Thinking of Ulrick only reminded Azalyn of yet another reason Keltor needed to regain consciousness—so he could use his diplomatic skill to keep the merchant an ally.

"Why didn't you want us?" Toralyn asked softly.

"It wasn't a matter of want. I was a seventeen-year-old unmarried female, carrying the children of the crown prince. To keep you would've put you in danger. Well, or so I thought. I guess Ulrick's power plays ended up doing the trick, even if it wasn't straight away."

Toralyn's gaze met hers, anger flashing. "That's not an answer. If you had truly loved us, you would've found a way to keep us."

She gave a sad smile. "You have no reason to believe me, but giving up my babies was the hardest thing I've ever done, Toralyn. You were the last pieces I had of the male I loved. Not keeping you threw me into a year-long depression. Even if I only believed I had lost one baby, it was enough. I tried to think of what I could do, but in the end, I was a powerless female who needed the protection of my adopted Sulani family to survive. Because if I had tried to steal you away, someone would've found me eventually, since I had no resources or people to protect me. I decided that watching Kelzal from afar was better than never seeing him ever again." She paused, and reached out a hand, but stopped shy of touching Toralyn's arm. "Not to mention King Kastor probably would've banished me, or worse, if he discovered the full truth. Until the laws change, many unmarried females end up with the same choices as I had—giving up their children for adoption, or risk the father stealing away the children and ruining your reputation, to the point someone could end up living on the streets with few options beyond selling their bodies or even their freedom."

Toralyn studied her face for at least a minute before she finally replied, "I have a mother, you know."

She resisted flinching. "I know."

"And no one can replace her."

Ignoring the twisting in her heart, she nodded. "Of course."

Toralyn's gaze moved back to Keltor's face. "I'm not saying that I'll stay on Keldera forever, but until I have all my questions answered, I'd like to see you and the king sometimes."

She did take Toralyn's hand. When her daughter didn't pull away, hope bloomed in Azalyn's chest.

After a few minutes, Toralyn tugged her hand out of her grasp, walked a few paces away, and turned to face her. "I have two more conditions for staying."

Azalyn's brows drew together. "I'm almost afraid to ask."

"The first is that I want my mother brought here as soon as possible. And second, I want to be kept informed of what's happening. Trying to shield me and Kelzal from pain only ended up creating this mess. We're no longer children, and we deserve honesty."

With Toralyn's chin thrust into the air and confidence in

her gaze, Azalyn could easily see Toralyn as queen one day.

Not that it was possible at the moment.

As she debated how to respond to Toralyn's request since she didn't like speaking for Keltor, the male in question grunted. Everything else faded away as she moved closer and placed a hand on his cheek. "You're awake."

✸ ✸ ✸

At the voices talking around him, Keltor blinked his eyes open. He was inside a hospital room of some sort, machines whirring, with tubes connected to his body.

It took him a few seconds to focus on the faces above him, his mind hazy from some sort of drug. Azalyn's beautiful face was frowning at another lavender-skinned female—their daughter.

His gaze drifted to the other side of the room, where Kelzal sat assembling some device in his hands.

He attempted to sit up, but a sharp pain exploded throughout his body and he grunted. Azalyn's gaze shot straight to his. In the next instant, she placed her warm hand against his cheek. "You're awake."

Keltor's voice was deeper than normal when he stated, "Yes, *zyla*. Now, tell me what happened."

Azalyn hesitated, and Kelzal's voice filled the space. "We're at the retreat complex just outside Cillaren. Your lower body was severely damaged by debris. They saved your leg, but it will always be stiff and you will need a cane."

For once, he was grateful for his son's straightforward manner.

The city of Cillaren nudged his mind, but he couldn't remember why the place was important.

Glancing down, he saw a series of rods and braces surround his left leg.

"But all that matters is that you're alive, *zylar*," Azalyn murmured.

He met his female's gaze. "And the attackers?"

"The unknown spaceship self-destructed before the army could capture it," she answered. "They're analyzing what they can of the debris, but it'll take some time."

"And the antimonarchists?" he queried.

"The army has captured everyone who was attacking the palace, but also quite a few more who had been en route."

She paused, and slowly he moved his hand to cover hers. "Tell me, love."

"The palace was mostly damaged or destroyed. General Morvel strongly suggests abandoning it."

Kelzal's voice rang out. "I'm not sure that's wise."

Keltor shifted his gaze, but Kelzal was already coming toward him with a notescreen in hand. Before Keltor could ask, Kelzal turned the screen toward him.

It was playing a video. The footage was of people slowly passing debris down a line outside the palace, until the last person on the human chain tossed it into an incinerator shuttle. The scene switched to one of builders delivering replacement materials to a confused-looking guard, and the builders merely leaving the materials and walking away. Not far from every person shown were signs saying, "We will help you rebuild" and "We stand with King Keltor."

Kelzal spoke again. "The day after the attack, citizens started showing up at the palace, offering their help. At first, the general tried to turn them away. But eventually, someone convinced him to let them help."

"Who?"

"Me," Azalyn stated. She smiled. "There are some people who hate you, but there are many more who love or at least admire you, Keltor. And even if you dismiss yourself as being too new, they respected your father and his role in winning the Brevkan war. I thought it wise to let them show their support. Between their public displays and the arrest of hundreds of antimonarchists, it should at least hold off a war or rebellion. Well, for the foreseeable future at any rate."

And to think he'd given up decades with this wonderful female. "You are amazing, Azalyn soon to be tro el Vallen."

Her cheeks flushed, and it was as if the years melted away and he was with her over two decades ago.

As much as he wanted to tell her how beautiful she was, he was keenly aware of his two children in the room. One of whom shouldn't have been there; Xerlig must've used his vague order to bring her here.

He looked at Toralyn. "Why are you here?"

"And here I thought you'd be happy to see me," she drawled. Azalyn opened her mouth, but Toralyn beat her to it. "Xerlig and Ervan brought me."

He almost smiled. "It's obvious someone brought you. But why? You were on an assignment, the last I heard."

She shrugged. "Xerlig pulled me out, something about my safety."

Keltor sensed there was more to the story than that. But before he could ask about Xerla, Kelzal grunted and said, "She didn't want to attack the palace when the antimonarchists asked her to. Xerlig took her to a safe house, but eventually realized she'd be safer here. Or, perhaps they realized she wanted to be here."

"Kelzal!" Toralyn hissed.

The younger male shrugged. "It's the truth. Why you pretend to hate them, I will never understand."

Keltor had no idea what had transpired, but it seemed Kelzal was now on his side.

Azalyn jumped in before the siblings could bicker further. "By the way, your father is safe here as well, Keltor.

Although it will take some time for him to recover whatever strength he has left."

His father. That was why Cillaren was important—one of his half siblings lived at the retreat complex. "I need to see him. With the aid of a hover chair, maybe the doctor will allow me to do it later today."

She arched an eyebrow. "We'll see about that. The doctor must sign off on you leaving this room."

When she hesitated, Keltor said softly, "Tell me whatever it is, Aza."

She blew out a breath. "We're at the retreat complex I mentioned, the one owned by Jalarra. Since security details have worked here before, it was the logical choice to temporarily stay here for your recovery."

Toralyn jumped in. "Who is Jalarra?"

Kelzal answered, "Grandfather's paramour and the mother of two of our aunts and one uncle."

"Wait, what?" Toralyn demanded.

Azalyn quickly explained the situation and then looked back to Keltor before Toralyn could ask further inquiries. "The problem is with your half sister, Kasarra. She's anxious to meet you and is giving the guards a headache with her attempts to sneak into this room."

"She sounds like my kind of person. Too bad she's so young," Toralyn stated.

Keltor switched his gaze to his grown daughter. "You've just volunteered yourself to tell your aunt that I'll see her as soon as I have a little more strength."

Toralyn scrunched her nose. "She's only sixteen. I'm not about to call her my aunt."

"I didn't say you had to," Keltor said. "But nevertheless, you need a new assignment. Kasarra may just end up being it."

Toralyn tilted her head. "Only if I have the power to order her around."

Keltor smiled. "Power must be dealt out sparingly. Xerlig and Ervan will oversee your assignment." She huffed, and he quickly added, "We can talk more once you return, as I sense you have questions. I look forward to getting to know you better."

The female looked to the side, clearly uncomfortable. "I'll return shortly," she murmured before racing out of the room.

Azalyn focused back on him. "I'm not sure what happened, but as soon as she walked in here right before you woke up, she's tried making an effort. She also seems okay being stuck here, rather than on a ship to Jasvar."

Kelzal chimed in. "Because she's even more curious than I am about you two."

Glancing to his son, Keltor said, "While I appreciate your honesty, sometimes it is better to keep the secrets of others for a short while. I'm sure Toralyn told you those things in confidence."

His son put aside the device in his hands. "Perhaps. But all three of you dance around the truth. I plan to speed up the process."

"I can't wait to see what that entails," he muttered.

Azalyn placed her other hand on Keltor's face, garnering his attention. "Are you sure you're all right? Tell me now if you're in pain so I can call the doctor."

He slowly raised a hand to cover one of hers, the slight twinge in his shoulder worth it to touch her warm skin. "At the moment, it's tolerable. Although a kiss would make me feel much better."

She smiled. "I'm sure it would." Lowering her head, she whispered so low only Keltor should hear. "Just as I imagine me being naked would cause you to jump up, fully cured, and be able to dance me off my feet."

He laughed, but it quickly turned into a groan. "Laughing hurts too much, *zyla*."

Pressing her lips to his, she lingered a long moment before pulling away. "I wish I could do more, but there are many people waiting for your orders. Kelzal is officially the heir, but without a formal document and announcement, some are leery of taking orders from him. The quicker you recover, the better. That means rest."

He glanced at his son. "Regardless if they're hesitant, you are the crown prince. You must act as if they must take notice of you."

Kelzal interjected, "They think me odd. Warriors and I have never gotten along all that well."

He was saved from replying by the door opening and the royal doctor waltzing in. The doctor fixed Azalyn with a look. "Remember our deal."

Keltor frowned. "What deal?"

"He keeps a secret if I allow him to examine you when needed."

"What secret?"

Azalyn shook her head. "Not now. I'll tell you later."

Since Kelzal remained quiet, Keltor suspected his son didn't know what it was, either.

After kissing him gently, Azalyn moved toward the door. "I'll be back the second he's done, *zylar*. Even if you're asleep, I'll wait by your side." She looked at their son. "Come, Kelzal. You can help me with those council matters we discussed."

"Yes, Mother."

As his bride gave one last loving look, they exited the room.

The doctor began his examination, but Keltor barely paid attention to the pokes, prods, and short bursts of pain. There was much for him to do with regard to securing Keldera, but all he could think about was the secret and the happiness dancing in Azalyn's eyes.

Chapter Twenty-Three

It was late the next day before Azalyn was with Keltor when he was both alone and awake.

The sound of the door closing echoed in the room. Facing her male, she took his hand and was content to register his warm weight in hers.

Keltor squeezed and she met his eyes. "What is it, *zyla*? Tell me."

"I—" What should be easy to say was proving to be harder than she'd imagined.

But as she started into Keltor's dark brown eyes, she found the courage to blurt out her secret, "I'm pregnant."

Happiness flared in his eyes. "Are you sure?"

She bobbed her head. "Yes."

He brought her hand to his lip and kissed her. "Now tell me why you aren't happier about this."

Of course he would be able to read her. She sighed. "It's silly, really. It's just that things are going so well with Kelzal, and now with Toralyn making an effort...I don't want to destroy the progress we've all made."

"While we work on building relationships and earning trusts, this can remain our secret for now."

Her eyes widened. "How, exactly? The doctor already knows, and I suspect it won't be long before others suspect it, too, especially if I get as ill as when I carried our other two children. It's partly why I was secluded in the middle of nowhere with my new Sulani aunt."

"Ill?" Keltor echoed.

Scrunching her nose, she answered, "Let's just say that unlike most females, I lost weight rather than gained it."

Concern filled his gaze. "Should you even be up and about? Let alone spending so many hours working with the council? And before you ask, Farren informed me of your long hours."

"I'm going to have to have a word with him," she growled.

"Feel free. But I won't allow you to change the subject. Tell me what you need Azalyn, and I'll do what I can, even if it means relying on others to help me until I can get out of this bed again."

"I'm fine for now, truly. But as much as I want to have another child with you and look forward to watching our child grow up, I don't want the other two to think I want them any less."

Keltor whispered, "Lay next to me."

Careful to stretch out against the side opposite his injured leg, she rested her head on his chest. The second his arm wrapped around her, she felt safe and warm.

No matter where she was, Keltor would always be her home.

As he traced her arm with his forefinger, some of the tension eased from her body. His voice rumbled in her ear. "You're tired, stressed, and probably not eating enough. And I know you're worried about Kelzal and Toralyn. But if we pace ourselves and share the news at the right moment, I have faith that they will feel joy and celebrate with us."

"Kelzal, perhaps, if it's a male."

"By all accounts, he's been slowly coming into the role. Not to mention a certain talented female has been helping him learn how things function and how to handle council meetings."

She frowned and glanced up. "How do you know so much? You're bedridden and have only been awake for less than a day."

The corner of his mouth ticked up. "I have my ways."

"And let me guess, you'll only share them once I'm your bride?"

"Perhaps. It depends if you promise to stay out of trouble until after our child is born."

Our child. Warmth bloomed in her chest at Keltor's words.

And yet, there was something more important she needed to discuss first. "I think the bigger question is whether I can still become your bride or not, given recent events."

"Of course you will become my bride. The Sulanis haven't reneged, according to my sources. Besides, they have been granted exclusive rights for the announcement. Everything is already in place."

She blinked. "What are you talking about?"

"Look inside the drawer next to the bed and see for yourself."

As much as she didn't want to leave Keltor's side, her curiosity was stronger. Sitting up slowly, so as to not jostle the bed, she finally opened the drawer and extracted a large, rectangular package.

The paper was striped in gold and lavender, the colors reminding her of Keltor's and Azalyn's skin tones respectively.

She carefully unwrapped the package and revealed a wooden box. The royal seal was stamped into the black wood with a green-tinged gold inlay, the official color used for all royal seals.

Taking a deep breath, she released the latch and opened

the lid. Inside were two ceramic mugs, glazed in a shimmery white. In the center of each was a face—one hers, with the words Queen Azalyn, the other Keltor's, with the words King Keltor. Emblazoned on the inside lid of the box was a date about two months in the future, coupled with a few sentences:

The claiming ceremony of King Keltor tro el Vallen and Azalyn Sulani will be broadcasted exclusively in Sulani Merchant shops around the planet. Join us for the celebration and activities to commemorate the happy event.

From her decades working for the Sulanis, she immediately recognized a marketing ploy when she saw one—never before had there been merchandise related to the monarchy for sale, not even for the coronations. "They're going to make a fortune off the merchandise."

Amusement tinged Keltor's voice. "I suspect so. The announcement sets are due to go on sale in a few weeks. Both Ulrick and I are confident that the first publicly broadcasted claiming ceremony of a king and his bride will be too good to overlook. Not to mention the public support of the Sulanis selling wares related to the palace will make quite a few think twice about rebelling."

The Sulanis were the exclusive vendor to many establishments around the globe, not to mention many corporations had loan accounts with them, too. "Let's hope so."

"Azalyn." She met his gaze again. "It will work. Even if I have to use a hover chair to attend a ceremony in an underground bunker, we are going to be married on that date. After all, that's the anniversary of when we had our real first kiss."

A long ago memory, of stealing a kiss under a tree, flashed into her mind. "How did you remember that? Not even I could tell you the date after decades."

"It was important to me, *zyla*. It was the date a female

stole my heart for the first time, and I never seemed able to forget her, no matter how hard I tried."

Gently placing the box on the shelf next to the bed, she slowly moved until her face was just above Keltor's. "I love you, Keltor tro el Vallen."

Reaching up, he cupped her cheek. "I love you more, Azalyn Rippak Sulani."

She raised an eyebrow. "So, this is to be a contest, now?"

"Not until I'm healed. Then we can try to outdo each other in the bedroom."

Snorting, she pressed her forehead against his. "You may be king, but you're still just a male."

He smiled slowly. "A fact I will remind you of often."

She felt something warm against her abdomen and looked down to see Keltor's hand. Without hesitation, she laid hers over his.

For a few moments, they remained that way, their hands protecting their unborn child, as if to ward off any threats that may come in the future.

And for the first time since learning of her pregnancy, Azalyn began to think that everything would work out.

Well, until the door slid open and all hell broke loose.

✵ ✵ ✵

Even with his hand over Azalyn's abdomen, it was still sinking in that he was going to be a father.

Again.

If not for his damn leg, he would've lifted Azalyn into the air, twirled her around, and shown her how grateful he was for the news.

But the moment was ruined by the door opening and a teenage female with golden skin and dark blue hair raced into the room. Close on her heels was Toralyn.

Toralyn growled, "You were told to wait."

The teenager somehow managed to keep enough distance from Toralyn so as to avoid capture. "He's my brother. I have every right to see him."

Keltor frowned and put the female's looks and words together. "Kasarra?"

At her name, she turned her head.

And Toralyn promptly tackled the girl to the ground.

With a sigh, Keltor mustered as much steel into his voice as he could. "Let her up, Toralyn. If she went to this much trouble, then she's earned a few minutes with me."

If looks could kill, Toralyn's would've sliced him in two. But she obeyed, and the female who was his half sister rose to her feet.

Dusting her skirts, she stuck her tongue out at Toralyn and Keltor immediately felt a headache forming behind his eyes.

Thankfully the teenager looked back to him and said, "Yes, I'm Kasarra." She stood tall, although it didn't help much since she barely came to Toralyn's shoulder. "And you are my brother Keltor."

He resisted a laugh at her words. "Yes, that is me. What is it you wish to discuss?"

"I—" She paused before finally saying, "I don't know. I just wanted to see you."

Toralyn muttered some choice words, but Keltor ignored them. After all, Kasarra was only sixteen. "Well, you seem fortunate to share my good looks. There's no denying we're related."

Regaining her composure and standing tall, she said, "I'm not so sure about that. Apart from my hair, I take more after my mother."

At the young female's firm tone, Keltor had to admire her.

It also reminded him of his father's long-hidden female and his multitude of secrets.

An older female rushed into the room. Short, with golden skin and magenta hair threaded with silver, she stopped at Kasarra's side and grabbed the girl's bicep. "Kasarra Mayven, you were told to wait."

Looking between the two, Keltor saw the resemblance. "You must be Jalarra."

At her name, the older female met Keltor's gaze. "Yes." After a second, she quickly bobbed her head, as if remembering her place. "Your majesty."

"No need for formalities. Keltor will do. I must thank you for allowing us to stay at your retreat." When Jalarra remained quiet, he added, "My father spoke highly of you to my bride." He gestured to his side. "This is Azalyn."

As if on cue, Azalyn moved to stand in front of Jalarra. "It's a pleasure to meet you, Jalarra."

Jalarra studied Azalyn's face before replying, "So, you found a way after all."

"Pardon?" Azalyn asked.

Shaking her head, Jalarra took a step back, taking her daughter with her. "Nothing. We should leave the king to rest."

"I hope we can talk more later, if you have the time," Azalyn said with a smile.

"Perhaps." Jalarra took another step back. "Congratulations on your upcoming claiming ceremony."

With that, Jalarra exited the room, her daughter in tow.

Toralyn spoke up. "I'm going to watch her more closely this time."

And before Keltor could say a word, his daughter left, too.

The room was almost too quiet. How quickly he'd grown accustomed to chaos with his ever-growing family.

Azalyn sat on the edge of his bed and took his hand. "You know what you need to do."

He smiled at his female. "Yes, I know. As soon as I can maneuver into a hover chair, could you arrange a meeting with my father, his lover, and my sister? Toralyn and Kelzal should be there, too. I only wish Korjal could join us, making the Kelderan-arm of my family complete."

According to reports, Korjal had disappeared. Keltor had a few of his guards searching for his brother, but until they could return to a newly rebuilt and secured palace, most of his resources were spent protecting the retreat complex and searching out more of the antimonarchist leaders.

Squeezing his hand, she said, "Of course. But I must say, I already like your sister."

"I figured you would say that," he drawled.

Azalyn laughed. "Well, you did say how you hated being alone and isolated. It now seems you have more family than you know what to do with."

He smiled. "Yes. As much as it will turn my hair gray, I wouldn't have it any other way." After kissing the back of her knuckles, he added, "But I think we should share some of the...boisterousness with Kason. The doctor said I could move about with a hover chair in a day or two. If we schedule a meeting with my father and his other family, and then a video one with Kason about fifteen minutes after that one begins, we can all talk to him and his bride. Kason will make sure that Kalahn is there, too."

"I still think Kalahn would be a better watch guard for your other half sister on Jasvar, Kajala, than Kason."

He grunted. "Kalahn can barely keep herself out of trouble. How is she supposed to do it with someone else?"

"You should at least give her a chance, Keltor. The responsibility might be good for her. Not to mention she and Kajala are only a little under four years apart; they have the greatest chance of bonding with each other. Because as much as I love my older male, two of your children are older than your half siblings."

"Did you just call me old, *zyla*?"

"Older, your majesty. There's a difference."

Tugging her hand, Azalyn leaned close enough so that her lips were only a few scant inches away. "I can't wait until I'm healed enough to leave this bed and show you just how many years young I still am."

She ran a hand down his body, under the sheet, and lightly brushed his semihard cock. At her light touch, he turned to stone. "I look forward to it."

He kissed her, stroking the inside of her mouth, and lightly nipping her bottom lip. No matter that he'd had Azalyn dozens of times over the last month or so, it wasn't enough.

As he groaned at her taste, he decided no amount of times would ever be enough.

Chapter Twenty-Four

Two days later, Azalyn walked alongside Keltor's hover chair and took strength from his firm hand holding hers.

Somehow she'd managed to convince Jalarra, Kastor, Kasarra, Kelzal, and Toralyn to all be in the same room at the same time. Since Kasarra lived to irritate Toralyn, and the pair of them made Kelzal shake his head and run for his ad-hoc research lab, it was no easy feat. "I still say my job was harder than yours."

Keltor had been responsible for setting up the meeting with Kason.

Her male chuckled. "You say that, but remember, Kason had to first locate Kalahn and then practically lock her in a room for a day so she wouldn't go wandering again."

"I somehow think Taryn will have a different story as I believe Kalahn is taking some lessons from her warriors."

"Perhaps, but she's also exploring caves and waterfalls, if the reports are accurate. So much so that it's delayed Syzel and Ryven's return trip home with the colony transport ship because of them having to search for her."

"Maybe one of them should remain and watch Kalahn clandestinely. I'm sure Kason's carefully vetted elite warriors can help protect the colony ship."

"We shall see. Depending on how he acts for the video conference, I will either make it easier or harder on my brother. As it is, our sister Kajala refused to attend."

According to Kason's messages, Kajala rarely left her quarters, apart from when her duties required it. "Give it time, *zylar*. I have faith that everything will work out in the end."

Her words implied more than just with his family. Information had started flowing in about disgruntled Barren thanks to Vala's contact. On top of that, Xerla had begun a secret investigation into the Sulanis. One day, Azalyn and Keltor hoped to be rid of their current partnership.

They arrived at the conference room, which was guarded by Xerlig and Ervan. Azalyn smiled at each of them. "Any injuries yet?"

Ervan grunted. "If so, Toralyn will be at fault."

She bit back a smile. "Is everyone else here?" When Ervan gave a brief nod, she looked to Keltor. "And so it begins."

Shaking his head, he entered the doors once they opened, taking Azalyn with him.

Kastor lay in a hover bed, with Jalarra on one side and Kasarra on the other. She noted that each female held one of Kastor's hands, which probably meant that they had made peace with the former king.

On the other side of the room, Toralyn sat on the edge of the table with her arms crossed over her chest. Kelzal sat at the table, taking apart a portable replicator machine.

Toralyn was the first to speak. "You're late."

She resisted a sigh. "Actually, we're on time."

Her daughter shrugged. Ever since Azalyn had explained that Dolvia Sulani wouldn't be allowed to see her until she passed a thorough background check, Toralyn had become more difficult than usual.

At least she hadn't tried to run away.

Keltor's voice filled the room. "I appreciate you all coming, especially you, Father."

Kastor gave a small smile. "I should be the one thanking you, Keltor. You're going to bring most of my family together today. I will forever be in your debt."

If Keltor were standing, Azalyn guessed he'd have shifted his feet. Praise from Kastor was never easy for him.

She lightly squeezed her male's hand and he continued. "The reason I wished to gather you all here, beyond allowing Father to see everyone, is to let you know what lies in our futures.

"As you know, Azalyn and I will be married soon. Provided it goes as planned and the planet mostly remains at peace, I intend to formally recognize Kasarra and Kajala." Jalarra's eyes widened. Keltor continued before she could speak. "As for Korjal, once he's found and hopefully can be swayed to accept us, I will work toward acknowledging him as well."

Azalyn jumped in. "Which brings us to our next point. Jalarra, with your permission, we'd like to make this retreat a permanent royal residence. That way, you and Kasarra can be protected but will still also have your home."

Jalarra frowned. "But what of my business?"

Keltor answered, "We'd still like to use it for international visitors and royal guests. If some of my plans are successful, we might be having more humans come to the planet. I think this would be an ideal place to welcome them, what with the forest and mountains in the distance."

"Will I still have full control of how this place is run?" Jalarra asked.

Azalyn was starting to see why Kastor adored his female—being royal meant little to her, in terms of ceremony.

She nodded. "For the most part, yes. Although the dietary requirements of humans can be slightly different. I hope you'll allow suggestions."

Bowing her head, Jalarra said, "Of course."

"Good." Keltor swung his head toward Toralyn and Kelzal. "Azalyn and I hope that both of you will attend the claiming ceremony."

Kelzal never looked up from his machine. "Of course."

Toralyn merely stared at her and Keltor. She held her breath.

"It's less than two months away, correct?" She and Keltor both nodded. "Then as long as I can see my mother before then and my image is out of the shot of the broadcast, then I will attend."

"Always the one to negotiate," Keltor drawled.

"Well, it's hard not to. What with my merchant upbringing and half of my genetics coming from a king."

Azalyn forced her voice to not sound overly eager. "We shall try, although with recent events, you must understand why we're being cautious with regard to inviting guests here."

"You know my terms," Toralyn stated. "Whether I attend or not is up to you."

Part of her admired her daughter's ability to stand up for what she wanted, and another part wanted nothing more than to scowl and order her to heed their request.

In other words, she felt like a mother.

She resisted placing a hand on her lower abdomen. Now wasn't the right time to share the secret.

The video screen flashed with a transmission request. Keltor glanced around the room. "That will be Kason, his bride, and Kalahn. The line is secure, so feel safe to speak freely."

As Keltor clicked the Receive button, Azalyn pasted a smile on her face. She had yet to meet Kalahn, either in person or via a video conference. And for some strange reason, she wanted Keltor's sister's approval.

Keltor may have survived the meeting thus far, but tension was thick in the room. For once, he hoped his sister Kalahn could act the part of a royal sibling and display at least some semblance of restraint.

Not that he wanted to change her completely, but the truce among the factions of his family was tentative at best. If she could avoid saying the first thought that entered her mind, it could save him a lot of trouble.

Kason, Taryn, and Kalahn's faces appeared on screen. Kason sat between his bride and their sister. Taryn was the first to speak. "Hello everyone. Greetings from Jasvar."

While accented, his sister-in-law managed to get the words correct in Kelderan. "And similar greetings from Keldera."

Kalahn rolled her eyes. "Do we have to be so formal? Keltor may be king, but he's still our brother."

He decided to ignore Kalahn's words. Instead, he motioned toward Azalyn. "Kalahn, may I introduce Azalyn Sulani, your future sister-in-law."

Kalahn scrutinized Azalyn's face before sighing. "You've made me out to feel old, what with a niece and nephew almost the same age as me."

He frowned, but Azalyn's voice filled the room. "Well, when there's already sixteen years between you and Keltor, it can't be helped."

Kalahn snorted. "Using facts against me. You'll fit right in with my brothers." Kalahn's eyes skirted around, no doubt taking in everyone in the room. "I'm guessing the male and female at the table are my niece and nephew, and the younger female holding Father's hand is my sister."

Keltor opened his mouth, but Kasarra beat him to it. "I'm Kasarra, although technically, you should call me Aunt Kasarra."

Kalahn laughed. "I see Keltor getting rid of me didn't calm things down, with regard to females related to him."

"I didn't get rid of you, Kalahn. You ran away," Keltor pointed out.

Kason jumped in. "Unlike you, we don't have an unlimited amount of power to use for this transmission. I shall be talking with Kalahn later."

Keltor was one of the few in the room who could understand Taryn's reply in CEL. "Both of you need to behave. Remember everything they've just gone through. I sometimes think when the tro el Vallen siblings get together, all reason goes out the window."

Kastor snorted, reminding Keltor that his father was probably the only other one to understand the Earth language. He replied in the same, "I'm glad to see someone can reason with them."

Taryn opened her mouth, but Kelzal replied in flawless CEL. "Reason isn't always the best way to handle a situation, although I wish it were."

Grinning, Taryn replied in her language. "It seems I have a father-in-law and a nephew who can understand me, in addition to Kalahn, Kason, and Keltor."

Kason grunted. "You still need to work on your Kelderan."

Azalyn squeezed his hand, reminding him she had no idea what they were saying.

He cleared his throat and switched back to Kelderan. "We shouldn't be rude. Taryn may not fully be able to reply, but thanks to the device in her ear, she can understand. So let's continue this meeting in Kelderan."

Kalahn spoke up. "What else is there left to say?"

"Kalahn," Kastor said, and everyone's attention shifted to the former king. "I know I have no right to ask you, especially since you're the child I neglected to visit the most after your mother's death, but I hope you can look after your sister, Kajala. She wanted to go to Jasvar to start over, and I made it happen. However, she could use a friend. Please visit her and give her a chance."

Kalahn's bravado faded, her eyes turning concerned. "Trust me, you don't want to give that task to me. Kason should do it."

"No, Kalahn. I'm asking you. Grant me one last favor before I die."

The room fell deathly quiet. The topic they'd all been avoiding—his father's mortality—was suddenly front and center.

"Father," Kalahn said as her voice cracked.

"Please don't worry about me, Kalahn. I have lived a full life, with plenty of children to carry on my name, and even grandchildren. I cannot make up for all I've done over the years with regards to my offspring, but getting my two families together is all I can hope for. Please, watch over Kajala for me."

Wiping her eyes, Kalahn bobbed her head. "I will, Father. I'm sorry I ran away without telling you."

Kastor smiled. "You get it from your mother. And in a way, that comforts me."

Within seconds, Kalahn, Azalyn, and Jalarra all started crying. As Kason comforted their sister, Kasarra comforted her mother, and Keltor put an arm around Azalyn's shoulders, he decided the meeting hadn't gone quite the way he'd planned.

Once the females calmed down a little, Keltor spoke again. "Kason and I will coordinate private meetings with

Father over the coming days. I think that might be best."

Kason nodded, even as he continued to hold Kalahn at his side. "I will ensure there is enough power to do so. I'll also send my report as soon as possible."

As understanding passed between him and his brother, the screen went dark.

He looked to his father with Jalarra and Kasarra. "You must be tired, Father. We'll leave you to rest and will visit you later."

Kastor smiled. "Make sure to bring my grandchildren."

"I will try."

Keltor motioned for Toralyn and Kelzal to follow as he and Azalyn exited the room.

Once in the hall, he stopped and turned his chair toward his children. "Thank you for remaining silent so that my sister and father could reconcile to a degree."

Toralyn shrugged one shoulder and looked to the side. "I have no wish to upset him."

"There was little for me to add to the conversation," Kelzal stated.

"Regardless, thank you."

His two children looked anywhere but at him. Thankfully his clever Azalyn spoke up and steered the topic toward something less emotional, knowing they all needed it. "Right, I know it's a little early for dinner, but that means you two can help me cook it this time."

Toralyn groaned. "I hate cooking. And if anything, I'll make it taste even worse than yours."

"Toralyn," Keltor warned.

Azalyn put up a hand. "I'm aware of my faults." She flashed him a smile. "And I adore that you still choke it down each time I attempt it."

Kelzal spoke up. "If you want your next training session with Ervan and Xerlig, Tora, then you must attend dinner every evening. Since your agreement was vague, helping to prepare it falls under the stated parameters."

Toralyn looked askance at her brother. "You're supposed to be on my side, Kel."

"I believe in facts and truth. I will protect you if needed, Tora, but this is an agreement you freely agreed to. You must accept the result."

"Fine. But I may need to alter my agreement going forward. I'm not about to cook every day," Toralyn grumbled.

Azalyn snorted. "That would be entertaining, but for now, let's just say it's for tonight." She released his hand and stood between the twins. "Now, I have a new recipe that requires some extra hands. Kelzal, I hope you'll help, too."

"What about Father?" Kelzal asked.

Keltor grinned. "There's not much for me to do until I can stand again."

"Nonsense," Azalyn answered. "If we place a chopping board on your lap, you can help just fine." She motioned down the hall. "Now, let's go. We're going to need as many minutes as possible to do what I have planned."

As they made their way down the hall, Azalyn and Toralyn argued about how many courses they needed. Kelzal wisely focused on anything but his mother and sister and remained quiet.

Keltor may be a long way from having a close-knit family that could talk and tease with ease, but it was a start.

And for the chance to experience emotions ranging from love to annoyance, Keltor would gladly put up with as many arguments as it took. He finally had a family of his own, one that would only grow. They would no doubt be his toughest challenge to tackle, but he looked forward to every second of it.

Epilogue

Almost Two Months Later

Azalyn darted into a side room with Keltor at her side. Once the door closed, she let out the laughter she'd been keeping inside. "I hadn't expected Farren to lead the other council members in a song."

Keltor sighed. "I sometimes second-guess my decision to put him on my council."

"That's silly. He's clever and full of knowledge. Not to mention he knows how to make people laugh when they need it."

"You laugh a little too often at his jokes," Keltor muttered.

Rolling her eyes, she said, "I just became your bride, Keltor tro el Vallen. I want you as my lord, not Farren."

Leaning on his cane, Keltor reached around her waist and drew her up against him. "I think there are more important matters to attend to than talking about Farren."

She placed her hands on Keltor's bare chest; he'd worn the formal attire of tight trousers and a long vest. As she rubbed her fingers against his hard muscles, she murmured, "I hope these matters involve us with far less clothing."

Heat flashed in his eyes. "Yes, although I'm tempted to

simply toss up your skirts and take you once to slake my desire."

She smiled coyly. "I saw how you looked at me in there. Considering you gave me this dress, you only have yourself to blame."

Wanting to tempt her lord, she backed away and twirled once, the long, silky skirts a light caress against her skin.

He growled. "I didn't think it'd be so revealing."

She smoothed the fabric of her dress, her fingers loving the embroidered birds flying over the colors of a Kelderan sunrise—yellow, blue-green, and purple. One of Veljan's prized new flowers, a small bloom in dark, iridescent blue, was pinned to one side of her chest, completing the outfit. "It's perfectly acceptable."

Keltor stalked toward her, each click of his cane hitting the floor making her heart pound harder. His voice was gravelly as he said, "I can see every curve of your body because of that damn material."

"Well, not quite all, thankfully." She stretched the material over her belly, which was a little rounder than it had been when she'd woken up inside the palace over three months ago.

All because of their baby, who had decided they liked food quite a bit and weren't going to let her forget it.

Her male stopped in front of her and lightly traced the curve of her abdomen, leaving a trail of heat behind. "The most important people know, and that's all that matters."

She smiled at the memory of Toralyn tossing her hands up in the air, declaring she had too much family as it was, what with both older and younger aunts and uncles.

However, after the initial outburst, both Kelzal and Toralyn had been supportive, stating as long as they didn't have to babysit or change diapers, they would enjoy a sibling.

The only person who didn't know was Korjal, but she was certain Keltor's men would locate him eventually.

Not wanting to ruin her claiming day with worries about a missing brother-in-law, she turned and slowly swayed her hips as she walked. Keltor followed.

Stopping at the edge of the bed, she kept her back to Keltor. She could tell he stood just behind her as his heat seeped into her body.

His breath tickled her ear. "Just for that, I am going to take you once while you're fully clothed and I'm not."

Glancing over her shoulder, she tilted her head. "You say that as if it's a bad thing."

With a growl, Keltor cupped her cheek and took her lips in a demanding kiss. Each stroke and lick was another brand, as if claiming her in front of most of Keldera wasn't enough.

Turning toward him, she threaded her fingers through his hair and met him stroke for stroke, letting him know that she wanted everything he had to offer.

Because she had just as much claim to him as he did to her. He may be king, but to Azalyn, he would always just be Keltor, the male who stepped on her foot inside a shop and ended up winning her heart.

And no matter what came, they could handle it as long as they were together.

Author's Note

The water maze Keltor showed Azalyn was inspired by the actual water maze at Hever Castle in Kent, England. While the one at Hever Castle is outdoors and lacks the statues of the one inside the Kelderan Palace, the concept and mechanics are the same. I had no idea when I went there on vacation in September 2017 and watched the children deliberately step on the wrong planks to get wet that it would play a role in a science fiction romance book! Not only that, but Veljan Ranna's character was inspired by my many visits to formal gardens in England and France in 2017. I hope to tell his story eventually and further use the knowledge I've gained about garden design and layouts. I may even need to visit a few more famous gardens for inspiration. :)

Another point I wish to bring up is Kelzal's character. During the editing and beta process, quite a few people caught on to his quirks and figured out what they were. If he were a human male, Kelzal would probably be diagnosed with Asperger Syndrome, which was folded into the more general autism spectrum disorder in 2013. I was lucky enough to spend a few years working as a substitute teacher in the USA and most of my time subbing was in special education classes. Some of my favorites were those for students on the autism spectrum, ranging from mild to severe. I never understood why so many people turned down jobs in those classes as a lot of the students had huge hearts and I always looked forward to going back. At any rate, those experiences influenced Kelzal's character. Since he's Kelderan, his condition is slightly different, but everyone will get to know him better when he has his own book!

And lastly, if you're wondering about how the laws will or won't change, or even about King Kastor, that is to come. The next book will be about Princess Kalahn and will take place before the epilogue of this book. My Kelderan series is turning out to be a saga, and change takes time. I hope everyone has a little patience. Especially since we have a lot of new characters to learn about in the future. :D

As always, there are several people I need to thank for getting this book out as it is:

- Becky and her team at Hot Tree Editing were amazing as always. I'm fortunate enough to have an editor that gets me and isn't afraid to push me to be better. Becky is the best.
- Clarissa Yeo of Yocla Designs produced another beautiful cover for me and I'm fortunate to have found her back in 2014!
- Finally, a big thank you to my beta readers—Donna H., Iliana G., and Alyson S. They help to catch some of the lingering typos and minor inconsistencies that true fans would notice.

And of course, I'm eternally grateful for my readers. This series pushes my creativity to its limits and I'm grateful that I can continue to write it, thanks to those supporting me. Writing this series helps refresh and renew my love for my dragon ones.

Princess Kalahn's book should be out in July, and toward the end of the year I hope to have a follow-up novella for either Taryn and Kason or Vala and Thorin. I know my readers love updates as much as I love writing them, and I can't wait to revisit some of our beloved characters.

BLAZE OF SECRETS
(Asylums for Magical Threats #1)

After discovering she has elemental fire magic as a teenager, Kiarra Melini spends the next fifteen years inside a magical prison. While there, she undergoes a series of experiments that lead to a dangerous secret. If she lives, all magic will be destroyed. If she dies, magic has a chance to survive. Just as she makes her choice, a strange man breaks into cell, throws her over his shoulder, and carries her right out of the prison.

To rescue his brother, Jaxton Ward barters with his boss to rescue one other inmate--a woman he's never met before. His job is to get in, nab her and his brother, and get out. However, once he returns to his safe house, his boss has other ideas. Jaxton is ordered to train the woman and help her become part of the anti-magical prison organization he belongs to.

Working together, Kiarra and Jaxton discover a secret much bigger than their growing attraction to each other. Can they evade the prison retrieval team long enough to help save magic? Or, will they take Kiarra back to prison and end any chance of happiness for them both?

CHAPTER ONE

First-born Feiru children are dangerous. At the age of magical maturity they will permanently move into compounds established for both their and the public's protection. These compounds will be known as the Asylums for Magical Threats (hereafter abbreviated as "AMT").

—Addendum, Article III of the *Feiru* Five Laws, July 1953

Present Day

Jaxton Ward kept his gaze focused on the nearing mountain ledge ahead of him. If he looked down at the chasm below his feet, he might feel sick, and since his current mission was quite possibly the most important one of his life, he needed to focus all of his energy on succeeding.

After all, if things went according to plan, Jaxton would finally see his brother again.

He and his team of three men were balanced on a sheet of rock five thousand feet in the air. To a human, it would look like they were flying. However, any *Feiru* would know they were traveling via elemental wind magic.

Darius, the elemental wind first-born on his team, guided them the final few feet to the mountain ledge. As soon as the sheet of rock touched solid ground, Jaxton and his team moved into position.

The mountain under their feet was actually one of the most secure AMT compounds in the world. Getting in was going to be difficult, but getting out was going to take a bloody miracle, especially since he'd had to barter with his boss for the location of his brother. In exchange, he had promised to rescue not just Garrett, but one other unknown first-born as well.

Taka, the elemental earth first-born of Jaxton's team, signaled he was ready. He nodded for Taka to begin.

As Taka reached a hand to the north, the direction of elemental earth magic, the solid rock of the mountain moved. With each inch that cleared to form a tunnel, Jaxton's heart rate kicked up. Jaxton was the reason his brother had been imprisoned inside the mountain for the last five years and he wasn"t sure if his brother had ever forgiven him.

Even if they survived the insurmountable odds, located Garrett, and broke into his prison cell, his brother might not agree to go with them. Considering the rumors of hellish treatment inside the AMT compounds, his brother's hatred would be justified.

Once the tunnel was big enough for them to enter, Jaxton pushed aside his doubts. No matter what his brother might think of him, Jaxton would rescue him, even it if took drugging Garrett unconscious to do so.

Taking out his Glock, he flicked off the safety. Jaxton was the only one on the team without elemental magic, but he could take care of himself.

He moved to the entrance of the tunnel, looked over his shoulder at his men, and nodded. After each man nodded, signaling they were ready, he took out his pocket flashlight, switched it on, and jogged down the smooth tunnel that would lead them to the inner corridors of the AMT compound.

If his information was correct, the AMT staff would be attending a site-wide meeting for the next hour. That gave Jaxton and his team a short window of opportunity to get in, nab the two inmates, and get back out again.

He only hoped everything went according to plan.

***

Kiarra Melini stared at the small homemade shiv in her hand and wondered for the thousandth time if she could go through with it.

She had spent the last few weeks racking her brain, trying to come up with an alternative plan to save the other prisoners of the AMT without having to harm anyone. Yet despite her best efforts, she'd come up empty-handed.

To protect the lives of the other first-borns inside the AMT, Kiarra would kill for the first and last time.

Not that she wanted to do it, given the choice. But after overhearing a conversation between two AMT researchers a few weeks ago, she knew the AMT would never again be safe for any of the first-borns while she remained alive.

The outside world might have chosen to forget about the existence of the first-born prisoners, but that didn't make them any less important. Kiarra was the only one who cared, and she would go down fighting trying to protect them.

Even if it meant killing herself to do so.

She took a deep breath and gripped the handle of her blade tighter until the plastic of the old hairbrush dug into her skin. Just as she was about to raise her arm to strike, her body shook. Kiarra closed her eyes and breathed in and out until she calmed down enough to stop shaking. Ending her life, noble as her reasons may be, was a lot harder than she'd imagined.

Mostly because she was afraid to die.

But her window of opportunity was closing fast; the AMT-wide meeting would end in less than an hour. After that, she would have to wait a whole other month before she could try again, and who knew how many more first-borns would suffer because of her cowardice.

Maybe, if she recalled the conversation between the two researchers, the one which forebode the future harsh realities of the other AMT prisoners, she'd muster enough nerve to do what needed to be done.

It was worth a shot, so Kiarra closed her eyes and re-called the conversation that had changed the course of her life forever.

Strapped to a cold metal examination table, Kiarra kept her eyes closed and forced herself to stay preternaturally still. The slightest movement would alert the researchers in the room that she was conscious again. She couldn't let that happen, not if she wanted to find out the reason why the researchers had increased her examination visits and blood draws over the past two weeks.

Most AMT prisoners wouldn't think twice about it, since they'd been conditioned not to ask questions, but Ki-arra had gone through something similar before. The last time her visits had increased with the same frequency, the AMT researchers had stolen her elemental magic.

Since then, no matter how many times she reached to the south—the direction of elemental fire—she felt nothing. No tingling warmth, no comforting flame. She was no dif-ferent from a non-first-born, yet she was still a prisoner, unable to see the sky or feel a breeze, and forced to live in constant fear of what the guards or researchers might do to her.

Of how they might punish her.

Dark memories invaded her mind. However, when the female researcher in the room spoke again, it snapped Kiarra back to the present. The woman's words might tell her more about her future, provided she had one after her treatment.

She listened with every cell in her body and steeled herself not to react.

"Interesting," the female researcher said. "Out of the ten teenagers, nine of them still can't use their elemental magic, just like F-839. Dr. Adams was right—her blood was the key to getting the Null Formula to work."

It took all of Kiarra's control not to draw in a breath. Her serial number was F-839, and all of the extra blood draws finally made sense—the AMT was using her blood to try and eradicate elemental magic.

The male researcher spoke up. "They're going to start a new, larger test group in a few weeks and see if they can stop the first-borns from going insane and/or committing suicide. If we don"t get the insanity rate below ten percent, then we'll never be able to implement this planet-wide."

"Don't worry, we'll get there. We have a few million first-borns to burn through to get it right."

Kiarra opened her eyes and embraced the guilt she felt every time she thought about what had happened to those poor first-born teenagers.

Because of her blood, not only had five teenagers already gone insane, but their insanity was driving an untold number of them to suicide.

And the researchers wanted to repeat the process with a larger group.

She couldn't let that happen.

They needed her blood, drawn and injected within

hours, as a type of catalyst for the Null Formula to work. If they didn't have access to her blood, they wouldn't be able to conduct any more tests.

There was a chance the researchers might find another catalyst within a few weeks or months, but it was a risk she was willing to take. Stopping the tests, even for a few months, would prevent more people from going insane or committing suicide.

Kiarra needed to die.

I can do this. Think of the others. Taking a deep breath, she tightened her grip around the shiv's handle and whispered, "Please let this work,'" before raising the blade with a steady hand and plunging it into the top half of her forearm.

Kiarra sucked in a breath as a searing pain shot up her arm. To prevent herself from making any more noise, she bit her lip. Despite the AMT-wide staff meeting, a guard would come to investigate her cell if she screamed.

You can do this, Kiarra. Finish it. With her next inhalation, she pulled the blade a fraction more down toward her wrist. This time she bit her lip hard enough she could taste iron on her tongue.

While her brain screamed for her to stop, she ignored it and gripped the handle of the blade until it bit into her palm. Only when her heart stopped beating would the other first-borns be safe—at least from her.

An image of a little girl crying, reaching out her arms and screaming Kiarra's name, came unbidden into her mind, but she forced it aside. Her sister had abandoned her, just like the rest of her family. Her death wouldn't cause anyone sadness or pain. Rather, through death, she would finally have a purpose.

This was it. On the next inhalation, she moved the blade a fraction. But before she could finish the job, the door of her cell slid open.

Kiarra looked up and saw a tall man, dressed head to toe in black, standing in her doorway and pointing a gun straight at her.

Shit. She'd been discovered.

———————

Blaze of Secrets is now available in paperback.

About the Author

Jessie Donovan wrote her first story at age five, and after discovering *The Dragonriders of Pern* series by Anne McCaffrey in junior high, she realized people actually wanted to read stories like those floating around inside her head. From there on out, she was determined to tap into her over-active imagination and write a book someday.

After living abroad for five years and earning degrees in Japanese, Anthropology, and Secondary Education, she buckled down and finally wrote her first full-length book. While that story will never see the light of day, it laid the world-building groundwork of what would become her debut paranormal romance, *Blaze of Secrets*. In late 2014, she became a *New York Times* and *USA Today* bestseller.

Jessie loves to interact with readers, and when not reading or traipsing around some foreign country on a shoestring, she can often be found on Facebook. Check out her pages below:

http://www.facebook.com/JessieDonovanAuthor

And don't forget to sign-up for her newsletter to receive sneak peeks and inside information. You can sign-up on her website:

http:///www.jessiedonovan.com